JINX AND TONIC

THE MAGIC IN MIXOLOGY SERIES *BOOK THREE*

GINA LAMANNA

For updates on new releases, please sign up for my newsletter at www.ginalamanna.com.

Feel free to get in touch anytime via email at gina.m.lamanna@gmail.com!

ACKNOWLEDGEMENTS

This book is for the you, Islanders.

Special Thanks:

To Connie Leap: Thank you for inspiring this book with your beautiful work. Without you, Jinx would not exist!

To Mom & Dad—For letting me stay in bed all day to read Harry Potter on its release.

To Alex—For making the simplest moments a little bit magical. я тебя люблю!

To Meg & Kristi—Jinx. You all owe me cokes.

To Stacia: For making sure the heads in this book are tilted all of the right ways.

To Kim: For your magical new hair, and your friendship.

To my Oceans Apart ladies: Joy, Asheley, and Monique—for bringing me into the magic of the book world!

To Miss Emma Hart—for having the most magical pink hair on this planet. X adores it. And you too, Olivia.

To Katie Hamachek: For being my only "real" friend to visit The Isle.

To Sprinkles On Top Studios, my awesome cover designer. Photo Courtesy of Deposit Photos

And last but not least, to all my family and friends, thanks for making me laugh.

Synopsis

THE TIME HAS FINALLY ARRIVED! The Trials are in full swing and celebratory parties fill The Isle as Candidates go head-to-head to prove themselves worthy of the coveted Ranger title. Drinks, dances, and masquerade balls set the stage for a glamorous series of events until suddenly, it all changes.

The most dangerous criminal on the island escapes from prison. Tragedy strikes. The Isle is thrown into chaos due to old, forbidden black magic, and only one person can help.

As the island's Mixologist, Lily is expected to step in and save the day. When she's forced to keep secrets from X while deciphering decades old clues, however, she's pushed to the edges of her sanity.

With the help of her family, The Core, and her new boyfriend, X, Lily must stop The Puppeteer from taking over the island before it's too late.

Because if she doesn't succeed, nobody will.

"Only at the end do you realize the power of the Dark Side."

Star Wars

CHAPTER 1

"WHAT DO YOU THINK?" RANGER X stared at himself in the mirror, his brow furrowed in concentration. "Be honest."

"I love it!" I said, clapping my hands. "Definitely the winner. Can we *pretty please* agree that this suit is perfect?"

"*No!*" Ranger X roared. He tugged on his shirt sleeves. "It doesn't fit right."

"Spin around." I made a twirling motion with my finger. "Let me see the back."

X shot me a skeptical glance. Then he did as he was told, rotating in a slow circle and gracing me with a 360-degree view of his body. It didn't disappoint.

"If I could whistle, I would," I said. "Unfortunately, that's not one of my skills. But you look great! What's wrong with this one?"

"It's something about *this*." He wrestled with the bowtie strapped across his neck. Light blue with polka dots. "It's not very... intimidating."

"You're going for a *welcoming* look!" I paced around the room, trying to keep my patience. If there had been any space left on my bed whatsoever, I would've plopped down and relaxed hours ago. As it was, there were enough suits on my comforter to outfit a bridal party. "It's the first public trial. You're allowed to look likeable instead of scary for once."

"My normal look is scary?" He raised his eyebrow at me in the mirror. "I like scary. Let's stick with scary."

I tried not to laugh and failed miserably. "Fine, you're right. Lose the bowtie."

Ranger X ripped off the bow tie, threw it out the window, and let out an incredible sigh of relief. "This is ridiculous."

"Take a break." I stopped my pacing, moving a few steps closer to him. I let my hands rest on his shoulders, frowning at the tension in his muscles. "You look good in everything. Just pick *something*."

"I'm sorry." The annoyance in Ranger X's face slipped away as his eyes fell on me. "I appreciate your patience. I don't know what's come over me."

My eyebrows shot up. "Believe me, watching you change clothes has not been a hardship. But next time you put on a fashion show, let's stick to three costumes instead of nine million and eight."

"It's not a fashion show."

"It's sort of a fashion show."

"It's not—" He broke off, winced at the bed laden with suits, and frowned. "I'm putting on a fashion show. What's wrong with me?"

"You're tense." I let my hands skim over his chest, pretending to smooth down his clothes. "You're cute when you're tense, you know that?"

The rest of his discomfort vanished, replaced by a gleam dancing in his eyes. "You don't say?"

I stood on my tiptoes, leaned in close, and allowed my body to do the talking. Pressing a light kiss to his lips, I let it linger until the frustration left his shoulders, his arms sliding around my waist as he kissed me back.

My hands slipped into his hair, massively disheveled after all the discarded outfits. He sighed at my touch, deepening the kiss until eventually, we were forced to step apart, breathless.

X's fingers skimmed down my arms until he reached my wrists. He hooked his hands in mine. Then in a single motion, he swiped all the clothes from the bed, sending them tumbling to the floor.

"We don't have time—" I started.

"I need to rest," he said with a passive expression. "That's all. We have time for a *rest.*"

I doubted his intentions, but I went along with them anyway. As I curled against his warmth on the comforter, he stretched his arm over my shoulder and we lay together in silence.

"You've already been running the Trials for weeks. There's nothing different about today than any other day, except a few extra people will be watching."

"Months."

"What?"

"We've been watching, analyzing, testing the Candidates for months. A Uniqueness can take years to surface."

"Exactly. This public Trial hardly matters at all." I gave him my biggest smile. "And neither does the suit you wear to it. Just pretend you're getting dressed for a party."

"I don't like parties," Ranger X growled before he caught himself and fought back the annoyed expression for a more patient one. "And it's still a Trial, even if it's *mostly* for show. How the Candidates handle themselves in front of a large audience is part of their overall rating."

"Fine," I said. "Then there's only one solution."

Ranger X's expression reminded me of a lion that hadn't been fed in weeks. "Is that right?"

"Go naked."

It took a moment for the joke to sink in, and when it did, he raised eyebrow. "That's your solution?"

"If nothing fits properly, then I see no other choice." I shook my head in mock severity. "In fact, I insist you remove your suit this very instant."

He leaned toward me, his large form an intimidating wall of muscle. He raised a gentle finger to my chin and tipped my mouth upward until his lips were an inch from mine. "You always know what to say. What would I do without you?"

I had a sarcastic response all lined up and ready to go, but the way his black eyes glimmered as they looked into mine wiped all of my breath away. He leaned in, pressed a kiss to my forehead.

"I know you're stressed about this whole thing. The Trials are intense, the rules are changing, The Faction... well, it doesn't matter," I said. "Just so long as you're sure about me and I'm sure about you. Everything else will work out."

He moved his kiss from my forehead to my lips, lingering there. "Some days," he whispered, "you're the only thing in this world of which I'm sure."

CHAPTER 2

AN HOUR LATER, WE'D PROCRASTINATED until we couldn't procrastinate any longer. Unfortunately, we were no closer to deciding on a suit for X, even though he had needed to be out the door five minutes ago. I fiddled with the heart locket around my neck, a gift from my mother. While I'd had half of it my entire life, the second piece had been passed down to me from my aunts on the day I'd found out that I was a witch.

"I feel like a professor," he said, shaking his head. "I'm a Ranger. I'm not an idiot with a bowtie. Rangers are tough and—"

"Yeah, yeah, you're all burly and manly and all of that jazz." I pursed my lips. "But you still need clothes over your body."

"Then you pick. What about this one?"

Pasting a smile on my face as he turned around, I gave him the hugest thumbs up I could muster. "It's perfect."

Then again, he'd looked perfect in everything, and this suit was no exception. In fact, it was the very first one he'd tried on *three hours ago*. If he'd selected it then, we would've been spared a lot of time and energy, but no, he'd thrown it on the floor because it looked too *stuffy*.

It was probably all my fault. I'd let X borrow my self-populating closet—a spell that, when performed correctly, provided a girl with enough options to dress in a different outfit every day of her life. Unfortunately, it had the unforeseen side effect of freezing Ranger X with indecision

While X had been busy preparing for the Trials, I'd been busy studying. I had taken full advantage of his extended absences to put my head down, study with Gus, and earn the Mixology title bestowed upon me.

The closet was just one example of how far I'd come—a Styling Spell wasn't the hardest tool to master, but to make it function properly for a third party was tricky. I'd tried it on Poppy, my bright, bubbly cousin, and she'd strutted out dressed like a peacock and clucking like a chicken.

I'd run a few more tests before offering to try the spell out for X. I didn't think he'd be amused if it malfunctioned on the morning of his big day. However, when I'd managed to make it work successfully last week, even Gus had been pleased.

"How is Zin feeling?" Ranger X had refrained from asking about her since the public Trials had begun. To be fair, he had limited his interactions with all Candidates to avoid any illusion of bias.

"She's. . . " I trailed off as a noise filtering through the open window drew my attention away from the conversation. I looked outside, sighing as I caught sight of my cousin. "I suppose you can see for yourself how she's feeling."

"Oh, no." Ranger X joined me at the window. He pulled me into a hug and rested his hands over my stomach, his chin on my shoulder. "That's not good."

Zin paced outside the bungalow. Her angular features were even sharper than normal—gaunt, as if she'd lost weight from the stress. Though she was completely human at the moment, the grumbles coming from her throat sounded distinctly animal.

I wondered if her Uniqueness—the very thing that would make her stand out from the other Candidates—had been unearthed yet. Was it her ability to shift into a jaguar? Or something else entirely?

Her short bob cut against her chin, her dark eyes flashing with a glimmer of gold. From head to toe, she'd dressed in poisonous black clothing. Everything about her was dark except for her mumbled words, which sounded like a very colorful array of expletives.

I raised my window and stuck my head out. "Zin, are you okay?" I called. "You're growling."

She looked up, her eyes clouding into a storm of nerves, worry, stress. Instead of answering, she frowned, glared at the two of us, and stomped away.

I turned to Ranger X and shrugged. "She's been on edge lately."

"I can see that."

"It's just a lot, you know? She's been training for this all of her life. She might be the first female Ranger. That's a huge opportunity, but also a huge burden. All eyes will be on her."

"I know. She can handle it, Lily. Trust your cousin."

I sighed. It was a day full of hope, and a day full of terror. Change was hard, and the Trials were no exception.

"Good luck today," I said, resting my head against his chest. "You'll do great. I'll walk over with you if you'd like."

He stroked a hand through my hair, and I felt him nod. Before he could respond, the Comm device around his wrist vibrated, signaling a private message.

"I'm sorry." He pulled his hand out of my hair, brushed a kiss against my neck, and stepped back from our embrace. "I have to take this."

"Of course. You stay here; I'm going to check on Gus. Come down when you're ready."

Ranger X dove into his conversation before I left, his voice rumbling through the room as I closed the door. I hurried downstairs as fast as my heels would carry me.

As this was a highly anticipated event, there was more hoopla scheduled than ever: ceremonies, fancy clothes and dinners, awards and celebrations. Even the spectators dressed up. My cousins had kindly informed me that flip-flops were a no-go, so I'd dressed in formalwear for the occasion.

To top it off, the Trials would culminate in a grand ball, a masquerade-type event with gowns and tiaras and gloves. Very fancy, very exciting, very dramatic. The Isle had positively lit up with gossip and festivities the last few weeks, spreading enthusiasm from shore to shore.

For now, I kept things simple with a spaghetti-strap black dress that landed just above my knees, and a pastel pink shawl draped across my shoulders for a pop of color. I topped off the outfit with a set of new booties borrowed from Poppy.

"Gus," I said, reaching the ground level of the bungalow. "You look nice."

He glowered at me, looking up from his seat at the table in the middle of the storeroom. "No, I don't."

He turned his attention back to the knife in his hand. The tip was jagged as broken glass, and looked just as sharp—even from a distance. His fingers moved in quick, dangerous motions as he sliced through an exotic fruit on the table. I had no clue what he was making, and he didn't offer any explanation.

Though Gus could never, would never, be the Mixologist, he was the most knowledgeable person on The Isle when it came to ingredients and potions. I'd been learning just as fast as I could, but it was hard to keep up. A few months on The Isle didn't compare to a lifetime of Gus's experience.

He lived in this storeroom, adored it. Every row, every shelf, every column. Jars and vials filled to bursting with bright liquids and shimmering gasses adorned the walls. Flower petals and herbs stuffed into glass canisters had been slotted carefully into every available nook and cranny. The room felt alive, filled with the ghosts of hundreds and thousands of formerly growing, breathing plants.

"What are you making?" I sat down next to him, the small patterns of cut vines and leaves a good distraction from Ranger X's murmurings upstairs. "I'd love to help."

"None of your business."

"It *is* my business. I'm the Mixologist. I should be learning from you."

Gus threw his hands up in the air. "Fine, then help."

I reached over, pulled *The Magic of Mixology,* my beloved spellbook, close enough to read. The book was open to a page titled *Spells for the Lost.* "Did you lose something?"

Gus's face reddened. "No."

"Then why are you making this potion?"

"*I'm* lost, okay? I'm not looking for anything."

"Is that right?" I ran my finger over the list of ingredients, trying to memorize the potion. "Well, where are you trying to go?"

"Nowhere."

"Sorry, I don't follow."

"It's not a destination. I'm lost—completely clueless—on how to use this stupid thing." Gus threw a bowtie in my direction. It landed on the table with a light *puff* of fabric against wood. "*Stupid dress code.*"

I hid a laugh, recognizing the bowtie as the very same one Ranger X had tossed out my bedroom window an hour before. Picking up the fabric, I easily adjusted it and leaned over Gus. I paused, my hands an inch away from his neck. "May I?"

He gestured to go ahead, although the look on his face was one of excruciating pain.

"Where'd you get your tie?" I asked, keeping my expression neutral, knowing full well he'd picked it up off the ground and recycled it. My voice chirped innocently through the silent storeroom. I patted the polka-dotted bowtie into place. "It's very lovely."

"The stupid thing fell from the sky. Mimsey told me I had to wear one or I couldn't sit with her, so I took it as a sign."

"That Mimsey is full of tough love, huh? It won't kill you to wear a bowtie for her, you know."

"Who said anything about love?" Gus sliced the fruit faster. So fast he nearly cut off his fingers. "Speaking of, where's your boy toy?"

"X is not a boy toy. We're dating. That's all."

Gus rolled his eyes.

I stood up and rested my hands on the table. "Let's call a truce. I'll leave your love life alone if you leave mine alone. Now put your potion stuff away, and let's get going. Mimsey and Poppy are going to meet us, and they won't be happy if we're late."

Footsteps sounded on the stairs, sparing us any further conversation. However, when Ranger X stormed into the room, I had a whole new reason to worry. X's face was dark and volatile, his pupils dilated. He hardly glanced my way as he swept through the room like a thunderstorm.

My heart pounded. "Is everything okay?"

He turned an unreadable expression toward me. "Let's go. Now."

I scurried behind him. Gus followed, locking up the bungalow. The three of us left the pink-and-purple beach house behind—in silence, since Ranger X clearly was not in the mood for small talk. Gus shot me a glance, but I raised my shoulders in confusion.

X's legs carried him much faster than either Gus or I could move, and eventually I had to shout for him to wait up. He turned around at the sound of my voice. "Sorry, I was preoccupied."

"What was the Comm about?" I asked, slightly out of breath as I jogged toward him. "What's wrong?"

"There's been an escape," Ranger X said after a long pause. "One of the most dangerous criminals on The Isle broke free from prison twenty minutes ago. The day of the first public Trial?" He shook his head. "I don't like it. This isn't a coincidence."

"You said security will be tight at the Trials. Surely nobody would try anything on the first day?"

His eyes roved over me, stern, even a little sad, and he shook his head. "You don't understand, Lily. All of the security in the world can't protect us from *her*."

CHAPTER 3

I DIDN'T HAVE LONG TO WONDER about who Ranger X meant by *her* before we were off again. Retreating into his own thoughts, X picked up the pace, leaving Gus and me struggling to keep close to his heels as we crossed The Isle to the arena.

Normally, the white sand beaches glistened like diamonds, the sky a cotton candy blue, the clouds fluffy and bright. Today, a dark haze hung low over the tide. The salty air had a bitter taste to it, and for the first time in a long while, the lake breeze sent shivers across my skin.

When we arrived, Gus clomped through the masses of folks—witches and wizards, fairies and elves, pixies and even a few Companions—to find Mimsey.

"Lily, wait." Ranger X reached out and grasped my wrist as I turned to follow Gus. "I need to talk to you."

I paused. "I know you're busy. I'll just join my family for now."

"I'm sorry." His apology was heavy. "I'm sorry I can't tell you any more information. I don't *know* much more than I've already said, and I'm…"

He trailed off, and I could see the physical signs of stress. Under his dark, ruffled hair were eyes that lacked their typical light. Even when he forced a smile it looked tired and weak, nearly breaking my heart.

"You don't need to apologize for anything." I rested my fingertips against his cheek and brought him closer. "I understand."

He swept his lips across mine, sending tingles through my

body. "There's one more thing. I've assigned a Companion to sit in your box, and that is final. I wish I could be next to you, but since I can't, this is the next best option."

"I don't need a Companion; my entire family will be there."

"He'll be watching over you, and it's his job. I'm sorry. Until I can explain about the prisoner, I need you protected."

"What about you?"

He frowned. "What about me?"

"Your safety."

His jaw tightened. "Let her come for me."

"But—"

"I need to address the Candidates." He pulled me in hard, fast, and held me as if he'd never let go. My fingers grasped at his suit, squeezing tight. "But first, there's one more thing."

"What is it?"

"*This* is why I didn't want to change the rules," he said, letting go of me. He moved a foot away. A foot too far. "I have half a mind to cancel the Trials and bring you home with me. For good. That option would never have crossed my mind if I hadn't fallen for you."

"You can't let this . . . whatever, whoever it is win," I said, my voice cracking. I felt empty without his body against mine. "Fear, or evil, or whatever you want to call it. If you cancel the Trials, she'll win."

He looked down at his feet and cleared his throat. "I have to go."

"Everything will be okay," I said as he turned to walk away. "I promise. The Isle needs to see you and your team more than ever. We need to see people who love this island enough to dedicate their lives to protecting it. With everything that's been going on lately, this is a bright spot, a ray of hope."

Without looking back, Ranger X nodded, and then stepped onto the stage.

CHAPTER 4

STILL A BIT SHAKEN FROM Ranger X's words, I took my time locating the special box seats reserved for families and close friends of the Candidates.

"There she is!" Poppy called, waving me over. "Right here, Lily!"

I joined Mimsey, Poppy, and the rest of the West Isle Witches except for my grandmother, who hadn't yet arrived. I did my best to hide any lingering emotion on my face. Not that it was necessary, since everyone's adrenaline was running high today.

The air was filled with nerves, excitement, danger, and most importantly, pride. Pride for The Isle, for the Candidates, for a glimpse of light in a darkening world.

"I can't believe she's doing it." Mimsey clasped her hands to her face. "Zin, a Ranger. Golly gee whiz, that has a nice ring to it."

"Candidate," Trinket said. "She's only a Candidate, not a Ranger."

I watched as Mimsey glared at her sister. The pair were as opposite as opposites could be. If Mimsey was jelly—sweet and mushy and bright—Trinket was the peanut butter at the bottom of the jar. A little bit crusty, sort of old, and sometimes quite dry. Where Trinket was tall and willowy like a cattail, Mimsey sat short and squat and round.

"It's the truth," Trinket said, returning Mimsey's gaze with a stern one of her own. "The Trials are challenging. Most Candidates never become Rangers, and that's just a fact."

I laid a hand on Mimsey's arm before she could respond.

Tempers flared easily in this atmosphere. Even Trinket was more on edge than usual; her face was a little too pale, her lips a little too thin, her hands a little too agitated... and she was the queen of stoicism.

"Let it go," I said softly, for Mimsey's ears only.

She frowned but didn't comment.

I glanced at the rest of the group. "Anyone caught sight of Zin yet?"

"There! There!" Poppy pointed behind us. "All of the Candidates are arriving on the stage!"

I turned around to watch the whole extraordinary scene unfold. We were somewhere in the middle of The Isle, somewhat near The Forest. Most likely enhanced by magic, the arena had seats as high as the eye could see.

Closest to the pitch sat an array of boxed-in seats, family names scrawled across the front of each enclosure. The sign plate on our box read "West Isle Witches." From our primo seats, we could see a raised platform in the center of a grassy field that resembled a football stadium.

"Have they announced what will be happening yet?" I squinted, wishing I'd brought binoculars strong enough to see the expression on Ranger X's face.

"They don't tell us," Poppy said. "It's a secret until the day of the event. Well, most of the Trials are secret actually, since they happen offstage. The Rangers observe Candidates in their daily lives, sometimes before the Candidates are even aware they're being considered."

"Times are a-changin', that's for sure." The words sounded wise, but they were a little hard to take seriously coming from the mouth of my pipsqueak grandmother, a feisty old witch named Hettie who'd worn light-up "Z's" strapped to her head like antlers. She stepped through the door into the West Isle Witches box and grinned. "This is the start of a whole new world."

"Hi, Hettie," chorused a handful of voices. I joined in, waving my grandmother up front to an open seat next to me.

Hettie poked her way into the box, brushing aside a few of Trinket's other children. All six of them were scrambling for a look at their oldest sister.

"Out of my way, munchkins." Hettie threw a few elbows. "I've got a granddaughter to watch."

The kids groaned, but they parted to allow their grandmother passage. Hettie, with gray hair marching across her head in curly little rows, was barely a head taller than any of the children. She was known to tweak noses and tug ears if the children didn't move fast enough.

For this occasion, she'd worn a particularly glamorous outfit. An all-purple suit with a violet bandana tied across her forehead, the glowing "Z's" bouncing enthusiastically over a glittery plastic headband. Her earrings dangled so low that the bottoms brushed her shoulders, the silvery strands *thwacking* anyone who dared move too close to her side.

"Nice shirt," I said, gesturing to the back of her velvet tracksuit. "Where'd you get it?"

Hettie pointed to her back where the word *Zinnifred* had been printed with diamonds. "Thrift store."

"I thought Zin's real name was Zinnia?" I asked, raising my eyebrow. "Who is *Zinnifred*?"

Trinket let out a long sigh. "Her name is Zinnia, mother."

"I got this on sale," Hettie explained. "If I wanted the real deal, I'd have had to order it special, and it would've cost extra coins. I'm not made of money, you know. It's not my fault she was named Zinnia instead of Zinnifred; that one's on Trinket."

I turned my attention back to the events on stage. All of the Candidates had lined up on the platform in a single row. They stood perfectly still, hands clasped behind their backs, postures rigid. There was something utterly military about the whole thing.

"There's my favorite tush in the universe," Hettie said. "He looks good up there, doesn't he, Lily?"

Scanning the arena, her eyes landed on none other than my boyfriend. She whistled so loudly everyone in the auditorium winced, including the person attached to said rear end. Ranger X squinted into the crowd in my grandmother's direction, looking for the source of the noise. I hid behind her small frame and stared directly at the word Zinnifred until the coast was clear.

"Nice, huh, Lily? I like that suit on him, even though he looks like a professor. I always did have a thing for teachers." My grandma smiled. "You picked a studmuffin."

I groaned, my face turning redder by the second as Trinket's children looked up at me, their faces filling one by one with disgust. At their age, cooties were real.

"Mother!" Trinket caught sight of her children's wandering eyes. She muttered a curse that made all the children under the age of ten clasp their hands over their ears. "Watch your language, or I'll have to keep the Earmuff Enchantment on them all day."

"Loosen up," Hettie mumbled, but she refrained from commenting further. She did, however, elbow me and point toward the stage. "What is that man doing up there? He looks like he's having a seizure."

My eyes were glued to Ranger X. He prowled through the Candidates like a ringmaster, sizing up the crowd, the Rangers, the arena. When he reached the microphone set front and center, he paused, hands hanging loosely by his sides. He looked calm and confident, and if I hadn't witnessed his anxiety minutes before, I would have never guessed anything was wrong.

"No, look to *the right*," Hettie said. "I *know* you like looking at X, but I'm talking about the guy at the end of the line. His name is Trent."

I followed her pointed finger. "What is he doing?"

"Heck if I know."

Hettie and I watched the last Candidate in the lineup. He was average in size, broad shouldered with a ruddy face and red hair. He was neither handsome nor ugly, but somewhere in between. It was the robotic motions of his hands, however, that held my gaze.

Trent's fingers jerked in twitchy motions, the polar opposite of the other Candidates' absolute stillness. Zin stood next to him, her posture so rigid her chest barely rose and fell with each breath.

Then Zin moved. Her eyes, ever so slightly, flicked toward Trent. They rested on him for a long moment as she watched his odd behavior. Even from here, I could see the passive, empty expression on Trent's face, his eyes staring into a realm nobody else could see.

"Ladies and gentlemen," Ranger X began, drawing everyone's attention. Even Trent stilled, the Candidate's gaze refocusing on X. "Today, we make history."

The audience quieted to nothing. Even the children were silent. We waited and watched, the air brimming with anticipation.

"Before you, we stand—ready to protect our island at all costs. Today we have ten Candidates, each with something unique to offer. They have trained hard. The process ahead promises to be a grueling one. Some of them have already sacrificed great things in the name of The Isle." Ranger X's gaze slid toward Zin so quickly I might have imagined it. "To be standing here today is a feat of its own, and I want you all to join me in welcoming our Ranger Candidates to the Trials."

"Let's get to the good stuff," Hettie muttered while Ranger X gave his prepared speech in a powerful, captivating voice. "I want to see some blood."

"I wasn't told there would be blood!" I bit my lip. Having heard bits and pieces of this speech a hundred times, I zoned out, focusing on Hettie. "I thought these Trials weren't dangerous."

"You're crazy," Hettie said, giving me a look of disbelief. "Of course they'll be dangerous. I mean, it's not like in the really old days when people died in these events left and right. But, you know,

I'm always hoping for a little smacking around. Makes for a more exciting show."

"I didn't think anybody was in danger of dying."

Hettie rolled her eyes. "They're *not*. That's what I mean, the Ranger program's gone soft."

A wave of nausea flooded my stomach as I surveyed the lineup. Zin was the smallest of the bunch except for one—short male with a missing front tooth, slanted eyebrows, and a smile that bordered on crazy. If things got physical, Zin's size wouldn't exactly set her up for success.

Ranger X continued on, introducing each of the Candidates. Zin was the only female in the lineup, as expected. I recognized two males from random run-ins around The Isle, but the others I'd only read about in the media. The local newspaper had posted continual Candidate coverage since the Trials had been announced; it was all people had been talking about for weeks.

When X finally wrapped up the introductions, he went on to explain what would happen next. There would be five public Trials, one per week. Closing ceremonies were to follow the final Trial, and the whole thing would culminate with a masquerade ball.

I glanced at the crowd, the seats filled to bursting with an excited sea of bodies pressed together. Rooting, cheering for the Candidates. It helped that there was no direct competition between the Candidates—all of them could become Rangers if they made it through the Trials. A highly unlikely event, but a possibility.

"It seems a little bit selfish to put the Candidates through this," I said. "If it's only for the fanfare. It feels a little like a dog and pony show."

"On the contrary." Hettie crossed her arms, looked up at me. Though her eyes were shining, there was an underlying severity that caught my attention. "These Candidates need to see the people they're protecting. They need to love The Isle more than anything. From the deepest, most primal level, they need to understand those who inhabit it—human and otherwise. They need to feel appreciated and essential. Otherwise, why would these men—and now women—give their lives to a career filled with danger?"

Her words soaked in as I caught a glimpse of Zin. Though she still hadn't moved from the militant position, she tilted her chin high, a calmness flashing through her eyes. Zin had been wired with nerves for the last few months but now, finally, she stood where she belonged.

Ranger X introduced the Trial Masters, a group of three judges dressed in all black robes, masks over their faces. Their identities remained completely anonymous for obvious reasons.

"Let the Trials begin..." Ranger X set the microphone down and stepped back.

The three judges strode to the center of the arena and moved back to back. Extending their hands, they spoke in low tones, raising their arms in sync with their words.

Black smoke rose from the outer edges of the pitch, masking the arena in clouds so thick I could taste bitter metallic flavors. Since I couldn't see anyway, I closed my eyes and waited.

It was only a minute before the smoke vanished as quickly as it'd arrived. I coughed and blinked a few times, along with those around me were also coughing, waving their hands, and struggling to see. When my sight finally returned, I blinked a few more times, unable to believe my eyes.

Where a patch of empty grass had been moments before, the arena was now filled with a series of obstacles. Flames shot from one end of the playing field, while boulders rolled across the other. Ropes appeared from the sky, seemingly attached to air, and swung violently back and forth over a spike-laden field.

"Omigosh," Poppy said, then keeled over in a dead faint.

I wouldn't admit it, but I was glad she fainted first because I was feeling light-headed, too.

"It's an obstacle course," Hettie said, rubbing her hands together. "Yippee skippee."

I bent over my cousin, pulling out a small vial of Antidote that I kept on me. Similar to Advil or Aspirin, it was a potion that had a strong healing vibe for any minor illness, including but not limited to nausea, fainting, cuts, and bruises. A quick sniff and Poppy was back on her feet and straightening her dress in no time.

"Whew," she said, taking a few deep breaths. "Guess I'm not cut out for this Ranger business."

I silently agreed. Once I was sure Poppy was fine on her feet, I turned to face the arena. Zin stood on top of a tall pedestal along with the rest of the Candidates, perched in her ready position. I held my breath as Ranger X raised a whistle to his lips and blew, the shrill sound echoing over the silent crowd.

As soon as the first reverberation left his whistle, the Candidates were off, racing through the minefield of obstacles. By the time the sound had faded into the distance, the crowd was going wild.

I froze, a hand clasped over my heart as the scene unfolded before us. No longer was I rooting for Zin to be the best, the fastest, the cleverest—now, I prayed that she would make it out alive.

CHAPTER 5

"HOW LONG DOES THE TRIAL last?" I asked. The large clock on the wall, a magic-enhanced version of a sundial, signaled thirty minutes had passed. "They've got to be exhausted."

"This is nothing." Hettie waved a hand at the arena. "I once danced for eight hours straight. And *that* is harder than it sounds. I had blisters for a year, and I think I'm permanently missing a toenail from that night."

I scrunched up my nose, watching as the Candidates scaled sheer rock faces, hurtled over moving boulders, dodged spurts of fire. "I'm not sure that's the same thing."

"Sure it is." Hettie did a little jig. "My feet were moving just as quick as theirs. Only the fire was missing from my performance. Maybe next time I'll get a fire-breathing baton. I wonder if there's a dragon trainer who'd—"

Hettie's recollections were interrupted by a huge, collective inhalation from the crowd. My heart skipped a few beats as Poppy grasped my arm, squeezing so tight I nearly lost the circulation in my biceps.

On the pitch, one of the Candidates, a handsome man by the name of Dillan Dartmouth, had scaled a wall, the highest wall in the arena, when a pile of boulders hurtled at him out of nowhere.

The boulders rolled from the far side of the arena, crushing paths in the grass, taking down small trees as they went. If the rocks hit the wall, the whole thing would surely crumble, and the Candidate would go down in a heap of rubble.

Dillan wobbled at the top, trying to steady himself and get a firm grip where he stood. He was in the lead, the rest of the Candidates lagging so far behind they'd never catch up. He stood alone, trapped. I wanted to help him, but I couldn't—nobody could.

I was actually thankful that Zin had struggled to cross the rope mine—a section of the course filled with heavy strings dangling from the sky. Spikes poked up from the ground below, forcing the Candidates to swing straight through.

The first boulder hit the wall with a resounding thud. Dillan wobbled, bending in half to grip the slick wall with his fingers. The second boulder hit shortly after, jolting him from his perch. He fell off the side, his fingers grasping at the wall, white as bone.

Poppy screamed as he swung. Dillan groped futilely at the air with his free hand while his grip with the other weakened. When the third boulder hit, the impact was too much, and he lost what little hold he had on the wall. With a gut-wrenching cry, he began to fall.

I shut my eyes and curled my body into Poppy's. I couldn't stand to watch, couldn't stand to listen.

"It's okay," Hettie said finally, shaking me by the shoulders. "He's alive. A bit broken up, but he'll be fine."

I peeked through one eyelid at the crowd, not daring to look at the fallen Candidate. "Why is everyone watching? This is horrible!"

"You forget, sugarpants. We have magic." Hettie winked. "The Healers are on hand, and they'll get to him quickly. We're allowed to be a little rougher than your human friends."

I allowed myself the quickest of glances toward the pitch, relieved to see the Healers had already arrived, strapped Dillan onto a stretcher, and carried him off of the field. Meanwhile the competition raged on.

My nerves, however, had shattered. The possibility of injury—

or worse—had become real. Too real. I excused myself from the group to go wait outside. I couldn't bear to watch the events unfold knowing that Zin was wrapped in the middle of it all. Ranger X had promised to watch out for her, but *how*? How could he promise that?

I'd stepped halfway out of the box when a patch of red hair caught my attention, stopping me in my tracks. At the far end of the pitch stood two Candidates—Trent, the one with the strange, robotic movements, and a second I didn't recognize.

They were tucked behind several obstacles that shielded them from Ranger X's view. I stepped back into the box, swiped a program from the closest seat, and matched the second Candidate's face to a picture that identified him as Raymon. If I'd seen clearly, Trent had just whispered into Raymon's ear.

I pushed forward until I reached Hettie's side, keeping my eyes locked on the scene before me. Trent's fingers snaked out, grasped Raymon's hand, and then let go just as quickly.

"Did you guys see that?" I raised a hand to point toward Trent and Raymon. "What is Trent doing?"

Hettie was focused on a section of the course currently sizzling under flames, while Poppy was busy examining her swimsuit tan lines. They looked to where I was pointing, but it was too late. The Candidates had moved on to the next phase in the Trial.

"But why would they stop to talk when flames are shooting everywhere and…"

Poppy looked at me like I was crazy. "Maybe they were saying good luck. It's not against the rules to *talk*."

"Maybe," I agreed, though something didn't feel right about it.

Although I'd intended to leave, I couldn't tear my eyes away this time. Zin and her fellow participants dipped, dodged, and ducked, while Trent and Raymon pressed onward until eventually, Trent pulled ahead and left Raymon behind. The latter's pace noticeably slowed, turning sluggish as he struggled to climb a tree.

My palms were slick with sweat as Raymon floundered, his arm movements clumsy and slow. When he finally summited the tree, he paused, sucking in oxygen as if he couldn't catch his breath.

My stomach plunged. If I had a way to contact Ranger X, I would—something felt *off* about this whole thing. The point was moot, however, since X's Comm device was set to a "Rangers Only" channel to stave off miscellaneous interruptions.

Similarly, the arena had a magic-dampening charm layered over the grasses to prevent the Candidates from using spells. During the public Trials, magic was not allowed for participants or spectators within the arena.

Ranger X stood at the head of the stage, arms crossed, focused thoroughly on the events before him. A sharp gasp rose from the crowd as Raymon reached a hand out to swipe for the first rope dangling from the sky. A sea of spikes rested below, and in order to cross, he'd have to use the swinging ropes.

But he missed the rope entirely.

It shouldn't have been difficult. Even I could've grabbed hold of the first rope but somehow, he missed—an inexcusable miss, considering that all Candidates were preselected, and peak physical fitness was expected from the Candidates at this stage of the Trials.

Even so, the next time he swung he missed again. And then again. Moving at the speed of molasses, he swung a fourth time, spiraling out of control.

He wobbled dangerously, drunkenly, on the edge of the tree branch. As the crowd's attention focused on Raymon and his struggle to remain upright, the rest of the Candidates were forgotten.

"What is he doing?" Poppy said in horror. "He's going to fall!"

Raymon reached a hand to his forehead. Sitting down hard, he balanced against the trunk of the tree and let his head sink into his hands, as if whatever was inside was hurting him so badly that he couldn't see straight.

My chest constricted, and I couldn't speak. Couldn't look away, couldn't move, couldn't respond.

Then a cry so raw, so soulful rattled through the crowd, beginning from Raymon and permeating the arena. Struck silent by fear, I couldn't move. Ranger X leaped from the stage, hurtling himself across the pitch. He sprinted faster than I'd ever seen him move before, bypassing one obstacle after the next as he raced toward Raymon.

If there were any doubt about X's physical prowess, it vanished after his showing in the arena. Pure athleticism and grace, he raced past the fire, the darts, the boulders, and pulled up to a stop below the tree where Raymon sat rocking, lost in the pain inside of his head.

Ranger X called up to him several times in a voice loud enough for everyone to hear, but Raymon gave no response. Someone in the crowd screamed. And then there was silence.

"Look!" Poppy pointed toward the center of the course in horror, and I turned to find Zin rushing back toward Raymon and Ranger X. She scaled the wall from which Dillan had fallen, moving as fast as she could toward the tree.

A cry froze on my lips as she reached for the ropes and began swinging back through the jungle of spikes. She moved fast, her small figure agile. The rest of the Candidates froze. Except for Trent, who moved onward. Forward. Never once looking behind as he pushed into first place.

Zin was mere feet away from the tree when it happened.

Raymon stilled on the branch for a long moment, a moment that'd be permanently frozen in time. The crowd inhaled as one when Raymon's body tipped left, farther left, his weight off-balance, and he fell, hurtling to the ground below.

Ranger X moved like lightning. Maybe he'd anticipated the fall, or maybe his reflexes were just that sharp, because he reached the place where Raymon would've landed on the spikes in an instant, catching the man's body.

X grunted under the impact. His knees bent under the weight as he staggered toward a patch of soft-looking grass and laid Raymon down. Kneeling next to him, X gestured for the Healers, who were already halfway there, to come assist.

From my seat far, far away, I could see the blueish tinge of lips, the emptiness across Raymon's face. He didn't flinch, didn't move, didn't breathe.

And then from somewhere deep within the crowd, a female burst into tears, a guttural cry that pierced the sky. She went hysterical, crying and screaming, until someone pulled her away from the auditorium.

But long after she was gone, the weight of her words hung heavy in the air.

"He's dead."

CHAPTER 6

THE CROWD MOVED AS ONE, a throng of bodies fighting to reach the exits. With the exception of one. While the rest of islanders evacuated, I reached over the edge of the box's railings, my fingers stretching into the arena as I called for X.

My cries were swallowed by the cacophony rising from the bleachers. The stands sagged under the stampeding feet, but I didn't move. Ranger X stood below, his eyes scanning the crowds as he blew his whistle and shouted instructions that only the Candidates could hear.

"X!" I yelled. "Please, X—"

My cries were cut short by a tree trunk–sized arm colliding with my stomach, crushing the air from my lungs. My breath whooshed out in a grunt, and before I could speak, someone had flung me over their shoulder and started a march for the exit.

"Apologies, Miss Lily, but you're coming with me." The man who'd scooped me up was big—broad-shouldered with lots of dark hair on his head, arms, and chest.

I'd forgotten about the Companion assigned by Ranger X. Companions were shifters of all sorts who went through Ranger training, and then typically entered the field of security, watching over high-risk targets—and now me, apparently.

As it turned out, I'd had more experience with Companions than I'd ever known. Just recently Hettie had explained that the man who I'd assumed was my father wasn't anything more than a randomly assigned Companion. It'd been a shock, but in retrospect, not as surprising as I'd once thought.

"Put me down," I said to the big hairball of a man. "I have to talk to Ranger X."

"I have instructions, Miss. I'm to bring you to the bungalow and stand watch until relieved of my duties."

"No! This can't *wait*. I saw something, and I need to talk to Ranger X."

As he lumbered forward, I realized he had many distinct mannerisms of a bear. It would also explain the dark hair everywhere. He didn't stop, so I pounded on his back. *Nothing*, not even a flinch.

"Hettie," I called. "Help!"

My grandmother licked her lips as if she wouldn't mind being strapped across the back of a big, strong man. "Look at that, we've got ourselves a lift home."

"No, Hettie, I need to get down!"

She reached a wrinkled hand out, grasping my wrist with surprising strength. The Companion kept right on marching, and Hettie kept holding on tight. Eventually, she just dragged behind us like a sled.

"Stop, you're hurting my grandmother," I said. "She's old and fragile."

The Companion looked over his shoulder, surprise blooming on his face when he noticed the gray-haired lady being dragged behind him. "Please let go, Miss Hettie."

My grandmother ignored him. She was a little old, but not the slightest bit frail, and her spunky spirit made up for the number of years lining her face. Rising onto her tiptoes, she whispered into my ear, "It has started, Lily. The beginning of the end."

"The end?" I echoed. "The end of what?"

"Don't fight it, just go with him," she said. "I'll explain later."

"But—" I started to argue, but Hettie pinched the Companion

on the behind and shouted for him to *giddyup*. The Companion lurched forward, leaving my argument trailing in the wind.

I looked for Poppy, X, Mimsey… even Zin, but there were too many faces blurring my view. Finally, we reached the clear pastures beyond the arena, yet he still didn't listen to my pleas to be set down.

Once at the bungalow, he dropped me inside the door. Then he stood, and he stared. Directly at me.

"Can you at least turn around?" I said. "You're not even blinking, and it's freaking me out."

He had the grace to blush. Without arguing, he turned to face the waters lapping against the shore, his body so large it barricaded the entire doorway.

"May I go out to the bar?" I asked. "I need coffee."

"No."

"What if I get customers?"

"They can come inside."

I slumped in Gus's normal seat at the storeroom table. My mind spun, working on another argument for why the Companion should leave me alone in my own house. Until my attention was stolen by something else entirely.

On the table sat a flower. A gorgeous, huge bloom—freshly picked, judging by the rich, full scent of the petals. It hadn't been here when we'd left; I had watched Gus clean up all the ingredients, sweeping the table empty before locking the door behind him.

No one should have been inside the storeroom during the ceremony. Only Gus and I had a key. Everyone else on The Isle had been occupied at the arena, and I was pretty sure Gus wasn't the flowery type of guy.

My fingers shook as I rested them on the table, bending closer to examine the flower. I used a special examination technique Gus had been teaching me, one which utilized all five senses.

After my examination was complete, I still couldn't find anything wrong with the flower. It smelled like a flower, it felt like a flower, it looked like a flower… it just didn't make sense why *this* flower was on my storeroom table.

On the mainland, we called this flower the lily. The calla lily, to be exact.

Gus had pulled this very same bloom out during my first day on The Isle, except his had been dead—dried petals contained in one of the hundreds of vials on the shelves. Even then, he'd instructed me to never touch it. One of his most valuable flowers, he'd said.

I wondered where this particular one had come from; I'd never seen these blooms on The Isle before. They were rare here, and not readily available.

"What is that?" Gus asked through the doorway. He was hidden behind the Companion's large frame. "Move, this is my storeroom. Please."

"I'm sorry, sir, but—" The Companion's explanation was cut short when Gus raised his cane and poked him in the stomach.

As the Companion bent over in surprise, Gus marched past him. He didn't gloat, nor did he apologize, he merely stomped right up to the table and glared at me. "Where did you get this bloom?"

"It was here when I arrived," I said. "I was going to ask you the same thing!"

"You watched me lock that door," Gus said, his eyes narrowed. "I always leave the table clean."

"I *know* that," I said. "But you and I are the only ones with keys to this place. If it wasn't either of us, then someone broke into the bungalow."

"To deliver a flower?" Gus leaned over the table, performing the same assessment as I had, using all five of his senses. I'd stopped at *taste,* but not Gus. He cut a small sliver of stem from the plant and licked it. "Yep. That's the real thing," he confirmed.

"Who would've broken in while we were away? And why?"

Gus sat down at the table next to me, his eyes so focused on the lily I thought it would wither under his gaze. "Where do lilies come from?"

"Um, are we talking about the flower?"

Gus raised his eyebrows and let my question linger. "It's a curious thing, this appearing here. Today, of all days."

"But—"

"Put it in water, care for it." He stood, stretching his creaky joints as he surveyed the single bloom on the table. "Just because we don't know where this flower came from, it doesn't mean that the bloom is any less powerful. Knowing its history won't change anything."

"Of course it changes things. Someone is sending us a message with this flower. But are they trying to help us or threaten us?"

"I'm here to help you in any way I can." Gus gave the faintest of smiles. "That doesn't mean I have all the answers."

CHAPTER 7

THE MOOD TURNED SOMBER WITH the onset of darkness. My ever-present Companion didn't once move away from his post at the door, except for a side-step to the left which allowed a few guests to pass through at my request.

Gus had arrived first, then Mimsey. They now spoke in low tones beside the fireplace, roaring flames crackling behind them. Poppy had arrived shortly after her mother and now sat across the table from me, her face white as sand, her fingers pulling apart a napkin into miniscule shreds. Darkness had set hours ago.

"Are you okay?" I reached over, sweeping the napkin pieces into my hand. She could've stuffed a pillow with how much paper she'd gone through. "You haven't eaten anything all day."

She scrunched up her nose. Even though Poppy was a vampire, the sight of blood made her nauseous. "I don't like violence," she whispered. "And Zin was right there…"

I stood up. "Since we're stuck here behind Bozo at the door, let's make the best of it. C'mon, let me show you something I've been working on the past few weeks."

"What is it?" A flash of interest appeared in her eyes. "A potion?"

"Remember that glowing tea you got from Harpin during my first week on The Isle?"

"Heck yeah!" She grinned enthusiastically. "I glowed like a lighthouse. I'm pretty sure everybody was jealous. They all asked about it."

"Yep, that's the one!" I forced a smile.

Poppy had glowed all right, but it'd been more of a toxic green than a healthy shine. Most likely, everyone had asked how she was feeling out of concern for her health, not out of envy.

Which was why I'd set out to fix it. "I've been working on something even better. I'm going to call it Glo. Without the "w" because that's edgier."

"Most definitely." She clapped her hands. "I need to see this."

I stood up to retrieve the potion from my shelves. Before my fingers found the correct bottle, the Companion stood to the side and allowed another figure through the door. The man we'd been waiting to hear from all afternoon.

"Hello," Ranger X said, his expression unreadable. His eyes found mine before continuing around the room. He gave a brief nod to my guests. "I'm sure you have lots of questions, but first, Zin is safe. She is with the rest of the Candidates at an undisclosed location this evening."

Relief washed over Mimsey's face, but Poppy looked more concerned than ever.

"Undisclosed... like a safe house?" she asked. "Why?"

Ranger X shifted his weight from one foot to the other. He murmured something to the Companion. The latter nodded, then stepped outside and closed the door behind him. Once the lock clicked shut, X addressed the group again.

"Raymon didn't make it." X's voice remained even, though an underlying anger slid beneath the calm surface. "The Healers were there immediately as you witnessed, but even so, it was too late."

Poppy sucked in a breath. Her face remained passive but her hands went to work tearing napkins like a paper shredder on steroids. "How did he die? Why do the rest of the Candidates need to be locked away? What's going on?"

Ranger X looked to me as he responded. "We made an arrest."

Mimsey leaped to her feet. "An arrest? But that means... that means someone did something wrong. Are you telling us this was *murder?*"

"This information must not be repeated. I have my men relaying the same message to the other families—" he paused, glanced at Gus, "—and friends, of the Candidates."

"I still don't understand. They were in the arena with everyone watching. *How* could this have happened?" Poppy's voice faded as she turned to look at me, understanding dawning in her eyes. "Lily, you saw something. She tried to tell us, to tell you, but she couldn't."

Ranger X's eyes flicked toward me, a hint of curiosity in his gaze. "We've arrested Trent and placed him in the most secure prison cell we have. When we watched the video recording of the Trial, we noticed Trent speaking to Raymon minutes before his death."

"They were not only speaking, they also made an exchange. Trent grabbed Raymon's hand, and I didn't realize it at the time, but I think he gave him something."

"A Poison Pill disguised as a Strength Solution," Ranger X said. "We're assuming Trent handed Raymon the pill, explaining that it would help him through the obstacles."

"Why would Raymon have believed Trent?" I shook my head. "That makes no sense. A random Candidate handed over a pill, and he just took it blindly?"

"I spoke to the other Candidates, and it appears Raymon and Trent formed some sort of friendship before the Trials—an alliance of sorts—thereby creating a trust between them."

"Lily's right, this doesn't make sense," Poppy said, tapping her fingers against the table. "Why would he take the time to befriend him?" Poppy paused, her eyes widening. "Unless that was his plan all along."

"I thought all of the Candidates were screened thoroughly," Mimsey said. "Wouldn't something have come up in Trent's background…"

As she trailed off, Ranger X's face hardened. "Everyone was

screened as thoroughly as possible. We've watched them for months, dug back as early as history would allow on each Candidate. I know Zin was allergic to blueberries for a year as a child and Dillan broke his arm in three places at the age of five. Nothing turned up."

"I didn't mean anything by it," Mimsey said quickly. "I just don't understand."

"Did you talk to Trent and ask him why?" I diverted the conversation away from Mimsey and back to the murder at hand. "Why he'd do such a thing in plain sight?"

"That's the oddity." Ranger X looked at the floor, his stance wide, shoulders straight. "I talked with Trent for a long time, and he claims to have no recollection of *anything* after he stepped foot in the arena."

I blinked, swallowing back my surprise. "And do you believe him?"

X sighed, the energy seeping from his very being. "I don't know."

"What does your gut tell you?"

"I don't have the answers," he said sharply. Then he ran a hand over his forehead and apologized. "It's *convenient* he doesn't remember anything, sure. But it seems like he believes it."

"Aarik said the same thing, you know," I whispered. During my first weeks on the island, someone who I'd called a friend had tried to kidnap me. His name was Aarik, and he'd very nearly succeeded. "You believed him."

Ranger X's stood straighter, and I watched as he sifted through his memories of Aarik and the poisoned smoke. "That was different. We could *see* the effects of the potion on Aarik. It ran through his veins, no doubt about it."

"Have you checked Trent?"

"He's healthy as a unicorn. Nothing in his veins that shouldn't be there," Ranger X said with a weary shake of his head. "Aarik went through an intensive detoxification process after we took him into custody to rid his body of poison. It altered his mind, and the recovery process is grueling."

"All magic leaves some sort of trace," I pointed out. "If there are no signs of magic, does that mean Trent acted on his own accord? Is he flat-out lying?"

"Trent will remain on high-alert lockdown until we can figure out the answer," Ranger X said. "All spells, all potions leave a trace, that is correct, but—"

Poppy jumped in before he could finish the thought. "How will you ever be able to tell if he's telling the truth?"

"Regardless of the *how*, or the *why*, Trent is responsible for the death of a Candidate, as far as I'm concerned. And that is an unforgivable offense."

The room fell into a somber silence. Gus threw another log on the fire, and Mimsey shifted, her flowing dress billowing about her body.

"What I still don't understand," Poppy said eventually, "is why you have to keep Zin locked away. If you've already found your murderer. . . "

"We *believe* we've found him. It's not absolutely certain. The investigation is ongoing."

"Are you afraid something else is going to happen?" I asked. "Is that why you're locking the Candidates away?"

Ranger X glanced my way, his jaw working as he debated which answer to give. "It's better to be safe than sorry."

"Well, we should be going," Mimsey said. "I wanted to make sure Lily wasn't alone, but now that X is here... let's go, Poppy."

"Do you want me to go?" Poppy asked me. She stood and nodded toward the couch. "I can stay if you'd like."

"She'll have a guard all night," Ranger X said, thumbing toward the door where the Companion waited outside. "He has been instructed not to leave."

I put my hands on my hips. "I'll be fine. You've already put Trent away."

Mimsey scrunched up her nose. "I really thought it'd be you staying, X."

X ran a hand through his hair. "I'm planning to stay as long as I can, but there's a lot of work to be done. I am needed at Ranger HQ."

"Okay, people, I'm an adult!" I waved my hands at all the guests. "Mimsey and Poppy, go home—your beds are much more comfortable than my couch. Same with you, Gus."

"I'll walk them home," Gus said. "Keep an eye out tonight, you hear me, Lily?"

I walked the group to the door, giving the Companion a polite elbow-nudge to the ribs until he moved out of the way. Standing next to him on the front steps, I waved, watching the retreating backs of my family. It wasn't until I returned to the storeroom that the strangeness of Gus's goodbye hit me.

It hit Ranger X, too. He leaned against the edge of the table, one eyebrow raised. "Since when do you and Gus speak in code?"

"What do you mean?"

"Keep an eye out tonight?"

"Cryptic? I think he was just being blunt," I said with a forced laugh. Since I had no clue what Gus was talking about, it wasn't hard to feign confusion. "You know, like saying be careful in Gus's own way."

"Mm-hmm."

Ranger X didn't sound convinced. I took my time shutting the door, leaving the Companion outside. I wasn't being entirely honest with X—not because I wanted to lie, but because I'd been *instructed* to lie.

A few weeks back, Hettie had introduced me to a small group called The Core—a company created to fight back against The Faction. My grandmother had expressly forbidden me to discuss it with anyone. Including X and my cousins. I hated keeping secrets from them, but for now, I couldn't figure out a way around it.

Though he didn't seem to buy my explanation, Ranger X moved on to greener topics. "Are you hungry?"

"I could eat."

"You can always eat." He smiled, the air warming as the tension dissipated. "Let's eat outside."

We made our way to the bar area attached to one end of the bungalow. It was mostly outside with an awning over the top boasting the words *Magic & Mixology*. The place wasn't fancy—a few barstools, a shining counter, several tables and chairs. The water was visible from here, the waves churning beyond the sand.

Cracking a few eggs over a pan, X set to work sizzling up an omelet while I put on a pot of coffee. We moved effortlessly together in the kitchen, a synchronized sort of dance that'd come from weeks of practice.

After a bit of silence, Ranger X threw a few slabs of bacon on the skillet and turned to face me. "What aren't you telling me?"

I focused on the water dripping from the kettle, seeping through the coffee grounds, drizzling into the pot. "What do you mean?"

Ranger X sucked in a breath and licked his lips, his eyes torn between amusement and concern. He sliced a few chives over the omelet. I could only hope that his hunger would overpower his curiosity, buying me time until after dinner to come up with some answers.

In the meantime, I opted for distraction. "What are we?" I blurted, turning to stare right back at him. "You and me. Us."

Ranger X blinked, his motions stiffening as he flipped the egg mixture over, sizzling it in leftover grease from the bacon. "What do you mean?"

I wasn't proud of using this technique, but the secret I was keeping from Ranger X was big. Huge. Important. And since I couldn't keep secrets, I had to avoid them entirely.

"Well, we hang out. We kiss. We do things like *this...*" I waved my hands at the way we'd seamlessly prepared a meal while hardly muttering a word. "*Couple* things."

"Yes," he said, sliding the eggs onto a plate and setting it on the bar. "Do you like couple things?"

"Yeah, I do." I grabbed some forks and the jar of sugar for the coffee. "But that doesn't answer my question. I called you my boyfriend today and honestly, it felt a little weird. We've never talked about it, and I didn't want to assume anything."

We each slid onto a bar stool, our elbows brushing against one another as we shared a meal from one gigantic platter. I picked at the bacon, he went straight for the eggs.

Ranger X chewed thoughtfully. "If you like doing couple things, then we're a couple."

"Does that mean you're my boyfriend?"

"Is that what you want it to mean?"

My face turned red, and it wasn't because of the heat swirling up from my food. "Um, I don't know."

"What's going on, Lily?" Though it looked painful, Ranger X set his fork down. "Did I say the wrong thing?"

"No, not at all." Spinning to face him, I sighed. "I like you *a lot*. I'm not trying to force you into anything, I'm just... I'm trying to understand what these new rules mean. You're allowed to have a relationship now. I'm just not sure if that's what you want."

He pulled me closer, chair and all. Running a hand over my cheek, a soft smile curved his lips upward. "I wouldn't have turned an entire set of laws upside down if I didn't think you were worth it." He paused, picking up his fork and stabbing his eggs to death. "If you want to be with me, then I would like to be your boyfriend."

Despite the crazy night, the horrible day, the fact that this island was tumbling out of control—none of it mattered. Somehow, the two of us had managed to find a lighthouse in all of these dark and stormy seas, the light keeping us on a path of good, a path of love and hope and all things bright.

I pressed my lips to his cheek and let the kiss linger until he relaxed, the fork dropping from his hand and clattering against the plate.

"I'd like to be your girlfriend," I said against his cheek. "On one condition."

"What's that?"

"I don't want anything to change between us. I love the way things are right this very second."

He pulled me onto his lap. My bar stool tipped over, crashing to the floor. We ignored it, and I looped my arms around his neck, nuzzling in close.

His lips brushed against my neck. "I can't make that promise, Lily. Things change. The world is always changing. Our journey together is just getting started."

"But I don't want *us* to change. I can't imagine things getting better than they are now."

"If nothing ever changed in the world, we wouldn't have butterflies. Without change, the caterpillar would never fly—they'd never blossom into the beautiful creatures they're meant to become. The best is yet to come, Lily. Trust me."

I blinked as he grasped my hand in his, holding it tight. So tight, I believed he'd never let go.

"I want to know every inch of you. Starting from here..." He kissed my forehead, my cheek, my shoulder. "Down to here." He tapped my toe. "With the new rules, we can savor what we have, enjoy each moment together. That's what this is all about, isn't it?"

I curled against his chest, my head resting against his warm, hard body. Finally, I cleared my throat. "Your bacon's getting cold."

He laughed. "Well, you'd better stay here, since your stool is on the floor."

We finished the meal in contented silence. I didn't move from his lap until it was time to clear the dishes. As I washed and he dried, it startled me how far we'd come in such a short time together.

Even though I'd only meant to distract Ranger X from talk of The Core with my questions, they'd served a double purpose. We'd suddenly entered into new territory, and I didn't know how to feel about it. A little bit scared, a little bit excited... the conversation had left a vulnerability shrouding the room, soothed only by our memorized motions around the kitchen.

"Unfortunately, it's time for me to go," he said, closing the cupboard on the last of the clean dishes. "I'm sorry to leave you here tonight. If you want me to stay, maybe—"

"No, *go*." I put my hands on his chest. "This is what I was talking about. I don't want *us* to change your work. You have your work, and I have mine."

"The Companion will stand guard through the night. You'll be safe, I promise."

"I wasn't worried." I grinned. "I can take care of myself."

X laughed, his eyes sparkling as they met mine. "Yes, I have no doubt. On the same subject, his contract terminates when I say, so don't bother to argue with him. Companions never break a contract."

"Does he have a name?"

"I'm sure he has one, but we don't use it," Ranger X said. "Like the Rangers, Companions are tools. They are disposable, as are the rest of the Rangers. Trust me, it doesn't help to become friends. This is his job and nothing more."

"I'm sorry." I flinched under his sharp tone. "I didn't know."

He wrapped me in an embrace, his hands stroking through my hair. "I didn't mean to sound harsh. If I did, it's only because I worry about you. You're trusting and kind, two qualities I adore in you. Unfortunately, they can also get you in trouble."

I frowned. "I just asked his name, it wasn't a big deal."

"Not yet, but the next thing I know you'll be inviting him

in for a Caffeine Cup, asking if he wants a bit of shut-eye on the couch." Ranger X shook his head. "We can't have that. The rules are firm for the Ranger program."

"The rules aren't so firm between you and me," I said with a coy smile and a bat of my eyelashes. "Lucky thing, huh?"

A smile crossed his face. "You have a point, Miss Locke, and I'm still wondering how that happened."

I did some spirit fingers. "Magic?"

He hooked a hand over my shoulder, pecked me goodbye, and took a few steps toward the door. "Lily, promise me one thing. Stay put tonight. Please."

"I thought the Companion was going to watch over me."

"Yes, but you're too smart for your own good."

I laughed and then curtseyed.

"You're dodging my question," Ranger X said, his eyes following my curtsey. "I want to hear you promise."

"I'm not going to sneak out my bedroom window and go traipsing across The Isle," I said. "Are you happy?"

He didn't look happy, but the Comm device on his wrist buzzed, and his business face took over again. Bidding me good night, he gave me one long, lingering look before he vanished into the darkness.

His absence was heavy. I stood for a moment, wishing he'd stayed longer. Wishing that he wasn't in charge of solving all the terrible, mysterious happenings on the island.

I turned to shut the lights off in the bar, telling myself to get a grip, when something brushed against my ankles. I yelped, jumping half a foot into the air.

The Companion came bursting through the front door, his eyes on high alert as he scanned me for injury. "Everything okay?" He surveyed the bar area, saw I was alive and breathing, and his shoulders relaxed at the sight of my smiling face. "I thought I heard something."

"Sorry," I said, caught in a stare-down with a brilliantly orange feline winding its way around my legs. "I didn't see this guy, and he caught me off guard."

"Do you want me to dispose of the creature for you?"

"What? No! It's just a cat." I waved him away. "Thanks for checking on me, but everything is fine. He's mine."

The Companion returned to his post as I surveyed the cat, wondering where he'd come from. I bent over to scratch his ears, sucking in a breath of surprise at the sight of a paper slip tied to his neck. I spread the small note on the bar before me, smoothing it with my palm.

On it were handwritten words.

Meet Tiger—tonight.

I frowned. *Tiger—tonight?*

"Is your name Tiger?" I asked the cat. "Does someone want me to adopt you?"

The cat mewed, but it didn't speak back. I shouldn't have been surprised, but I was disappointed all the same.

"So you're just a regular old cat, aren't you?"

The cat looked up at me with his bright gray eyes. I scratched his neck some more.

"Are you going to stick around here?" I asked the cat. "You can be my guardian kitty. Hettie has a tiger, and I have a…*oh*."

It hit me all at once. The note was from Hettie, a secret code of sorts. Both she and Gus had been particularly cryptic about this evening, telling me to keep an eye out… for *Tiger*. If I was correct in my assumption, then Hettie wanted a meeting with The Core—tonight.

CHAPTER 8

"**H**ERE YOU GO, BUDDY," I said, placing a dish of milk on the floor. "You know, when Hettie told me she had a guard tiger, I never expected you to be so cute."

Tiger glared at me. Like Ranger X, he probably didn't appreciate being called cute. *Men.*

"Fine, I will leave you alone. As it turns out, I have someplace to be this evening." I made sure there was enough milk and food for the cat, and then climbed the stairs to my bedroom, my gut churning.

I wished, not for the first time, that the group meant to save The Isle didn't require me to keep my boyfriend in the dark about its existence. I'd promised that I wouldn't leave tonight, and now I'd have to break that promise. Although it was for a good cause, the deception didn't sit well in my stomach. Maybe tonight I could convince Hettie that it was time to bring Ranger X on board.

I changed into more sensible clothes—a pair of black jeans and a dark gray sweater—and debated my exit strategy. When I'd promised Ranger X that I wouldn't climb out my bedroom window, I'd left myself a teensy-tiny loophole—and climbed out the kitchen window instead.

I expected it to be harder to get away from the Companion, but as it turned out, Tiger was there to help. The Companion reached over to pet the kitty, and I bid him goodnight, pretending to retire to my room. Instead of climbing the stairs, I veered toward the bar. I slipped out of my Comm device, leaving it on the table. This meeting was private, personal, and I didn't need interruptions.

I'd also promised Ranger X that I wouldn't traipse across The Isle. So instead of *traipsing,* I strolled. Quickly. Keeping to the main path, I remained on high alert, winding my way across the moonlit beaches. Waves tossed and turned as if the very atoms of the water could sense the unrest. Even the palm trees, normally so bright and sunny, were skeletons against the stars.

The Isle was split in two sections by a channel bubbling with clear blue water, filled with vibrantly colored fish, sea creatures, and jungles of cattails. The only crossing points were two bridges—the more commonly used Lower Bridge, which was where I headed now, and the far more dangerous Upper Bridge used mostly by Rangers.

I headed somewhere between the two, keeping to the West side of The Isle. Hettie's enchanted labyrinth, her pride and joy, sat closer to The Forest than was probably safe. Then again, most of the creatures were probably more afraid of Hettie than she was of them.

I reached the outskirts of The Twist, its vibrant branches bursting with fruits and laden with flowers, spiraling every which way. As I stepped underneath a trellis of sweet-scented roses, I was confident that my West Isle Witch blood would lead me through the ever-changing path without incidence.

The first few minutes passed quickly, the scenery familiar. However, after swatting aside leaves the color of roasted pumpkin, I came face to face with a brand new clearing. I whirled around, wondering how I could've made a wrong turn, when a voice spoke, the words falling from the sky.

"Finally!" Hettie called. "I thought I made it crystal clear we were meeting at the treehouse. I've been waiting for twenty minutes, girlfriend. Did Tiger get lost?"

I tilted my gaze upward, following the outline of a thick tree trunk. There in the treetop perched a miniature house made from all sorts of recycled materials. Two by fours, blankets, ropes, pots and pans, and random kitchen utensils—all of it mashed together to create a grand fort, the likes of which might be found deep in Narnia.

"Climb aboard, girlie," Hettie called. "We don't have much time. You've got to make it back before that man of yours is done with his duties for the night."

"How do you expect me to get up there?" I scanned the trunk, but there was nothing remotely resembling a ladder. "We have longer than you think. Ranger X will be gone most of the night on business, and he left a Companion to watch over the bungalow."

"That doesn't matter, he's always suspicious," Hettie said, tinkering with something in the canopy of leaves. "It's in his buns."

"Excuse me?"

"Oh, did I say in his buns?" She fanned herself. "I meant his bones."

"Sure you did." I crossed my arms and took a step back. "I still don't know how you expect me to climb up there. Unfortunately, Gus hasn't gotten to the potions on *flying* yet."

"Don't be silly, you can't fly." Hettie pulled her head back, disappearing somewhere in the inner workings of her fort. There were a few scuffling noises, some creative language, and the next thing I knew, she was back. "Catch," she said, about thirty seconds too late.

By the time she called *catch*, a huge bundle of ropes had already hit me in the head. The sound made a *thunk* against my skull, and I crumpled to the ground.

"Sorry," Hettie said. "But you should really be aware of your surroundings these days. Not my fault you were daydreaming."

I pulled myself back onto my feet, holding the ladder straight.

"Come on already, I'm getting old just watching you."

Sucking in a breath of air, I shimmied up the rope ladder as fast as I could. My foot got stuck, my hair blew in every direction, and my palms burned against the rope. But I made it to the top without breaking any of my limbs.

"So?" Hettie raised her hand and bounced her hip a few times. She was dancing to some music I couldn't hear and looking thrilled about it. "What do you think?"

I turned in a slow circle, looking around the tree fort. Even though I was annoyed at my grandmother for whacking me in the face with a rope, I couldn't deny the awesomeness of the place. "Did you make this by yourself?"

"No, your grandfather was the mastermind." Hettie spoke with an undercurrent of happiness, a warm tone I'd never heard her use before. "He built it for me to escape from the kids."

"The kids?" I stifled a laugh. "Mimsey and Trinket and my mother?"

"Mimsey and Trinket and Delilah," she echoed softly, one of the rare occasions on which she spoke my mother's name. Then her smile returned, and she shook her head good-naturedly. "They gave me headaches. If they try to tell you they didn't cause me any trouble, they're lying."

"Huh. I wonder where they got *that* trait from," I mumbled, turning away so Hettie couldn't catch the words. "This is incredible; I love it here."

From the bottom, the fort's floor had looked like a flimsy wooden panel fashioned into a rickety platform. My first impression couldn't have been further from the truth.

The treehouse had been built by someone who'd never lost the imagination of a child. Burrowed into the expansive canopy, the setup expanded along dozens of branches. It was larger than the storeroom in the bungalow, lined with trinkets and knickknacks on every available surface. Like *The Little Mermaid's* collection of goodies, except this version lived in the sky.

Different platforms at different heights made for a split-level house. One of the platforms had been used for something that looked like a book nook—fluffy white blankets, fat pink pillows, piles and piles of warm things that would make for the most perfect cozy evening.

There were also the workings of a kitchen, minus the obvious appliances. A small, handmade cupboard held things like bottles of water, cans of juice, and wine. Lots and lots of wine.

The other platforms were just as unique, just as incredible. A rope swing sat high above the ground, while a hammock dangled across the center. A more formal dining area sat on the highest platform, the treetop opening so the starlight spilled onto the table and surrounded us in a hazy glow.

"I think I could live here," I said, turning to Hettie. "Nope, scratch that. I *know* I could. Have you told anyone else about your secret hideaway?"

She shook her head. "Until now, it's been a secret between your grandfather and me. If I'd told the girls about it, they would've never left me alone. Even now, they'd ruin the peace and quiet. Can you imagine Mimsey puttering around up here?"

"Yeah, but it's a sin to keep this place a secret."

"Of course it isn't. If I *hadn't* kept it a secret, we wouldn't have a secure meeting room for The Core."

I made myself comfortable on a pillow that was placed around the rugged excuse for a dining room table. "Are we waiting for someone else?"

"Yes, of course," she said. "Didn't you get the message?"

"From Tiger? Yeah, but it was pretty cryptic."

"We're waiting on The Core, Lily. That includes Gus and Harpin."

"Does Harpin have to come?" I despised the man more than I'd ever thought it possible to dislike another person. "I don't understand why he's in the group in the first place. He's nothing but trouble."

"It's not for you to understand." Hettie's gaze landed firmly on me. "If you'd like to continue participating in The Core, you need to be a team player."

"I'll be a team player with *anybody* on this island except him. With anyone in the *world* except him." I had a sudden thought. "And anyway, it's not too late to kick him out. He doesn't know that you head the group—only Gus and I were there when you explained everything. To him, you're still anonymous. We could meet without him, and he'd never know."

"My decision is final," Hettie said. "And Lily, I expect you to trust me, even if you don't understand. We're all each other has. As for my identity as head of The Core—I revealed it to him shortly after I explained things to you. It was only fair."

"I trust *you*, I don't trust him," I grumbled.

"I knew my ears were tingling. You can't be talking about me now, can you?" Harpin alighted on the platform behind me. The rope swung ever so subtly from a nearby branch, and I wondered if Hettie had sent Tiger to guide him through The Twist. "How unfortunate. After all, Lily, as your grandmother said... *I'm all you have.*"

"You are not." My fists clenched as I leaped to my feet. The hairs on the back of my neck rose at the sound of his slithering voice. "If it weren't for Hettie, I'd never speak to you again."

"I've noticed." Harpin wore his Cretan robes, a band of bright fabric around the top of the hood. "You haven't been by the tea shop to visit. I'd give you a discount because of our... relationship."

"No need," I said dryly. "I have no interest in your hokey tea leaves."

A flash of anger sizzled in his eyes, but he refrained from commenting and merely adjusted his robes. "Thank you for hosting, Hettie."

I sat back down, my gaze burning holes in the man's forehead. Harpin and Gus had graduated from the same, somewhat controversial, school for wizardry. Whether that had anything to do with Harpin's seat in The Core or not, I couldn't say. Neither of the men talked about their past.

Hettie handled the situation by ignoring it completely. "Speaking of tea, who wants some?"

I raised a hand and Harpin nodded.

Hettie hung a teapot from a spindly branch. Underneath sat a small tealight candle. She lit the magically enhanced wick by snapping her fingers and tossing a ball of blue light onto it. When the pot was situated and heating properly, she plopped down next to me at the table.

"Isn't the fort wonderful, Harpin?" Hettie asked, directing her question across the platforms. "Harvey built it with his bare hands. No magic whatsoever."

Harpin cleared his throat. "Harvey was a talented man."

"He was." Her voice turned soft, muted under the starlight. "A good man, too. I miss him."

With those three little words, Hettie laid to rest the tension between Harpin and me, at least for the moment. A somber minute passed in which she blinked a few times, her eyes damp with tears.

"Hettie—" I started, but the *snap* of a hefty branch broke my concentration.

"Ah, there's Gus." Hettie tilted her head upward, swiped a hand against her cheek. "Now that we're all here, let's begin."

CHAPTER 9

"RAYMON WAS MURDERED," HETTIE SAID, once tea had been served around the room. "Can we all agree on this?" She didn't leave time for a response. "Good talk. Can we also agree that there is more to the story than arresting Trent?"

"What do you mean?" I set my cup down on the table. "Ranger X said they arrested Trent because he gave Raymon the Poison Pill that killed him."

"The Rangers needed a face to pin this on, and Trent was the best option," Hettie said. "I highly doubt Ranger X believes this is the final story."

"That doesn't seem fair to Trent."

"In Ranger X's defense, Trent *did* serve a Poison Pill."

"He says he doesn't remember anything after stepping into the arena."

"Hard to say if that's true or not, isn't it?" Hettie raised an eyebrow. "And if the Rangers *didn't* make an immediate arrest, The Isle would be in a panic."

"Whatever the final story, Trent is not innocent," Harpin said as he held a cup of untouched tea in his hand. "He brought the Poison Pill *into* the arena, did he not?"

"There are ways of making someone perform actions they disagree with." Hettie cast him a warning glare. "You should know this, Harpin. Some of your very own tea leaves have the ability to. . . shall we say, alter one's decision-making abilities?"

Harpin's face turned red, and he fell silent. I made a mental note to never cross Hettie. Her ability to silence grown men with a few words was impressive.

"Do you have any thoughts as to why someone wanted Raymon dead?" I asked in the ensuing silence. "Why him, why now?"

"I believe I might." Hettie averted her eyes, focusing on swirling the tea leaves in her cup. "I was watching Raymon."

"Why?" I asked. "What did he do?"

"Nothing," she said. "He was a good boy, growing into a fine young man. I thought he might be the perfect recruit to join us. To join The Core."

"Did they know about this?" I nodded to Harpin and Gus.

"No, of course not," Hettie said. "I have always worked independently in selecting new members to join The Core. It must be an objective decision; personal feelings cannot enter the equation, and it is not up for debate. However, I did utilize one contractor in the process."

"Contractor?"

"A freelance Companion who is known for his surveillance skills," Hettie said. "The process of vetting a candidate to join The Core is a long and thorough one, and I needed help, so I hired an outsider. It was a necessary risk, and it failed."

"That still doesn't explain why someone would want him dead," I said. "So what if he joined The Core?"

Despite Hettie holding her chin high, the tiniest gleam of disappointment sparkled in her eye. Heartbreak for Raymon seeped through the cracks of her brave face. "If you found out someone was investigating you, what's the first thing you would do?"

I shrugged. "Find out who they were and why they were following me, I suppose."

"How would you begin?"

I bit my lip in thought. "Well, I guess I'd ask for help first. Maybe reach out to you, or Poppy and Zin. Maybe Ranger X."

Hettie nodded. "I'm guessing Raymon mentioned that he was being followed to a friend."

"Except this friend wasn't as trustworthy as Raymon thought," Gus said. "And this *friend* spilled the beans. Word made it back to The Faction that we were recruiting."

"The Faction might not know our name or our faces, but we have to assume they know about us," Hettie said. "Our group. Hence the reason they've got their blacklist. The price on my head is ten million coins, and I'm pretty proud of that number. I'm quite expensive."

"But how—"

"They're recruiting, we're recruiting," Hettie said before my question finished. "That's the name of the game. It's a race to secure the best teams before the battle begins."

I swallowed a warm gulp of tea. "So, if Raymon hadn't been killed, do you think he would've joined us?"

Hettie paused, sipped from her porcelain teacup. It was empty, but she didn't notice. "I had planned to extend him an invitation next week."

"I thought you didn't allow Rangers into The Core." I sounded a bit defensive. "Or has that changed?"

"It has not." Hettie kept a blank expression on her face. "Raymon would've had to choose between us and the Ranger program. I believe he would've chosen us."

"We have to assume The Faction knew this, too," Gus said.

"If The Faction couldn't have Raymon," Harpin said, "they weren't going to let him come to our side either."

"Bingo." Hettie finally realized her tea was empty and poured more hot water over the leaves. "Trent delivered the Poison Pill, but we *must* assume someone else was behind the decision. We need to find out who."

"How do you suggest we do that?" Harpin strolled along the edge of the dining room, looking through the cracks in the platform to the ground below. "We can't exactly run around The Isle asking questions."

"No, of course not," Hettie said with a frown. "We'll ask *one* question, to the right person. However, I can't do it. I have a more urgent matter to address—I must get in contact with my other recruit and ensure her safety."

"Another recruit?" Gus raised an eyebrow. "Do we know her?"

"You'll find out in time," Hettie said. "Lily, can you—"

Harpin crossed his arms and interrupted, "I'll handle it."

"I think not." Hettie smiled, her lips a thin line. "One of us knows the person with whom we need to speak. Lily, I imagine you know who I mean..."

CHAPTER 10

"To what do I owe this visit?" Liam rose from the table and air-kissed me on each cheek. "My dear, I never expected we'd be dining in the middle of the night again so soon."

"Neither did I." I sat across the table from him in Midge's dining room at the only B&B on the island. A successful businessman, Liam traveled often, and was a frequent guest of the inn. "I only wish the circumstances were better."

"As do I. Then again, when people ring me in the middle of the night, it's hardly to share good news." Liam forced a smile. "However, that may just be the nature of my business."

"I'm really glad you were on the island already. Thank you so much for dragging yourself out of bed. I know it's an inconvenience, but I can explain."

"It's hardly an inconvenience." Liam gestured to his long-sleeved button-up flannel pajama top and the swishy pants that went along with it. Underneath the table he wore two gigantic slippers—black, in the shape of panda bears—over his feet. "I'm quite comfortable and not inconvenienced whatsoever."

"I didn't take you for a flannel guy," I said as Midge approached. "A cappuccino for me, please, and for you, Liam. . .?"

"You know what I'll have." Liam gave Midge a wink.

Midge, the owner of the B&B, was hardly four feet tall. She doubled as the hostess, waitress, bartender, and concierge. But most importantly, her macaroni and cheese was to die for. Literally, if the rumors were to be believed.

She nodded, retiring to the kitchen to put in our orders. I turned back to Liam, hardly able to believe my luck. From the treehouse, I'd used Hettie's Comm device to ring Midge at the B&B. She'd said that yes, Liam was staying with her and yes, she would knock on his door to see if he was around. Then Liam had agreed to see me, and *voila,* a mac and cheese meeting had been arranged.

"What can I help you with tonight, my dear?" Liam offered that charming smile of his, the smile that made me feel safe and confused all at once. "Name your worry, and I shall do what I can to make it go away."

"I imagine you've heard about the Trials."

"Why, of course. In fact, I was there. That's the whole reason I'm on the island in the first place. I couldn't miss it—I booked my room *weeks* in advance. Midge is completely full tonight, never seen anything like it."

"Then you saw Raymon—"

"I saw everything, start to finish," he said crisply, sparing me the details. "I sat next to the lovely Madam Xiong; she was kind enough to offer me a seat in her box. It's a shame, isn't it?"

I tapped my fingers against the soft, white tablecloth. "Yes, it is. Any thoughts on what happened?"

Liam leaned forward, *tsking* as he shook his head. "I didn't become the most trusted businessman on The Isle by sharing *my* opinions, Lily Locke. I'm here to listen, and I imagine you have something to tell me."

Taking a deep breath, I began my story. I didn't stop until I'd finished everything. Of course I left out the exact details about The Core, and the bits about Ranger X and myself. Everything else—from Raymon being watched by a Companion, to our theory that he'd mentioned this to the wrong person and subsequently been killed for it—was accurate.

"I won't ask for your sources," Liam said when I lapsed into silence. "I assume this is confidential?"

"Yes, it's private."

"No problem, most things of great importance are. Now, you are wondering *how* it happened. Beyond the Poison Pill. Who was really behind the whole scheme."

"Yes," I said, my heart racing at his tone. "Do you know something about it? It's very important you tell me everything. I *promise* you it's essential."

"I understand that this is important. That doesn't mean I want you anywhere near it."

"Why would you care?" The question came out sharper than I intended. "It's my decision."

"I have a vested interest in your safety."

"What is that supposed to mean?"

Liam raised an eyebrow. "Don't ask questions you don't want the answer to."

"I didn't."

We stared eye to eye for a long time, Liam's bright eyes boring into mine. He was a handsome man, and charismatic. It wasn't his face nor his intelligence that had me captivated, however. There was something in the way he spoke. The way he carried himself with a calmness on the exterior and something deeper underneath. Passion, maybe. *Passion for what?* I wondered.

"I care about you and your safety," he said finally.

"I'm sorry, Liam. This whole thing has me on edge. But I am begging for your help. I'll do anything."

"It's called mind bending," he said abruptly. "The type of magic used to murder Raymon. I'm almost sure of it, but that's the thing—it's *impossible* to be sure of it unless you find the source."

My jaw dropped. This conversation had raced through twists and turns like a high-speed car chase, and I could hardly keep up. "What did you call it?"

"Ahh, thank you, darling," Liam said, turning his attention to the owner of the B&B. "This smells exquisite."

Midge's head barely came over the edge of the table as she unloaded a cappuccino, the macaroni and cheese, and shakers of salt and pepper onto the table. I took a sip of the cappuccino, giving Midge a huge thumbs-up in the hopes that she'd leave us alone.

Apparently, Midge had other ideas. Either that or she was lonely, because she plopped down next to Liam in the booth and dived into a plate of curly fries that she'd brought along with the other items.

"Midnight munchies," she said as an explanation. "Carry on talking, I didn't mean to interrupt."

The next twenty minutes were a work in self-restraint. The cappuccino was smooth with a caramel finish that I would have normally savored to the last drop. However, this time, I downed the froth in one gulp, tapping my foot for the next nineteen and a half minutes. Midge didn't get the picture, not even when the conversation ran out and we fell into silence.

Finally, just when I was about to explode from impatience, she kissed us each on the cheek and said goodnight. This required us to bend halfway to the floor so she could *reach* our cheeks. Then Midge swiped the last of the fries and told us to take our time.

"I want to get one thing straight," Liam said when the room was empty. "In no way am I endorsing your involvement with anything in this realm of magic."

"You mean mind bending? Is it *that* bad?"

Liam shook his head. He pushed the remains of the mac and cheese away from him, leaning back against the booth. "It's worse."

"Why haven't I heard about it if it's so bad?"

"It's not often discussed for many reasons." Liam rested his hands in his lap. "The only reason I'm explaining it to you now is because you're an adult, Lily, and you're the Mixologist. If you're going to experience the darker side of life, it's best if you're prepared."

"Mind bending. What is it?"

The light vanished from his eyes. "An illegal form of magic. It is banned across the world, not only on The Isle."

"Does that include The Faction?"

He inhaled a shuddery breath. "I can't speak for the group as a whole, but it appears someone has unearthed the dark magic form for the first time in years."

"How do you know it was The Faction?"

"I don't."

"But...?" I prompted him.

"There is only one person in the world with a nearly complete mastery of mind bending."

"Someone in The Faction?"

"Someone who escaped from prison this morning."

"No wonder X was upset," I breathed. "I've never seen him so uptight."

"I imagined he might not be thrilled." Liam paused for a dark, almost eerie smile. "This woman has been locked away for years, and quite honestly, I believe most people have forgotten about her."

"Why was she in prison?"

"She broke the mind bending laws, of course."

"But *what* is it? Similar to telepathy?"

Liam chewed on his lip for a second, sizing me up as he considered his response. "On the street, it's called *blood magic.*"

"How does it work?"

"Have you heard of voodoo?"

"Like the dolls? Yes, of course. I mean, in the movies. I don't believe in it, personally."

"You don't need to believe in voodoo, but you should start believing in blood magic." Liam reached for the salt, sprinkling it on his leftover macaroni and cheese. "She calls herself The Puppeteer."

"The prisoner?"

He swirled the mac and cheese with a fork. "Yes. She has a

collection of dolls made from yarn—the most extensive collection on The Isle, and most likely in the world. She's believed to have a doll for nearly every person on the island. They're essential for her to perform magic."

"Where are they? Someone must have taken them from her when she went to prison."

"Nobody could find them. She claimed they were hidden somewhere safe, somewhere they'd never be discovered."

"I'd have thought the Rangers would make her give up the collection when they arrested her."

"They tried." He poked a few noodles, but at this point, they looked like shredded cheese. "The Rangers offered to cut her sentence in half if she turned over the dolls. She refused."

"Why would she do that?"

"Your guess is as good as mine. I imagine it took her years to create her collection. It's not a simple process. Do you know where the term blood magic comes from?"

My stomach churned. I'd never liked the idea of blood. "Do I want to know?"

"These dolls are created like any normal doll—at least, in the beginning. Everything changes once they become enchanted, however. The spell is a difficult one. Complicated largely by the fact that the final ingredient in the potion is a drop of blood from the person for whom the doll is created."

I fought back a wave of dizziness. "How does she go about getting people's blood?"

"There are ways," he said. "It's a miniscule amount—nothing more than a finger prick."

"No wonder they locked her away," I said with a blink. "She sounds like a psychopath."

"She is incredibly dangerous, and many have debated about her mental state," Liam agreed. "But it's more than that. Mind bending affects the user on a fundamental level—it crawls deep under their skin and lingers, like smoke after a fire. Sometimes, the effects never go away. It changes a person's soul."

"Is that what happened with The Puppeteer? She changed?"

"I can't say." Liam cleared his throat, increasingly uncomfortable with the topic. "The Puppeteer has the power to influence a person's mind, their heart, their actions. It's completely within the realm of possibility that Trent was under the influence of blood magic when he delivered the Poison Pill."

"Let me guess—it leaves no trace of magic behind."

"That's a complicated question," Liam said. "All magic leaves a trace, you know that."

"That's what I *thought*. But according to X, they thoroughly checked Trent when they arrested him. There were no signs of magic whatsoever."

"As I said, it's complicated." Liam stood, leaving the soggy mess of salted macaroni on the table. "When a person performs blood magic, they lose a piece of their soul to the person on the other end of the spell."

"Those are steep consequences for a spell."

"Try to imagine performing a spell, *knowing* that you are losing a piece of the very thing that makes you... *you.*"

"I don't understand why anyone would do that. And what happens if a person gives away too much?"

Liam hooked his arm around mine, pulling me up from the table and leading me to the doorway. His slippers shuffled across the floor, the panda heads bobbing as he walked.

"That is precisely why mind bending is illegal." He spoke softly, his breath whispering across my neck. "Nobody wants to lose their soul."

I shivered at his tone of voice. We lingered in the lobby, his flannel-clad arm looped through mine. "Who can show me how to find her?"

"No, Lily, I can't allow—"

"Please help me, or I'll find another way."

Liam unraveled his arm from mine, taking a step back. Waves of emotion washed over his face. "There is one person more knowledgeable than I on this subject."

"Thank you," I said. "I will be careful."

"She is called the Witch of the Woods."

"Can you tell me where to find her?"

"Goodnight, Lily."

CHAPTER 11

MY THOUGHTS DEVOURED ME WHOLE as I sidled across the desolate beach, taking the long way home to let my mind wind down. I didn't look up until I was halfway across The Isle, my footsteps clanking on the wooden plank of the Lower Bridge. The *thunk* startled me back to reality.

A *crack* sounded in the distance, and I froze. I didn't move, didn't breathe until I located the sound. When I did, I exhaled in relief. Nothing but a tree branch banging against a boulder on the shore.

I took a step toward the railing, watching as the bright orange fish circled below, moving faster and faster and faster until...

"Ahh!" A pair of large hands muffled my scream. The hands were male, judging by the size and strength of their grasp.

A low, rumbling voice whispered in my ear, "What if it wasn't me who was out looking for you tonight?"

The hands left my mouth, and I whirled around coming face to face with Ranger X. "What in the world do you think you're doing?" My chest heaved with panic. I felt my heartbeat in my eardrums. "You nearly killed me."

"I could say the same thing about you," he said. "And you didn't answer my question."

"I was just..." My explanation disappeared into the night sky. "I had to do something."

"I thought I told you to stay in the bungalow tonight."

"You don't get to *tell* me what to do," I said, instantly regretting the harsh clip to my words. I pressed a hand to my forehead and sighed. "I'm sorry, I didn't mean to snarl at you, and I shouldn't have left, but I did. And I can't tell you why."

"I worry about you."

"I'm sorry," I said as his arms wrapped me in an embrace. I stared into his chest, my heart sinking at the look of disappointment I'd glimpsed in his eyes.

"I'd say I'm not angry, but I am—I can't help it," he said after a pause. "Not at you but at myself. I should never have left you alone."

"You didn't leave me alone! You left the Companion. It's not your job to watch over me all day, every day. You have a real job, an important one."

"It *is* my job to keep you safe."

"No, your job is to be a Ranger, and you should act like one. If we weren't dating, you wouldn't even have stopped by my place tonight."

"But we *are* dating, and that means something to me." He tilted my chin up until my gaze was forced to meet his. He watched me through dark, wary eyes. "Life isn't fair. It's not fair I can't be with you through each night. It's not fair that Raymon died."

"X—"

"But he *did* die, and now I have to deal with all of the consequences. And I have to do it while keeping you safe. Why did you leave tonight, Lily?"

"It's not your job—"

"I don't want you to tell me what my job is or isn't. I make my own decisions. When I first kissed you, I dragged you into the world of the Rangers, and I will protect you from it as much as I can."

My fingers toyed with his shirt. "When we discussed the possibility of us having a relationship, it was with the understanding that you'd continue to do the job you love. I can't be the one to take you away from it."

"I am still doing the job I love!" X ran a hand through his hair. "Don't you see? The problem is that you're a part of it now."

He fell into silence. My fingers slid from his shirt, the same shirt he'd agonized over choosing from my closet just this morning. Such a trivial decision in retrospect.

I rested my cheek against the crisp fabric underneath his jacket. "I don't know if I like that things are changing. It's hard, and it's a little scary."

"It's also good."

"Good?" I raised my head the tiniest amount. "How is any of this good?"

"I care more about you with the passing of every day. I wouldn't give that up for anything."

I smiled as one of the gigantic orange fish leaped from the water, splashing back to its home a second later.

"But with that change, I'm more terrified than ever to lose you." Ranger X took a step back and held my shoulders. "It's hardly been a month and already I don't know what I'd do without you. When you do things like this—" he gestured to me, widened his arm to encompass The Isle. "When you leave in the middle of the night without a word to the Companion, it tears me apart. You left your Comm device at home. I assume you didn't *want* me to find you."

"I'm sorry."

"Don't apologize, just tell me where you went."

"I had to do something." I stared at the ground, hating the fact that I couldn't ease his worries. "It was nothing."

"Nothing?" Ranger X's arm dropped, as if his very limb couldn't believe my answer. "You specifically went against my wishes, escaped from a trained Companion, and traveled across the island for. . . *nothing?*"

Hettie hasn't prepared me for this, I thought, unable to suppress a flash of anger.

"I followed you back from Midge's place," Ranger X said. "I'm sorry. I'm really, really sorry I did that, but—"

"You've been following me this whole time? Why didn't you say something?"

"I can't explain how it felt to receive a Comm that you weren't home. I asked the Companion to check on you, knock on your door. When you didn't answer. . ."

My rush of anger was replaced by a heavy dose of guilt. For terrifying X, for drawing him away from his work to come find me, and now, for failing to explain my whereabouts.

"I met with Liam," I said finally. "At Midge's place."

Ranger X didn't look surprised. "I figured."

"I thought he might be able to help, but he didn't want me to get involved, either." I reached for X's hand and squeezed it. "I'm really sorry."

He kissed me on the forehead. "Leave a note next time, please."

"For what it's worth, I didn't *technically* break your rules," I said, testing out a small smile. "I *didn't* climb out my bedroom window."

"Kitchen window?"

"Maybe." I laughed. "I'm not going to be able to get away with that again, am I?"

"Not a chance. Though I *did* tell you not to leave."

"We'll call it a tie." We resumed walking, our clasped hands swinging between us. A few steps later, I nudged him. "So, was this our first argument?"

"If that was an argument, I think we'll be okay," he said with a measured smile. "As long as we end on this."

"End on wha—?"

I couldn't finish the question because his lips were already pressed to mine—an urgent kiss brimming with need. As if he'd funneled all of his anxiety into this very moment.

Finally, he paused with a whisper. "I love you."

My eyes stung, the lashes sticking together as I blinked. "I love you too."

It was the first time we'd told each other these three little words. The moment felt right. I didn't have to think. I just knew it with every inch of my being.

Then Ranger X scooped me up, the aftertaste of our kiss swirling through the night air like a dandelion gone to seed. Despite the darkness all around us, a tiny shimmer of something—hope, maybe—burned bright.

CHAPTER 12

66 "I NEED TO ASK YOU A favor," I said once we reached the outskirts of the bungalow. "Please."

He raised an eyebrow. "Tonight?"

"I need to speak with Zin."

"Zin is safe, I promise. I've taken care of it."

"I know, it's not about that, I just need. . . " I trailed off. I didn't know exactly what I needed; all I knew was that my cousin had been in that arena today with the other Candidates. I couldn't imagine what that had been like, but I could guess she needed someone there for her. "Please?"

He sighed, pulled my hand tighter. "Tell me what you were doing with Liam."

"We weren't doing anything besides talking," I said. "I was curious about what sort of magic could kill someone without leaving a trace on its user."

"And did he have an answer?"

I looked up at him, hesitating a second too long.

"He explained about blood magic." Ranger X's voice was monotone. "Did he tell you anything else?"

"The Puppeteer," I said, watching his face for a reaction. "I know she was the prisoner who escaped this morning."

"Ah, I see."

"Do you know where she is now?"

"Unfortunately, no." Ranger X shook his head. "Due to her magical. . . persuasions, she is difficult to find."

"Have you ever experienced mind bending? Liam made it sound horrible."

"Every Ranger experiences it," he said, his words crisp. "It is unpleasant, but it is necessary to know how to defend against it."

"How do you defend against it?"

"You don't."

"What do you mean? Every person, every sort of magic has a weakness," I said. "There must be—"

"There *isn't*," Ranger X said flatly. "And if that's not enough of a deterrent to keep you out of things, then I should explain that the last time we tracked this woman down, one of my men never recovered."

"She killed him?"

"No, he's alive, but mentally he'll never be the same." Ranger X's shoulders stiffened in the way that meant he was hiding his emotions behind the sturdy exterior he'd been perfecting his whole career. "He'd been the lead Ranger on the investigation; he'd hunted The Puppeteer, tracked her for years."

"Did he find her?"

"I wish he hadn't." Ranger X's eyes shut for a brief second. "He closed in on her, and she used mind bending on him—she convinced him that they were in love."

"She can do that?"

"So much that when this Ranger returned, he dropped the investigation completely. Packed up and left before I could find him."

I made a noise in my throat. "Was it possible they *had* fallen in love?"

Ranger X's eyes flicked toward me, his gaze calculating. "I've wondered," he said finally. "But either way, he'd so convinced himself that it was love that he could no longer do his job. He knew it, so he left. I've heard he's on the mainland, but I can't be sure."

"Wouldn't he come back to his senses after the magic wore off?"

"That's the thing. She warped his mind so thoroughly with her blood magic that even when she let him go, the effects lingered."

I shivered at the venom in Ranger X's voice. He loved his men like brothers. He'd never say it, but I could see it in every breath, in every word, in every one of his actions. Losing a Ranger for any reason was like losing a family member, and he'd never get over it.

"I'm so sorry."

"Stay away from her." His eyes, filled with hurt and anger, turned toward me. "Do you understand me? I can't have you searching for her. That's why I didn't explain about the situation this morning."

The hard edge to Ranger X's voice threw me off balance. Not because he scared me—he'd never hurt me, of that I was sure. But somehow I sensed he was on the verge of losing control, and Ranger X had never lost control. The thought chilled my skin.

"Let's go find Zin," I said. "I need to make sure she's okay."

"Fine," Ranger X said shortly. "However, I will have to blindfold you. Close your eyes, Lily."

CHAPTER 13

"YOU KNOW, UNDER DIFFERENT CIRCUMSTANCES, this could be romantic," I said as Ranger X guided me over uneven ground, a makeshift blindfold strapped across my eyes.

He leaned in, whispering in my ear, "If I wanted this to be romantic, you'd know it, princess."

I shivered. "Warn me when you're going to do that, your breath tickles!"

Ranger X laughed, the sound a relief after the tense conversation. The other sounds of the night were amplified due to my lack of sight. Water gurgled in the background, leaves rustled overhead. Somewhere in the distance, a sweet-scented flower bloomed.

"How do you do it?" Ranger X asked a moment later. "Make me laugh in times like this."

"No idea. I've never considered myself to be funny."

"Here we are," he said, a few moments later. "But before you take off the blindfold, hold on for one second. . . "

His kiss took me by surprise. It wasn't the kiss itself, but the emotion behind it. Soft, sweet, almost tender. So very different from the kiss we'd shared earlier, but so very much the same. When he released me from the blindfold, I left my eyes closed and wished the world away, if only for a few more moments.

Even the best moments had to end. I opened my eyes to find Ranger X's dark hair and dark eyes blending in with the night sky. Bright stars pierced the blackness above us.

"We call this The Oasis," he said, straightening. His voice had a lingering huskiness to it as he took my hand and guided me forward. "Don't bother asking where we are—it doesn't matter anyway."

"The Forest?" Around us, trees loomed high.

"I meant it; don't bother asking. It won't be here tomorrow."

"Then why the blindfold?"

"Can't be too careful. With you, anything can happen."

"But what about the Candidates?"

"They won't be able to find this place either. That's why we call it The Oasis. It's a peaceful place."

"Peaceful because nobody can get to it."

Ranger X smiled. "Just how I like it."

The line of trees formed a circle, and for the first time since the kiss I let my eyes adjust to the darkness. The sight was something else.

"I thought you called it The Oasis because of all this. . . " I gestured to a pool so still, so clear it might have been sea glass. A waterfall flowed over the edge of a cliff, the spray carrying on the evening breeze across splotches of bright flowers and long, green grasses. "This place looks like the Ritz."

Beyond the pool rose a modern-looking building—sheer glass all around. The building was made of cubes and resembled a tower of dice stacked two by two for at least five stories. Inside of the cubes were people. More specifically, the Candidates.

"What is that?" I put a hand on my hip and faced Ranger X. "It looks like a prison!"

"It's a hotel. I told you, it's called The Oasis."

"No, that's a prison," I argued. "You can see everything! These rooms have no privacy."

Each cube appeared to be a small, luxuriously decorated suite outfitted with the basics: bed, chair, and desk. Through the clear walls, eight heads—each belonging to a different Candidate—bobbed along with their nightly routines. Most were in sleeping, though one or two sat up reading, doodling, writing. Not a single Candidate looked our way.

"It's for their safety." Ranger X crossed his arms over his chest. "I didn't bring you here to criticize. And I promise you, they've been treated like royalty. Good food, fresh linens, fantastic service—"

"So can I stay here tonight?"

He coughed. "No, sorry."

I counted ten different cells but only eight heads. The top two rooms were empty. One for Trent and one for Raymon, most likely. "Can I at least talk to Zin? It'll only be a second. We'll be right in front of your nose."

Ranger X hesitated. Then finally, he nodded. "Wait here."

Damp grass brushed across my toes as I scuffed my sandals against the earth. After making his way across the manicured grounds, Ranger X kept his face passive as he knocked on Zin's door.

She looked up from where she'd been doodling in bed. Her gaze swiveled toward me, and I waved. She squinted, but she didn't wave back, and I wondered if she could even see through the glass.

Ranger X helped her down, and I pasted a smile on my face as she made quick work closing the distance between us.

"Lily." She approached slowly, stopping an arm's length away. "Thanks for coming."

I shifted my weight from one foot to the next. "Are you all right?"

She nodded and then glanced at Ranger X, who hovered a foot from her shoulder.

"Could we have a bit of privacy?" I asked Ranger X. "Girl talk."

He rolled his eyes to the sky. However, he didn't argue.

When he'd moved a few steps away, I faced Zin. "What's wrong?"

"Why are you here?" Zin went straight to business. The tips of her short, black bob stuck to her neck, her skin pale. So very pale, she looked more vampire than shifter. "Why did he let you come visit me?"

"I don't know," I said. "I asked, and he agreed."

Zin frowned. "What does he want?"

"Nothing, I asked to come. How are you doing? Do you need anything?"

"They spoil us senseless." Zin waved a hand. "I had someone offer to comb my hair for me. I hardly have long enough hair to comb."

"Sounds like an Oasis."

Zin curled her lips into a smirk. "They make this place beautiful on purpose. Too gorgeous. Look around, Lily—any place this stunning couldn't be a prison, right? *Wrong.*"

"I'm sorry you're stuck here. But if there's anything I can do to help, tell me."

She looked nervously over her shoulder at X, then turned back. "I need you to look into one of the Candidates for me."

"Trent?"

"No, Camden," she said. "The baker's boy."

"Why? He's one of the two I've met in person. He seemed so nice. And polite."

"Polite?"

"Yeah, courteous," I said. "You know, please and thank-yous."

"Polite people can't be dangerous?"

"I suppose they can," I said. "What makes you think he's dangerous?"

The Candidate in question was one of the leading favorites to make it all the way through to the Ranger program. He had tall, lean, movie-star good looks. His smile came fast and shined bright, his eyes holding a gleam of humor in every interview.

"It was something at dinner tonight," Zin said, her voice low. "They fed us like kings—a huge feast at a long table. Camden sat across from me and two chairs down. We'd talked before, and I liked him. Most of the meal we were chatting, actually."

"I'm not seeing the danger, here."

"Wait," Zin instructed. "Dane, Dillan and Layton were part of the conversation, too. We were all sitting together."

"And?"

"There was one odd moment in the middle of the conversation. Camden all of a sudden..." she paused, searching for the right words. "He looked straight at me, but it wasn't *him.*"

"What do you mean?" My pulse sped up, and I leaned forward. "What happened?"

"His pupils were dilated and. . . I don't know, I can't explain it. I'm probably sounding crazy, but I know what I saw. He was empty in there, almost like his soul had left his body."

"What did he do then?"

"Well, a few minutes later he just seemed to snap out of it. One second he had that crazy look in his eyes and the next. . . we were talking about the type of olives he liked best."

"He didn't do anything besides look at you?"

"I told you it sounds crazy, but I swear it happened. All I know is that I don't want to be around the next time he turns weird."

"What makes you think there'll be a next time?"

Zin looked down, the starlight reflecting off her milky white skin. "You weren't there, Lily. You didn't see the look in his eyes. It was empty, yes, but there was something more—a hunger. The way he looked at me, it was like I had a target on my forehead, and he zoned in on it."

"I'll tell Ranger X," I said. "Maybe he can do something about it. Look into Camden, or—"

"No! Don't say anything." She raised her hands, pleading with me. "He can't know about this. He can't know I told you. If I'm wrong, if what I saw was my imagination. . . "

"It wasn't," I assured her. I couldn't explain about mind bending in the amount of time we had left together. Ranger X had strolled a good distance away from us, but he had begun to head back. "X can help, I promise."

"No. Camden could get disqualified or treated unfairly. And for what? Me thinking he looked hungry? No. Just... just look into him, Lily. Don't say anything, please."

Ranger X approached faster and faster, and I only had seconds left to ask my final question. "Zin, will you consider dropping out? The Ranger Trials can't be worth all of this. The danger, the fear, the stress... please, consider it."

"No," she said, her eyes holding a touch of disappointment. "I've worked my entire life for this. A Ranger never gives up. I don't plan to, either. Sorry."

I sighed. "I knew you'd say that. Worth a shot, I suppose."

She gave me a smile tinged with stubbornness. "Thanks for coming, Lil. I knew you'd understand."

"I do understand, trust me. But you need to understand where I'm coming from," I said. "I am the Mixologist, and I've taken an oath to *Do Good*. This is not a job to me, it's more than that. It's who I am, and I can't let myself keep this a secret if lives are at risk. If *your* life is at risk."

"Let's compromise." Zin responded so fast, I imagined she'd already planned her words. "The next public Trial is approaching quickly. Look into Camden—if you find something suspicious, if you uncover any evidence he has a reason to hurt any Candidate, you can tell Ranger X everything."

"Deal." I stuck my hand out eventually and shook my cousin's, her fingers cold to the touch.

"It's time to go, Lily," Ranger X called, ignoring Zin. "I'll walk you home."

"Exciting." I turned to face him. "Will we be needing the blindfold again?"

"Zin," he said, this time ignoring me, "we'll escort you to your room on the way."

CHAPTER 14

"**S**IR, WAIT."

We'd hardly dropped Zin off at her room before another Ranger called to us, jogging across The Oasis and gesturing for X to stop. When he reached us, he fixed me with a frown, waiting until I excused myself and stepped away before he started speaking.

The two Rangers held a brief, murmured conversation. I tried not to eavesdrop, but a few words made it through. Something about Healers, pain... *someone was injured.* My heart thudded—it couldn't be Zin. She'd been standing here just minutes before.

"Lily, join us, please." Ranger X waved for me to join them. "Do you have your Aloe Ale with you?"

"Yes, of course. I always carry it."

"Would you mind taking a look at Dillan's arm? After he fell during the Trial, he's been in constant pain. We released the Healers for the evening, but apparently it's acting up now, and the closest Healer can't be here for another hour."

"I'll do what I can."

Ranger X brought me around to a tent set up in the corner of The Oasis out of view from the rest of the Candidates. X tapped on the entrance and waited for a greeting before entering. "Dillan, I have someone here to help you."

Dillan looked up in surprise as we stepped through the door. He'd been in the cubes when I first counted heads, which meant he must've just arrived at the tent.

His face was contorted in pain, and he held his arm pressed across his chest. It'd already been bound, but whatever he'd been given to dull the pain had clearly worn off. "The Mixologist?" he grunted. "Sorry, ma'am, I didn't mean to bother you. I thought a Healer—"

"She was in the area, and she's as good as any Healer," X said. "Do you mind if she takes a look?"

"I'm nowhere near as skilled as a Healer, but I do have something to dull the pain," I said. "Until more qualified help arrives. May I?"

He forced a smile, his teeth gritted. "That would be great."

I sat down, murmuring words I hoped were sympathetic. For all X's confidence, I was no more a Healer than he—but over these past few weeks, I had been learning to Mix basic medicinal potions. I carried several essentials with me at all times, including the Aloe Ale, which was a stronger, magical version of painkillers.

"This might hurt…" I unwrapped a portion of his arm to apply the Ale. "Sorry. Hang in there."

He hissed, jerked back, and then came to a stop. "Sorry."

"I'm sorry. I saw the fall, and it looked excruciating," I said. "Try and think of something else while I get this applied. It won't take long to begin easing the pain."

"You could say it hurt." His eyes flicked toward the ground as he spoke. "It certainly wasn't fun."

His gaze landed there only for a second, but it was long enough for me to follow his line of sight. A slip of paper fluttered to the ground. I reached for it at the same time as X and Dillan, but I got there first.

"Ouch." I winced, holding the slip in one hand and pressing the injured finger to my shirt. "Paper cut."

"I'll take that," X said, pulling the note from my hand.

I caught a glimpse of numbers and letters, but nothing that made sense before it was whisked away.

While Ranger X read over the paper, I dabbed a bit of ointment on my finger, then continued to apply the salve to Dillan's arm. His shoulders tensed, and it wasn't until Ranger X handed the paper back to the Candidate that he relaxed.

"It's from my mother," Dillan explained. "It's the only thing I have of hers. She left me that note the day before she died."

"I'm sorry," I said, meaning it. "I heard she passed away when you were young."

"Of course you did," he said, a note of bitterness to his voice. "The media's been running stories about my history for months, just like the rest of the Candidates and their families. Some things are better left private."

The media had featured a story about Dillan, as it had with every other Candidate. They'd focused on the fact that Dillan had grown up in a single parent home, his mother having passed away while he was just a child.

I finished applying the salve and rewrapped his arm. "Better?"

"Much," he said. "Thank you for coming, Miss Locke. Goodnight."

"Goodnight," I said, watching as he walked out of the tent, followed closely by a Ranger escort.

As I cleaned up my supplies, I murmured to X. "Did you understand the note?"

"I read it," he said. "A series of numbers and letters, but it didn't mean anything to me."

"Do you think it was actually from his mom?"

"It's hard to say."

I let the subject drop, since clearly X didn't want to talk about it. "Well, I hope the salve helps until the Healer arrives."

"I'm sure it will." X tucked me under his arm, leading me out through The Oasis and into The Forest before he stopped with a thoughtful expression on his face. "So where did we land on the blindfold?"

CHAPTER 15

ONE WEEK LATER, I HAD no new information on Camden, but I did have more doughnuts, croissants, and cakes than I'd ever need. The number of trips I'd made across The Isle to the bakery had run into the double digits. Except for an overload of carbs, I hadn't gained anything from my visits.

I reread all of Camden's interviews. I watched the replay of the first Trial a hundred times, and I spoke with his friends and family. Nobody had a bad thing to say. Even his family was sweet—his father had given me baskets of baked goods, and his mother had hand-written me six recipes for how I could use the leftovers.

All this brought me right back to square one—back to the very theory I'd hoped to disprove. If Camden was acting strangely, it was likely due to mind bending. A part of me had hoped for a different explanation, but the second public Trial was approaching quickly, and I had no evidence to the contrary.

During the past week, I also hadn't rested in my investigation surrounding The Puppeteer. It was hard to unearth information about someone who'd been locked away for years, and even *harder* because everyone clammed up once I mentioned her name.

I was in the same place I'd been the night I'd visited Zin. I'd even tried to scribble down the numbers from the note in Dillan's pocket, but I couldn't remember most of them. From what I could tell, it wasn't a phone number, a location, or a code. Maybe, as Ranger X suggested, it was nothing.

Now, the second Trial would begin in ten minutes, and I had nothing. Absolutely nothing.

"Wait!" I called, scurrying after Ranger X as he strode toward the stage. We were back at the arena, the memories of last week heavy in the air. "One more thing before you go."

"What's wrong?" He stopped, despite the roar of the crowd pulling him forward.

Wringing my hands together, I debated for one final second. Though I'd promised Zin not to say anything, I couldn't do it. "It's about Zin."

Some of the tension left his gaze, though his muscles were taut, his posture stiff. "You have nothing to worry about. We've given each of the Candidates a thorough screening. Security has been increased tenfold. We have the entire Ranger staff working this afternoon—at least half will be on the pitch itself, and the rest interspersed throughout the island. There *won't* be trouble."

"But—"

"We can't hide from this, Lily. You said so yourself." His fingers traced tender lines across my cheek. "What message would it send if we canceled the event today? If the Rangers went into hiding?"

"I'm not asking you to *cancel* anything!" I sighed, tilted my head against his hand and relished the warmth of his skin against mine. "But I'm not sure that'd be such a bad thing. Surely you've already adjusted the Trials in one form or another."

"What do you mean?"

"You've said a hundred times that the public events are just a tiny snapshot of the entire Trial process. They're more for fun and island bonding. I thought you were supposed to be monitoring the Candidates on the streets as they went about their business, not keeping them holed up in some Oasis!"

"Some adjustments have been made admittedly, but this is different. Cancelling the public Trial would be admitting defeat loud and clear. It'd be sending a message to the Islanders—and The Faction—that we're scared. I'm not willing to do that."

"Well, how will you select the appropriate Candidates if you're keeping them locked up?"

"Lily, please. Take a deep breath—the Candidates have been under surveillance for months, and I promise you we won't make our choices until we're sure. The Trials will last as long as we need them to last."

"But Zin—"

"—Zin can handle herself."

"Just... keep an eye on her, okay? I know I've already asked you to, but I'm more worried than ever."

Discomfort crept onto his face. "We keep an eye on all of the Candidates equally, and their safety is of utmost importance. Zin is no exception."

"I know, I believe you, but. . . "

"Good." Ranger X leaned toward me, his lips brushing against my cheek. "I love you, Lily."

"I love you, too," I said, my hand sliding around his neck. I held him close. I held him so close that he couldn't help but hear as I whispered Camden's name in his ear.

Ranger X straightened at the name. "What about him?"

I released X and stepped back. The crowd swarmed in the distance, emotions running higher than ever. The Candidates were lined up in the wings, awaiting the starting whistle.

"That's all I can say," I said, turning to leave before he could ask more of me. "Good luck, X."

"Lily, wait—"

A throat cleared behind Ranger X. It was Elle, a stunning woman who ran Ranger HQ. Though she was hundreds of years old, she didn't look a day over thirty, thanks to Fae magic. She flicked her shimmering blonde hair over her shoulder.

"Hi, Lily, Ranger X," she said, her voice a thin melody over the roar of the crowd. She tapped her slender fingers against the clipboard in her hands. "I'm sorry to interrupt, but we're ready for you, X. It's time."

I waved goodbye to both, leaving Ranger X to stare as I hurried away from him.

"X, is everything okay?" Elle asked. I could hardly make out her words as I rushed to the stands.

"It's fine," he said, his voice gruff. "It's time to start. Security is in place?"

I wormed my way through the crowd, making it into the West Isle Witches box just before the beginning whistle sounded. I'd missed the announcements on my trek through the audience, but I needn't have worried. The second I took a seat next to my family, Poppy launched into her play-by-play.

"Did you see what Camden is wearing?" She sighed, fanning herself. She wasn't the only girl who'd had her eye on that particular Candidate with his movie-star good looks. "His... pants are nice."

I stared at Camden, pretending to analyze his pants. Instead, I watched his face, waiting for something, anything to happen. Except for his look of intense concentration, however, there was nothing—no emotion, no reaction, no empty, vacant expression.

The Candidates were spaced equidistant from one another around the outskirts of the arena. Though the starting whistle had blown, none of them moved. From the edges of the arena, a thick, dark smoke began billowing up—so thick that as it rose and covered the arena, we lost sight of the Candidates.

It took less than three minutes before the entire pitch had been covered by this smoke.

"What are they doing?" I tried to keep my voice steady. "I can't see anything!"

Trinket and her children sat on the other end of the bleacher, all of them watching with rapt attention. Mimsey sat next to them, just to the right of Poppy. I was last on the bench, though Gus and a few other friends wandered around behind us, too nervous to sit.

A man who was most likely a Companion, a different Companion than last time, perched near the rear of the box with his eyes trained on my back. Probably X's doing.

"Just watch," Hettie said. Her eyes didn't once leave the smog, though I couldn't figure out what she was seeing. "It'll go away."

It did. The smoke vanished as quickly as it'd arrived. The Candidates looked slightly stunned to be standing in bright daylight again, and even more surprised when they realized that a door had materialized next to each of them.

"What the heck?" Poppy said. "What are they supposed to do with a bunch of doors?"

I shrugged. Apparently the Candidates had no clue, either. A few of them tentatively tested their respective handles. One or two gained confidence and rattled the knobs, while the boldest of the group shoved their shoulders against the wooden panels. None of the doors budged.

"*Physical* fitness is only one part involved in becoming a Ranger," Hettie explained. "It's the mental Trials that are the most challenging."

Poppy frowned. "Well, what are they doing?"

"That smoke in the arena forced each Candidate into a deep sleep. If you look, you can see their eyes are closed." Hettie paused, letting us see for ourselves. "They've been forced into an individual nightmare based on their worst fears. The clock has begun its countdown, and they must escape before the time is up."

Sure enough, a large timepiece had descended in the middle of the arena. It was in the shape of a cube, hovering over the center for all to watch. Just under ten minutes remained.

"Ten minutes isn't a long time," I murmured.

Hettie snorted a laugh. "I don't know about you, but ten minutes inside of my worst nightmare is plenty long."

"How do they escape?"

"Well, at the end of the day, they are merely under a spell. In order to escape, they have to pull themselves out of the fog." Hettie's gaze bored into my head. "This Trial is meant to test the Candidates' mental power—we all know that magic exists in this world that can cause hallucinations or alter one's mind. It doesn't matter how big a Ranger may be on the outside—if their brain is weak, they can be controlled. The bigger they are, the harder they fall."

"Are you talking about mind—"

"No," Hettie cut me off with a quick glance at Poppy. "That is impossible to fight. I'm talking about simple charms; you know the ones, Lily. A light love spell or a Persuasive Potion. What you're referencing is different—that takes a piece of one's soul and gives it to another."

"What are you talking about?" Poppy leaned forward and threw a few kernels of fresh popcorn into her mouth. "I don't like the sound of it."

I left Hettie to explain, turning my focus back to the pitch. I watched Zin as she leaned against the door, her face pained while an unseen battle raged behind her eyelids. To the left of her station stood Camden.

He, too, crumpled in front of his own doorway. Eyes closed, arms shaking in what I could only imagine was terror. Then his whole body began to tremble, wracked with shivers until suddenly—he stopped moving.

Goosebumps raced across my skin. He stood still, so still I couldn't tell if he was breathing. I watched him carefully, the eerie stillness making me wonder if he'd become unconscious.

Then all at once, his eyes flashed open, revealing black pits in his handsome face.

My heart raced. My arm flew out and clasped Poppy across the chest. "Did you see that?"

"What?" Poppy tilted her head back, throwing popcorn into the air. "I've caught fifteen in a row. Don't break my streak."

Hettie stood abruptly. "I need to go. Lily, come with—"

A strangled cry bubbled in my throat. I lunged for the edge of the railing, my arm outstretched. The rest of the viewers in the box stared in mute horror as I leaned over the edge as far as I could go, screaming for Ranger X at the top of my lungs.

Everything happened fast. Too fast. Camden's eyes dilated. His hands jerked with robotic movements, sliding an item from his pocket. He swiveled to face Zin, his eyes filled with the same hungry expression she'd described.

"Zin!" The cry caught in my throat.

There was no way she'd heard me. Her body sagged against the door, her eyes scrunched closed against the nightmares holding her captive as Camden marched swiftly toward her.

Ranger X broke into a sprint, his lips moving with unheard words. Camden flinched as X closed the distance, but the magic-free arena muted the effects of any spells.

Camden reached Zin before X. A glint of metal in his hand reflected sunshine. A knife.

"Lily, do something!" Poppy's fingers closed over my shirt, shaking me. "He's going to hurt her!"

Camden stood over Zin. Sweat glistened on her forehead while she lay on the ground, oblivious to the man standing over her. As he raised his arm, the tip of the knife flashed, then soared through the air and straight toward Zin.

Poppy screamed as panic erupted in the stands around us. My eyes remained glued open, fixed on the commotion below, watching as Ranger X dove toward the pair.

At the same time, Zin shifted from her human form.

Her sleek, jaguar body leaped for the doorway behind her just as Ranger X hurtled toward Camden. X missed the Candidate, but the distraction was enough to knock him off balance and allow Zin to crash through the doorway and onto the other side.

Camden recovered, lunging for her, but he was too far behind. Zin had already begun shifting back to her human form, a limp figure on the ground as X tore Camden away from her, pinning him to the ground.

My breath came out in a whoosh, and I shook Poppy. "It's okay, they're okay."

Ranger X ripped the knife from Camden's grasp and flung it to another Ranger. The rest of the Rangers had rushed onto the arena, now flanking the fallen Candidate. One of them clasped Camden's hands in a pair of magic-proof handcuffs.

Zin stood on the other side of the door, her face pale. Her body trembled from head to toe as Rangers surrounded her. I couldn't pull my eyes from her face, my mind plagued with thoughts of *what if*. What if Ranger X hadn't been fast enough? What if Camden had struck one second sooner? What if...

"Lily," a soft, male voice whispered in my ear. "Come with me—there is work to be done."

I turned to find Liam's arm grasping mine. The Companion who'd been situated near the rear of the box was no longer in sight, and I wondered if that'd been Liam's doing.

A fury burned in his eyes. "This is a one-time offer, and it expires in ten seconds. If you ever want to find The Puppeteer, follow me."

CHAPTER 16

"WHERE ARE WE GOING?" I asked for the third time. "Nobody is around, you can speak, Liam."

He marched ahead, ignoring my questions. The day after X caught me outside of the B&B, I had updated Hettie on my meeting with Liam. She hadn't seemed surprised by anything he'd told me. Almost as if she'd known what he would say before he'd said it.

If I'd thought Liam had been emotional last week, it was nothing compared to now. Anger ran in his veins, radiated from his eyes. His words were short, piercing the air like gunshots. "I'll explain when we've arrived."

He'd taken me on a roundabout path outside of the arena, avoiding the stares of curious onlookers. We walked for nearly thirty minutes in zigzags until I finally recognized our location—Midge's B&B.

"She keeps this route quiet." Liam fished a key out of his pocket and unlocked the back door. "Private business matters, you see, so please don't announce this entrance to anyone else."

"I understand."

Liam marched up the spiraling staircase that wound through the rear of the inn. When we reached the top, he stopped and turned to me. "I apologize in advance."

"For what?"

In answer, he knocked three times on the door to the highest room in the building. It was the only room on the floor, and as

I waited for something to happen, I glanced uneasily around the empty hallway.

"Nothing to be nervous about yet," Liam said, a tight smile on his lips. "In fact, it might just be a pleasant surprise."

Then, someone answered his knock, and the door opened from inside.

"*Ainsley!*" My heart pounded at the sight of my former assistant. "What are you doing here?"

She rushed to me, opening her arms wide and bringing me in for a long overdue hug. "Hi there, boss. It's good to see you."

A burst of happiness had me staring dumbly back at her. "What are you doing here? I heard about everything. You were working for MAGIC, Inc. the whole time?"

She nodded. "I'm sorry I couldn't say anything to you sooner, but it was my job."

"I understand," I said. "When Hettie told me, I was shocked."

On the day Hettie had invited me into The Core, she'd explained that Ainsley—my former assistant at Lions Marketing, Inc.—was a Guardian witch. The whole time she had been my assistant, she'd really been working for the paranormal version of the FBI, tasked to keep me safe until I reached The Isle.

She grinned that familiar, mischievous smile. She'd always been a little bit different; her hair boasted a streak of purple, her arm a sleeve of tattoos, and her sense of humor was a little off-color. She'd been my best friend. "I've missed you, boss."

A blush of embarrassment crept so far onto my cheeks it might have reached my forehead. "I can't believe I ever asked you to help me with expense reports!"

Ainsley waved a hand. "It was fun. Turns out I have a knack for marketing, I'm pretty sure."

"So, what brings you to our lovely island?" I asked. "New assignment?"

"Nah. In fact, I'm funemployed at the moment."

"You quit your job at MAGIC, Inc.?"

"I'm in between gigs," she said, waving a hand. "I've started to use the term *freelancer*."

My eyes widened. "Was it because of me?"

"Nah, I'm just kidding. You were my last target, and I haven't been reassigned yet so I built in a little vacation to the island. You know, beaches and whatnot."

"The beaches?" I raised an eyebrow. She didn't seem like the beachy type.

"I asked her to come by." Liam stepped forward. "I'm about to disclose incredibly dangerous information to you, Lily, and you'll need help on your journey."

"My journey?" I looked between the two. "What journey?"

"I am going to tell you the location where you'll find the Witch of the Woods," Liam said. "And I knew you wouldn't ask for help. I'd also heard the two of you were good friends, and when I asked Ainsley about it—"

"I said *rock on*," Ainsley finished. "So, who's the Witch of the Woods, and why are we going after her?"

"She is one of only two people in this entire world who thoroughly understands the power of mind bending." Liam cleared his throat. "I know Camden personally, and I know his father. I was there in the stands today watching, and that... that monster in the arena wasn't Camden."

"The Puppeteer," I said. "She's back."

He gave the subtlest of nods. "Camden's family does not deserve to be disgraced in such a way. He'd never..." Liam paused to clear his throat. "Camden will never forgive himself once he hears what happened—I think it's safe to assume he won't remember anything after the Trial began."

"You want us to set the record straight," Ainsley said. "And the only way to do that is to find this Puppeteer."

"These matters should not be discussed in a hallway." Liam pushed past us and into the room. "Close the door behind you."

I'd expected the room to be Liam's, but once I stepped inside, I realized it belonged to Ainsley. A funky suitcase sat on the bed, her clothes spilling out of it. Pink frills lined every surface of the room, complemented by airy yellow walls—the exact opposite of everything Ainsley stood for with her dark hair and tattoos.

"Sit anywhere," she said. "Make yourselves at home. I have wine or more wine. Midge really stocked the room for me."

I passed on the wine, as did Liam. A small desk was pushed against the corner—old school and antique looking, and it was the perfect height for me to lean a hip against. Ainsley plopped on the fluffy white comforter draped across a bed accented by pastel pillows.

Liam stood next to the window, staring out over the water while we got situated. The anger he'd carried into the room seemed to have burned away, replaced by a glimmer of uncertainty when he turned to face us. "It's not too late to say no. That goes for both of you."

I folded my hands over my lap. "Zin is my family. I won't stand around and watch as the Candidates are picked off one by one."

"I'm not the beachy type." Ainsley eyed the bottle of wine, and then turned her attention to Liam. "And anyway, vacations are overrated. Tell us what to do."

"You may want to write this down," Liam said. "I will only explain the instructions once."

I dug in the old desk, finding a quill and a piece of parchment inside. The top of the paper was decorated by a letterhead that read *Midge's Memos.* "Ready."

"Through the trees and to the peak,
Where you must find the will to speak
To the Witch of the Woods who rules this place,
If the test is passed, you'll find her embrace."

Ainsley snorted. "Really, Liam? Rhymes?"

"He always does rhymes," I said. "He did this last time he sent me into The Forest, too."

"Directions through The Forest are liquid," he said. "Poems are like music—they may use the same notes over and over again, but each time they're played something is a little bit different. An accent here, a trill there, a tiny, itsy bitsy breath that wasn't there before. Just like The Forest."

Ainsley held out her hand, and I tossed her the notepad. She read the directions over. "I have no clue what this means, but I suppose we'll figure it out. Can we get a few snacks to take with us? We might get lost."

Liam's face paled. "I can't believe I'm sending the two of you into The Forest. Together."

"Come on, Lil," Ainsley said. "Let's go before Liam changes his mind."

"I'll catch up with you in a second," I told Ainsley as she bolted for the stairs. "I forgot one thing."

Once her footsteps had disappeared and her low murmurs with Midge in the lobby floated up the staircase, I faced Liam. He'd resumed staring at the lake beyond the window.

"Hey," I said, taking soft steps toward him. "Is everything okay? I've never seen you like this before."

When he turned back, his face was a mess of frustration and anger and sadness. "I hate asking you to do this, to find the Witch of the Woods. If I thought I could do it, I would, but I don't have the skills."

"I asked you for this information. You're hardly forcing it on me."

He looked down and stared intently at the floor for a long while before speaking. "We're dealing with dangerous magic, Lily. I don't know what will happen. I don't have the right answers."

"Nobody does. That's why we have to work together and figure it out."

"I am *never* emotional. Never. That's why I'm good at my job. It's the same reason my business has succeeded beyond my wildest dreams, and it's the reason that I can keep a secret. I care about neither fame nor glory. I don't even particularly care for money, so long as I have enough of it. I don't—"

"Liam, stop." I cut him off and moved farther into the room, closing the door behind me. "What do you care about, then? What's making you so upset?"

He inhaled, long and slow. Obviously stalling. "I don't know."

"Guess."

"I broke down just now and gave you directions to someplace you should never have to venture. For the *wrong* reasons—because I was angry, upset at what's happening to the Candidates. Raymon didn't deserve to die. Neither does Zin, and Camden... none of them deserve what they've been put through. It has to stop!"

I remained silent for a long second, the aftershocks of Liam's frustration fading into the air.

Then I took a chance and stepped forward. Liam didn't have an opportunity to move before I wrapped my arms around him and hugged him tight to my chest. He didn't return the embrace for a long time, until finally he relented, his shoulders relaxing.

I didn't know what it meant, or why I'd done it. All I'd known was that Liam needed someone to lean on, and I was there to help. I said goodbye, brushing an echo of a kiss against his cheek.

"Everything okay?" Ainsley asked as I joined her out front a few minutes later. "I don't know Liam all that well, but... he seemed upset."

I nodded. "I think he'll be fine."

"Then let's find this Witch of the Woods."

CHAPTER 17

"**H**OW DO YOU KNOW ALL of these things?" I asked, not for the first time, as Ainsley knelt against the forest floor. "I'd have been lost a hundred times already if it wasn't for you."

"Stuff sinks into my brain over time." She fingered the petals of a leaf, her face scrunched in thought. "Okay, we're headed in the right direction. I'm assuming that 'the peak' in Liam's stupid poem is the top of the volcano. These Fire Bird flowers can only grow if there's heat under the ground. We follow these, and we're good to go."

I looked down at unique flowers that I'd never seen before, neither on The Isle nor on the mainland. They looked like miniature roaring lions—the mouth of the flower opening and closing as Ainsley pinched the base of the bloom.

"Watch this," she said, holding the mouth of the flower open. "Watch closely, don't even blink."

As she squeezed the lip of the bright red flower, the tiniest noise erupted from it. Like a garbled hiccup. At the same time, a tiny blip of fire shot out of the flower and blossomed into the air above it.

I didn't know whether to laugh or look amazed.

"Cool, huh?" She stood up and didn't look the slightest bit unnerved by the fire-breathing flower. "Really handy to know if you're ever lost in the woods. If you find one of these guys, you can use it to get your bonfire going. Most people are scared of 'em, but if you treat them correctly, they just might save your life. Anyway, they grow near volcanoes. I think we can continue on this way."

"So, how have you been since…" We walked in silence for a moment. "Well, since I left?"

"Oh, I've been good," she said, her smile faltering a bit.

"C'mon, Ains. You worked next to me for years. I can tell when something's on your mind. Spill!"

She grinned. "There's a boy."

"I knew it! Tell me all about him."

Ainsley filled me in on a long, drawn-out story about a human policeman who'd accidentally knocked Ainsley right off her new broomstick. From there, it'd been love at first sight. Sort of cute, in a strange way.

"It's just challenging because he's a mortal. There's always a bit of a learning curve when you break the news to a human about being a witch and whatnot. I mean, you know the drill. Anyway, is island life treating you well? You look great, all tan and stuff."

"There's a boy for me, too," I said. "His name is Ranger X—"

"Okay, I knew about the boy," Ainsley said. "He's a hottie. I approve."

"Who told you?"

Ainsley gave me a skeptical glance. "Lil, when you snag the hottest, most unavailable bachelor on the island, people are gonna talk."

The back of my neck burned. "Oh."

"Don't be embarrassed; it's all good talk," Ainsley assured me. "Plus, how sweet is it that he changed laws that were hundreds of years old just so you could be together? Hello, Romeo."

"He is wonderful," I said, but when I smiled, it was forced. "Sometimes, I think he's too good to be true."

Ainsley stopped to burp another Fire Bird, this time lighting a strange little cigarette. I'd only ever seen one like it in Ferrah's hand, the fairy who'd greeted me during my first visit into The

Forest. "Why the long face? Of course you deserve him! Is there something you're not telling me?"

I hesitated. "I can't say."

"Is it about The Core? If so, I know about it."

"What?" I stopped walking. "How? When? *What?*"

She winked, plucked a Fire Bird, and put it behind her ear. "Your grandmother met with me this morning and filled me in on everything. She invited me to join, and of course I accepted."

"Seriously?" My jaw dropped. "She'd hinted about a girl joining The Core, but I never once thought it'd be you!"

"I'm happy to help however I can. Keep talking, though. If we stop now, we'll be here all night, and you don't want that."

It didn't take much prompting to get me going. Before I knew it, I had gushed to Ainsley for the next mile about how guilty I felt keeping The Core a secret from X.

"Here I am, sneaking around," I said, "while he worries and does his best to keep me safe. I don't know what to do. My grandmother and The Core are on one side, a very important side. Then equally important, I have Ranger X, who is convinced I'm lying about where I've been all night. If I were him, I'd be concerned, too."

Ainsley frowned. "That's tough."

"What would you do?"

She bit her lip. "Well, you did say that Ranger X tells you everything he can. I'm sure there are things about his job that he can't tell you, or chooses not to. You don't have to tell him everything about your life, either. There are reasons some things need to be kept confidential."

"Yeah, but that doesn't help when he catches me out all night and I can't explain where I've been."

"Well, maybe you should talk to Hettie and tell her exactly what you told me. In the meantime, I guess... well, I guess you should just *show* him how you feel."

"I told him I loved him."

"That's a good start! But you know that old saying—actions speak louder than words, and all that jazz. Plan something, do something special. He'll appreciate it, and it might help ease the tension until you can talk to Hettie."

"But—"

"Hold that thought," Ainsley said. She knelt down, her hands skimming over bunches of Fire Birds. We'd emerged from the trees into a valley.

Behind us stood a mountain covered with thick trees. I hadn't realized our ascent or descent, mostly because I'd been too worried about staying alive for the last few hours. I inhaled a deep breath and looked forward. After the darkness of the thick trees, this place was a haven.

Fire Birds bloomed in all directions, like the field of poppies in *The Wizard of Oz*. Red flowers coated the ground, a small dirt trail winding through the blossoms. The field rose before us in a steep ascent. At the very top, a light twirl of smoke rose from the final peak.

"We're here," Ainsley said. "The peak. We've just got to climb the volcano, and we'll be there."

"Nonsense," a voice said from behind us. "You've made it already. *Usually* my army of deadly beasts scares off the unworthy folks, but it seems they didn't bother you."

"She has an army?" Ainsley muttered. "Liam's stupid poem forgot to mention the *army*."

Together we turned to our right to find a woman standing there—old, hunched over a cane, her hair in two gray braids that fell halfway down her back and swished around her body as she hobbled forward.

She gave a smile that'd been practiced for years, peeking through her layers of wrinkles. "Welcome to my home."

As she approached, I held my ground. "Are you the Witch of the Woods?"

"Are you looking for her? If so, you're in the right place." The Witch clomped across the dirt path, stopping a few feet before us. She didn't speak another word, but her eyes scanned Ainsley from head to toe.

Ainsley shivered under the intense scrutiny, and then the Witch of the Woods turned her eyes to me. Suddenly, I understood.

Chills wracked my limbs as her eyes pierced my body like an x-ray. From the tips of my toes, she dragged her gaze up, goosebumps erupting across my skin with every inch her eyes traveled. When she reached my face, she looked straight at the center of my forehead and the sudden, intense pain was almost unbearable.

I doubled over, let out a cry as fire exploded in my head. Stars burst, darkness beat out the light. My hands covered my face as I fell to the ground.

"Are you okay?" Ainsley's hands clasped me, held me. She turned to the Witch. "What did you do to her?"

The Witch of the Woods merely shrugged. "You've both passed, now bring yourselves here for a hug."

As quickly as the pain had come, it subsided. Still shaky, my knees wobbling, I stood and met the old woman's eyes. An expression of interest rested on her face, and though there wasn't a whisper of an apology in sight, she opened her arms.

Liam's words rang through my head, and I realized that her offer of an embrace meant we had passed the test—I just hadn't expected the *test* to be so painful. I stepped forward first, and accepted the hug. Ainsley was more hesitant.

"Why should we trust you *now?*" Ainsley stood a foot away from the Witch. "We hiked half a day to get here through the most dangerous parts of The Isle, and now you're crippling my friend with some strange magic?"

The Witch's eyes flashed at Ainsley. "I'm pleased with you."

Ainsley shook her head, confused. "You're pleased with *me?*"

"You're a good companion for Lily," she explained. "She's too trusty, you're too crusty. It evens out."

"I'm not too crusty," Ainsley said. "I'm just careful."

"I'm not too trusty!" I said. "I'm optimistic."

"Okay," the Witch agreed. "Whatever you say. Now, are you going to come with me or not?"

"Do I have to hug you?" Ainsley looked a little mortified at the idea.

"Yes," The Witch said. "A big fat hug."

Ainsley shot me a look of frustration, but she did as the Witch said. When she stepped away, she shook her head. "What do hugs have to do with anything?"

The Witch of the Woods cackled. "Oh, nothing. But I live all by myself with only the beasts for company. This old lady gets lonely, and I love a visit from a friend."

Ainsley covered her mouth, hiding her surprise. The old witch continued cackling, and eventually Ainsley joined in, too.

"Don't get too attached to me," the old lady said. "I know I'm lovable, but neither of you will last here for more than a day."

Ainsley frowned. "That's harsh. You don't know how persistent I can be."

"The secrets I am responsible for keeping are too much for any one person to bear—except me, and that's why I'm the only woman for the job. I know the folks on the island say I'm nuts."

"No, that's not true—" I started, but she waved me off.

"It's okay, I happen to agree. The lifestyle suits me."

The Witch of the Woods gently moved branches out of her way with the tip of her cane. Ainsley and I followed close behind, and as I peeked over my shoulder, the flowers and branches mysteriously covered our path. If I hadn't walked along it moments before, I would've never known it existed.

"It's not *magic*," the Witch said, catching my look of surprise. "Well, I suppose it is, but it's not *my* magic. It's The Forest."

"The Forest has its own magic?"

"But of course," she said. "I expect Liam gave you directions to find me?"

"Yes, he did."

"I like that man," she said with a coy grin. "He's cute, don't ya think?"

I widened my eyes at Ainsley, who looked just as shocked. "I suppose he has nice eyes," Ainsley agreed. "Good hair."

"I was thinking about the whole package, but I suppose the eyes aren't bad, either," the Witch said. "Anyway, did he tell you much about me?"

"Not really."

"I suppose that was for the best. Well, I live here, obviously. It's my job to protect the secrets of this island. The Forest is my baby, and although I take care of it, it takes care of me, too."

I looked behind us and sure enough, our path was completely invisible. The Forest protected its own, and I doubted that *anyone* would be able to find the Witch of the Woods without an invitation.

"I hate to seem impatient, but we are sort of in a rush," I said, after waiting to see if she'd continue her explanations. When she didn't, I tried again. "There are bad things going on back home."

"I know it, I feel it," she said. "But true understanding can't be rushed, I'm sorry."

"Of course," I said quickly. "I want to do things right, it's just. . . . . ."

"I know," she said quietly. "I understand, I truly do."

We turned a corner, and the most incredible sight rose before us. Trees, rocks, lush greenery—a place far more spectacular than any I'd laid eyes on so far rose from the ground. A waterfall crashed from thousands upon thousands of feet in the air. The stream below it bubbled and gurgled through rocks the color of emeralds, sand that flashed the palest of pinks. Thick, luxurious trees twisted themselves into a sturdy fortress around it all, concealing an intimidating castle built into the rock.

"This is my home, and it is the heart of The Forest," the Witch said with reverence. "You must respect it, or you will die. It is really that simple."

My heart skipped a beat, and Ainsley's eyes widened.

"Use your common sense, and you'll be fine." The Witch smiled at us. "I didn't mean to scare you, but if you're smart, you'll be cautious."

Ainsley made a disgruntled noise, picking up her feet as if walking on eggshells.

"Now follow me and I will show you to the Library of Secrets. There, you will find everything you are looking for—and more." The Witch of the Woods turned to me. "You'll find more than you ever dreamed possible, Lily Locke."

CHAPTER 18

THE WORLD HAD NEVER BEEN more silent.

Ainsley and I climbed up the stairs, hundreds of them. We curled our way through the winding stone passageway for nearly an hour. My legs ached, calves burned, but I didn't complain and neither did Ainsley.

Despite her advanced age, the Witch plowed on ahead of us with impressive vigor. My breath came in loud huffs. Ainsley's choice of relieving frustrations was an array of creative expletives. The Witch of the Woods cackled at a few of Ainsley's more entertaining turns of phrases, but I didn't have enough energy to laugh.

As we climbed higher and higher, the air grew damp. Except for our gasping breaths, the only sound to reach our ears was the trickle of water in skinny rivers down the sides of the walls.

Despite the stillness in the gray passage, lit only by candles every few feet, there was something more happening, something greater than us all. It wasn't a sound, but a *feeling*; a feeling that ran beneath our feet, the vibrations consuming the mountain until its very stones trembled.

"Just about there, don't stop now, girls." The Witch of the Woods plucked a torch from the wall and circled to face us. "Keep up, children."

Ainsley winced. "I'm beginning to think it would've been easier to get eaten by a lion in The Forest."

"Or get attacked by poisonous bugs," I added.

"Or lay down to sleep with the Fire Birds," the Witch agreed.

"But since you didn't succumb to any of those obstacles, you obviously would prefer to be here. Don't worry, I guarantee you won't be disappointed."

"How many people have been here besides us?" I gasped. "I can't imagine anyone would come here without a very good reason."

"Oh, I have an elevator." The Witch turned to face us, a gleam in her eye. "I just thought we'd take the scenic route."

"You!" Ainsley gaped like a sunfish. "You! You *batty*, old—"

"Stop!" I lunged for Ainsley, yanking her back.

We were so exhausted that my tackle didn't work the way I'd planned. Our legs gave out, our bodies crumpling into a heap on the floor. Neither of us moved, except for our heaving chests.

"It was a joke," the Witch of the Woods said. "I don't have an elevator. You two need to relax. Anyway, what do you think?"

From our place on the floor, I turned my gaze upward. Her finger pointed toward the mouth of an enormous cave. I scrambled to my feet, pulling Ainsley up with me. She'd grumbled the whole way up, but as soon as she caught a glimpse of the room before us, she swallowed her words.

"Wow," Ainsley whispered. "*Incredible.*"

The Witch of the Woods beamed. "I think so. I don't get a chance to show it off very often. It's unfortunate, really."

"Maybe if you had an elevator, people would stop by more often," Ainsley said. "So folks wouldn't have to worry about *dying* on the way up."

The Witch's mouth formed a thin line. "Is that what you think?"

"I think. . . " Ainsley trailed off. "No, I suppose not."

"Most people can't be trusted with the information inside this room. Don't let me believe you're like the rest of them."

Ainsley's face reddened. She gave a single shake of her head. For now, that seemed to satisfy the Witch because she turned and gestured for us to follow. "Good. Let me show you the Library of Secrets."

The library was more of a cavern than a room, its beauty too impossible for words. Built from stones of all shapes and colors, the ceiling rose high above us, the walls thick with reds and grays and browns. Our footsteps echoed as we stepped through the dark opening.

"I don't know what to say..." My eyes traced the edges of the room. The walls went up, and up—so far up that the stones didn't begin to curve into the ceiling until the shadows engulfed their edges.

In the center of the room sat one long, wooden table. Ten stools sat on either side.

"If this is a library, where are the books?" Ainsley asked. "Or am I missing something?"

"You haven't even seen the beginning of this place." The Witch of the Woods scurried toward the farthest side of the room. The light didn't quite reach her, the room fading into blackness and hiding her small form. "Here you are, my dears. The Library of Secrets awaits."

She pulled back a black curtain that'd shielded the main portion of the library. She pulled so hard that she stumbled, bracing her body against the wall as the emptiness exposed a room ten times the size of this one.

My mouth fell open. "Oh, my. . . "

Ainsley reached over and squeezed my hand.

More shocking than the room's size, however, was the lack of a fourth wall. Straight ahead, the mouth of the cave opened to pure sky, the blue and white of the clouds marred only by the rush of water. Tons and tons of water pouring from the roof of the cave.

I moved closer, Ainsley following my lead. It felt like Niagara Falls streaming over our head, crashing hundreds of feet to the ground below, housing a secret library brimming with magic.

"The books are here, please help yourself." The Witch gestured to the sides of the room. Along the stone walls were hundreds of books stacked atop each other. "I'll leave you to your work."

Without further explanation, she ducked through a small side door carved out of stone.

"She's one strange lady," Ainsley said, her eyes glued to the waterfall. "Is it just me, or does this seem incredibly dangerous? There's not even a safety rail."

We crept as close to the waterfall as we dared. Though we left at least ten feet between us and the falls, the thunder of the water shook every atom of my being, dragging me toward it. I rubbed my sweating hands against my legs.

"I'm not a huge fan of heights," I said as Ainsley pointed out just how far the drop down went before a pool of lagoon-blue water blossomed at the bottom. "I mostly imagine all the ways I could accidentally fall off the edge and die."

"Are you doing that right now?"

"Yes," I admitted, my heart going through major palpitations as the hundreds of gallons of water washed past us. "One false step, and. . . " I tried to whistle, making a diving motion with my hands. The motion ended in a splat at the bottom.

Ainsley offered her most reassuring smile. "Let's start with the books. I don't know if we're welcome here overnight, and it's already late. If we don't hurry, we'll be making our way back in the dark."

The thought of re-entering The Forest was enough to bring on a wave of exhaustion.

"Maybe there's a hotel nearby," I said wistfully, ignoring Ainsley's eye roll. I sighed. "Let's get started."

CHAPTER 19

OURS LATER, THE SUN HAD begun to set.

Ainsley and I sat at stools across the table from each other. The only time either of us rose was to grab a new book. Once in a while Ainsley meandered toward the waterfall. I'd bite my tongue as long as I could as she stood there, staring over the edge, lost in thought.

Finally, my heart would beat too quickly and I'd yell at her to get back from the edge again. This process went on for hours, and yet we still hadn't found anything of use in the hundreds of books we'd skimmed.

Ainsley whistled a low tune to herself as she paced a row of books, her finger dragging lightly over their spines. "What titles might be relevant that we haven't thought of yet?"

"I don't know. Look for the words *mind bending, blood magic,* or *The Puppeteer*. Not that I've found anything on them."

"I'm hungry," she said. "Do you think the Witch will come back? I could use a Pop-Tart."

"I'm not walking all the way down those stairs to find her," I said. "I'll starve before I climb those stairs again. Let's just find the book and get out of here."

Ainsley's stomach rumbled in argument. She exhaled. "We've been looking for hours, and the most interesting thing I've learned is that bulberries are edible."

"It doesn't do us any good to know that if we never make it out of here. There's nothing in your section over there?"

All at once, Ainsley's spine went rigid. "Wait a second. I might have found something."

"What is it?" I stood, my stool scratching against the rocky floor beneath our feet. The water pounded in the background, pulsing against my eardrums. "Bring it here."

She moved quickly, holding the book before her like it was boiling hot. She dropped it on the table, her hands shaking as if she'd been burned.

I looked down at the cover. The book was black—the outside slightly scuffed, as if it'd been made from charcoal. Ainsley was staring at her fingers with a confused expression.

"You okay?" I asked. "What's wrong?"

"I don't have a good feeling about that book," she said. "I don't like it at all. If you're going to open it, I'm getting out of this room."

"Are you kidding? This is what we came here for!"

"I came here to learn about magic and to protect you." Ainsley crossed her arms. "I didn't come here to dabble with black magic. I may be impulsive and stupid, but I know my limits."

I stared at the book's cover, a slight haze surrounding it—as if its very existence was a figment of my imagination. "Go on, then, and leave. I'm reading it whether you're here or not. I didn't come here expecting to play with fairies and love spells, I expected the magic would be dark."

"Yes, but—"

"You weren't *there*," I said, my voice more forceful than I'd intended. "You can't understand what I saw, what we all went through watching one of the Candidates die on the pitch. Raymon is not coming back, Ainsley, don't you understand? He's *dead*!"

"Look, I'm sorry." Ainsley raised her hands, her face pale. "I'm not going to leave, Lily, I never would have left you. But I don't like it. I am here to protect you, and I will do that until my last breath, but I will not touch that book again."

"I understand," I said. "And you don't need to stay here. I

wouldn't blame you if you left. Liam shouldn't have asked you to come here in the first place."

Ainsley's jawline was firm. "You're stuck with me, boss."

I gave her a wry smile and reached for the book, hesitating just before I touched the edges. Swallowing hard, I debated pushing the book away, forgetting it ever existed. But I didn't.

We'd come here for a reason. If the Witch could've told us the answers she probably would have. Since she hadn't, that left just me, Ainsley, and the books.

As my fingers sank around the book's spine, I understood Ainsley's shock. Inky, invisible fingers of black magic seeped through my skin. The magic leaked into my veins, coursing through my body as I opened the nameless cover.

The first page had no words on it.

To my horror, there was a single droplet the color of rust on the yellowed page.

Blood.

"Lily, look down." Ainsley said, her warning strangled. "You're bleeding."

I glanced at my hands, surprised to find the tip of my right pointer finger pricked. The blood on the page was *mine*.

When I'd opened the book, the edge must have given me a paper cut. It wasn't painful, but it was enough to leave a mark.

"Put it back," Ainsley said in a shaky voice. "I don't have a good feeling about this."

I considered listening to her. My entire body ached to be rid of this terrible, evil book. Before I could push it toward her, the image of Raymon falling from the tree flashed through my mind. I raised my eyes, held Ainsley's gaze, and gave a single shake of my head.

She didn't argue when I flipped to the next page.

The words there blurred before my eyes, but I pressed on, whispering them in low tones:

"*With this blood, you shall be mine.*

A single drop, and I'll redefine
Your hopes and dreams, your loves and fears,
I'll make you laugh, or shed your tears.
And in exchange, my soul will break,
A piece of me, for you to take. . . "

The rest of the words swam before my eyes. The spell continued. My lips might have moved, but I couldn't control them any longer. I felt my body sway dangerously close to the table. I couldn't move my arms, couldn't brace my body as I fell to the cold stone floor.

My head hit hard cement, the crack sharp, though I didn't feel pain. Somewhere far away, deep in a vacuum, shouted a voice. Ainsley. I couldn't tell what she wanted or what she was saying as the world turned into a fuzzy, soul-wrenching blackness that dissolved my mind until I couldn't feel, couldn't think. . .

The next moment I was standing. I moved stiffly, as if watching a robotic version of myself from above. Ainsley lay at my feet, not moving. I didn't know what happened, or how she got there. All I knew was that the look in her eyes was confused, hurt.

Some force moved my feet forward. I stepped over Ainsley's head. A tiny place in my soul wanted to help her, but I couldn't— something prevented my heart from feeling, my mind from thinking. I marched forward, following orders from someone— *something*—else. Marching, marching, marching until I reached the edge of the cliff.

I hated heights, but it didn't matter to me now. I stood one inch from a thousand-foot drop, the water spraying in every direction. Mist hit my face, soaked my clothes, the lagoon looming hundreds and hundreds of feet below, the sky stretching upward to the heavens.

Jump, the voice told me. *Jump, Lily.*

I took one step forward.

A different voice called even louder this time... it sounded like

Ainsley, but I couldn't be sure—she was interrupted by the louder, more persistent voices in my head telling me to *jump.*

I took another step forward, wobbling over the edge.

Do it now, the voice said.

Somewhere inside, somewhere tucked deep in the safest recess of my heart, I wanted to stop. To go back, to find Ainsley and make sure she was okay. To be rid of the horrible book forever.

Jump, one voice called, while Ainsley whispered for me to *Stop!*

I reached a hand upward, my feet inching toward the edge of the waterfall. My hand landed on the necklace dangling over my chest, the heart locket from my mother. When I touched it, the voices in my head quieted, and I took a step back.

Jump, the voice said, sounding more enraged. *Now.*

I clasped the necklace tighter, and a third voice spoke—a new voice, made of the voices of everyone I'd ever cared about in this world. Ranger X, Poppy, Zin—Hettie. Ainsley. The image of their faces blinked into my memory ever so briefly, but it was enough.

Ainsley called for me to *stop,* and this time, I did.

My body collapsed to the floor, the blackness seeping out of my mind, leaving my head pounding and my body shaking with exhaustion. The black magic had sapped my strength.

All at once, I realized that I'd experienced mind bending.

Someone had controlled me with blood magic, and I'd nearly died because of it.

I tried to roll to my feet, but my body was too weak. As I pulled myself to a sitting position I slipped, one leg swinging over the edge of the cliff.

The wall, slick with spray from the waterfall, did nothing to stop my slide.

The next thing I knew, I was falling, falling over the side.

Ainsley reached for me, lunged, her eyes bright.

But she was too late, and I fell anyway.

CHAPTER 20

MY LIFE DIDN'T FLASH BEFORE my eyes.

Which was probably a good sign, because I hadn't ended up dead. A soft, fluffy sort of thing had caught my fall. I patted the air some more, and then looked down, realizing that it was some sort of cloud-like material perched just on the other side of the cliff. If it hadn't been there to catch me, I'd certainly have tumbled to my death.

With all the caution in the world, I pulled myself upward, moving with painstaking slowness back to the edge of the cliff. Ainsley popped her head over the edge, her eyes wild. As soon as she saw me, her face changed.

"Lily? You're alive! What happened?"

"Help?" I reached for her. My arms shook as she grasped them, pulling me over the edge. It wasn't until I managed to roll my way far, far away from the cliff that I could find the breath to mutter a thank-you.

"What was that?" Ainsley asked. "You were just reading the book, perfectly normal one minute, and then the next... it was like someone had taken over your body. Your eyes got all black and empty, and when you spoke, it was in this weird intonation that wasn't you."

"Blood magic," I said. "I sliced my finger on the edge of the book, and then when I flipped to the spell and started reading it... I must have invoked the spell."

"You've survived your first, and hopefully only, experience with mind bending." The Witch of the Woods spoke from a seat at the head of the table. "And I must say, I am tickled pink. You are... you are one of a kind, Lily Locke. A pure anomaly. I've never seen the likes of it before."

"Did you do this?" I stood, my hands resting against the wall of stone. "Why?"

"It's quite peculiar." She ignored my question. "You should have jumped—they all do."

"Were you trying to kill her?" Ainsley moved toward the Witch, the aggression seeping from her very pores. "Are you insane?"

"I'm well aware of my actions." The Witch of the Woods didn't seem the least bit bothered by the venom tinging Ainsley's words. "This needed to happen."

I shook my head. "You could have warned me!"

"I can't teach about blood magic until you've experienced it for yourself." The Witch of the Woods stood, her joints creaking in the echoing chambers. "Now that you know how powerful of a spell we're dealing with, I will answer all of your questions. I needed you to know the horrors mind bending can bring—personally—so you will never be tempted to use it for your own gain."

"I almost died," I said, my voice hoarse. "I almost leaped off that cliff."

"And I would've caught you," she said. "Just like I did when you fell off—the cloud was there for a reason. The others who have jumped? None of them have *died*. It's just to prove a point."

"Prove a point?"

"The thing people want most is what?" The Witch asked, and then answered her own question. "To stay alive. By showing that mind bending can cause a person to take their own life—well, one doesn't mess around with magic like that."

"But—"

"You, Lily Locke, are the only person in my long, difficult

life who I've seen fight off mind bending," she said. "Especially without training."

"I hardly fought it off—I fell off the cliff anyway."

"You did," she said. "If you hadn't succeeded, you would have jumped. You fought off the spell, but not before your friend took a tumble."

"My friend took a tumble?" My voice came out weak. I turned to face Ainsley, my words hollow. "Did I hurt you? Is that why you were on the ground?"

She averted her eyes, the action itself enough to send tendrils of pain through my stomach. My head ached as I remembered her lying on the ground, but I had no memory of how she'd gotten there.

"It was nothing," Ainsley said, speaking to her feet. "I'm fine."

"Look at me," I instructed her. "Ainsley, I need to know."

She looked up, and for the first time, I noticed a slight rim of darkness around her eye. I stepped closer, horror spreading through my body as I realized she'd fallen because of me. *What had I done?*

"I am so sorry," I said, tears heavy in my eyes. "I never meant to, it wasn't me, I'm so. . . I'm so sorry—"

"I know, it's okay." Ainsley reached out and gave my shoulder a light tap with her fist. "Your right hook needs some work. You're just lucky I slipped and fell, knocked myself pretty good on the head. If I'd been prepared, I would've had you in handcuffs in no time, boss."

A sob disguised as a laugh warbled in my throat, but it did nothing to help the sick feeling twisting in my stomach. The pain only escalated as I realized this sensation must be what Trent was feeling—but worse. Trent first, and then Camden. Now me.

The most frightening thought hit me then. Who would be next?

"I can read the fear on your face," the Witch said. "I can assure you it's in our best interest if we can move quickly. I don't know if The Puppeteer will wait until the next Trial to attack or if the strike will happen sooner. Either way, we need to prepare you as much as possible."

"It's late," Ainsley said. "Are we going back through The Forest tonight, or can we stay here?"

"You'll go back when you're ready," The Witch of the Woods said with a tilt of her nose. "Now, take out a quill and write down everything I say. Let me start by explaining how The Puppeteer got her name."

CHAPTER 21

HOURS LATER, I SCRATCHED MY head. "Sorry to be impatient, but when does The Puppeteer come into all of this?"

Ainsley traced her quill loosely over the parchment before us. We sat at the long table in the Library of Secrets, the Witch of the Woods at the head of it. She folded her hands before her, a look of strained patience on her face. "I'm getting to that."

I sighed. "I'm sorry, it's just—"

"Knowledge cannot be rushed," the Witch said. "If I give you bits and pieces, you'll run around like a chicken without your head."

"Yes, but if I'm too late to help, no amount of knowledge will help at all." We'd spent the past hour learning every teensy tiny detail about the history of mind bending. Details so insignificant, I couldn't see how they'd ever help us. "We're here to learn about The Puppeteer."

"Well, it's dark outside, and I'm not risking The Forest tonight." Ainsley tapped her fingers against the parchment. "So we've got until morning."

"The Puppeteer is a complicated woman," The Witch said, leaving me to lean back in my chair and resume my doodling. "Quite tragic, if you ask me."

"No amount of tragedy is an excuse to kill someone," I said. "Not like she did."

"She loves the power." The Witch made eye contact with both

Ainsley and me before continuing. "The control that comes with black magic."

"Which is why she's created an army of voodoo dolls," I said. "Liam said she has one for every person on The Isle."

"We do not use the term voodoo." The Witch of the Woods raised a finger. "And that is but a rumor. Nobody has seen this collection, including Liam."

"So nobody knows the truth? Why is this woman so hard to catch?"

The Witch's eyes scanned me hungrily. "That is where you come in, Lily Locke."

I didn't look up. Ainsley's eyes bored into the side of my head as I stared at the papers, avoiding them both. "What exactly are you suggesting?"

"Find The Puppeteer," The Witch hissed. "And ask her. The truth can only come from the source."

I'd known the task was coming, but it didn't make things any easier. "What is she like?"

"She is a great beauty," The Witch of the Woods spoke with hushed reverence. "Her hair is black, and they say it curls down her back like the ocean waves at midnight. She smiles with lips as red as blood, her skin pale as the moon. In her eyes are pieces of starlight."

"That sounds a little far-fetched," Ainsley said. "Sort of sounds like one of Liam's poems."

"Liam knows more than he's letting on, so I'd watch what you say around him." The Witch of the Woods smiled, a smile tinged with sadness. Behind that sadness was a secret that she wasn't willing to divulge. "He is a valuable resource, and you'd do well not to speak ill of him. He, too, has had a difficult life."

Ainsley's lips formed a tight line. "Of course, sorry."

"What happens when I find this collection?" I steered the subject away from Liam. "The dolls, I mean. She must have one for me, too, I suppose."

"No, you'll not yet have a doll, Lily. You're new to The Isle; anyone who arrived since she was locked in jail will be free... for now. And of course, The Puppeteer will not have a doll for Poppy—"

"Poppy was born here," I said. "Why wouldn't she have one?"

"Poppy is a vampire. Vampires are immune to blood magic."

"Anyone else?"

"Liam," she said. "I'm not sure there will be one for Liam."

"Why not?" Ainsley asked. "He's not new—"

"I'm ignoring your question because the answer is not mine to give," she said shortly. "And Lily, one more thing."

I raised my eyebrows.

"The spell you experienced today is a pale imitation of true mind bending. Blood magic, *true* blood magic, touches your soul. Today, this spell merely touched your mind."

"Like a hallucination?" Ainsley asked.

"A strong one," the Witch agreed. "Because I am not willing to give up a piece of my soul, and that—my dear, is the cost of blood magic."

"Why did The Puppeteer go to jail?" Ainsley asked. "I know it was for using blood magic, but I haven't heard the full story."

"That is all the information I have to offer." The Witch of the Woods folded her hands in front of her body. "I must take my leave. Have a safe journey home, girls. The Forest and I will assist you on your way."

"It's the middle of the night!" I stepped back so quickly my stool tipped over. "You can't send us on our way now."

"I *said*, The Forest will guide you." The Witch blinked as if that explained everything. "You will be safe. Follow me, please. The Library of Secrets is closed."

The way down the stairs was much faster than the way up, but even so, my legs ached when we reached the pool of water at the bottom of the falls. The Witch turned to face us, peppy as ever, while Ainsley looked half-dead.

"Good night, girls." The Witch of the Woods smiled at us, her old face crinkling with the effort. "Come back to visit when this is all over."

"Fat chance," Ainsley mumbled. "The only time I'm coming back to visit is when someone starts allowing broomsticks on this island. My legs are killing me."

I opened my mouth to agree, but I spluttered instead. A big bug had zoomed straight toward my mouth, and I'd nearly swallowed it. I coughed and waved a hand in front of my face, pausing only when a tiny voice began to scream profanities in my ear.

"What are you thinking, lady? You got your nasty spit all over me! What is this mess? So inconsiderate." A tiny little Forest Fairy zoomed away from me, shaking her small body. "You lunatic."

"I'm a lunatic?" I thumbed at myself. "You flew straight at my mouth."

"You didn't have to open your huge trap! I was going too fast and lost control when you sighed," the Forest Fairy said. "Cripes! That mouth of yours is huge. It's like a tornado, sucking me right in."

Ainsley stopped my argument with a touch of her hand on mine. "Who are you? What do you want?"

"I work with Glinda," the fairy said. She was about the size of my pointer finger, her wings fluttering in the air before us. "I'm out on a special favor for the Grandmother of the Woods."

"Can I talk to Glinda?"

"I'm not good enough for you?" she spat. "Fine, here you go, but I expect a good review on my customer service report when this is all over."

The fairy reached up to her head. There was a bandana there with a tiny little gadget attached that worked sort of like a magical camera. The Forest Fairies worked for Glinda, specializing in communication techniques across the island. They might be annoying little buggers, but they got the word out, and fast.

There was a crackle, a pop, and from the back of her bandana projected an image of Glinda behind her. Glinda's official title was Emergency Contact Specialist, but that was a big title for a little witch who adored glitter and eyeliner and clothing a few sizes too small.

"Chickies! How are you my lovelies?" Glinda sat on a bed with her hair wound in bright pink curlers. Her eyes, normally lined in thick, smudged mascara were clean of makeup. It made her look about thirty years younger than the last time I'd seen her. She wore a fluffy pink bathrobe and a bright smile. "Is Jessie treating you well?"

Ainsley snorted, but I waved her off before the fairy got mad. "Jessie is lovely. Five stars for customer service. But Glinda, how did you know we'd need help tonight?"

"My babies live and breathe The Forest," Glinda said. "My snuggy-wugglums know when the Grandmother needs something."

"Grandmother?" I asked. "Who is this grandmother?"

"You may know her as the Witch of the Woods," Glinda said. "But to us, those who dwell in The Forest, she is the Grandmother of all life here. She's the only soul on the island who can control the lions and the tigers, the beasts and the fairies, the trees and the flowers."

I raised my eyebrows. "I had no idea."

"Meeting her is the greatest honor for any creature in The Forest, and we dare not disobey her. Though the rest of the island may be terrified of the creatures in the woods, she's the gentle, guiding hand that rules us all. She's the voice of the ugly, the forgotten, the frightening."

"You're not any of those things," Ainsley said. "In fact, I think you're very pretty, and I love that robe on you."

"Isn't it darling? It's new." Glinda blushed. "Thank you, Lily's friend. You must come to the island more often."

"I'd love that." Ainsley grinned. "We should do a ladies' night sometime, the three of us. Wine, cheese—"

Ainsley stopped talking as Glinda stiffened. "*No.*"

"What's wrong?" I leaned closer, watching as Glinda's face went pale. "What happened?"

"Something is wrong. You're needed at your grandmother's house. Go, Lily. Now!"

Jessie the fairy lost all signs of sass, flipping the projection off. She waved an arm. "Follow close behind," she said. "The Forest will guide us home."

CHAPTER 22

NAVIGATING THE FOREST HAD NEVER been easier. We skirted the mountains, dodged the driftwood and fallen trees, and waded through gurgling streams in record time.

When we burst out of The Forest's darkness, I surprised myself by recognizing the location. "There's Ranger X's cabin."

The fairy glanced in the direction of my pointed finger. "Sorry, no time to stop."

"But—"

"I have my orders, straight from Glinda herself. To The Twist—*no stopping* for any reason at all."

Ainsley and I picked up the pace. There was an urgency in the fairy's voice driving us forward, pressing us through the last leg of our journey. When we reached the outside of The Twist, our new fairy friend bowed her head. "I must take my leave here. My business is done."

"Of course," I reached out and gave the Forest Fairy the tiniest of fist-bumps, since her hand was too small to shake and I was afraid I'd squish her with a hug. "Thanks for everything. Glinda, too."

The fairy zoomed off, leaving Ainsley and me at the entrance to the labyrinth.

I grabbed Ainsley by the wrist and dragged her through the convoluted maze. Flowers bloomed under the starlight, reaching toward the heavens as we dashed passed. Fountains spurted water into the sky, dancing to soundless music. The scent of lilacs was heavy tonight.

Due to my West Isle Witch blood, we made it through the maze without error, emerging in front of the babbling brook outside of Hettie's cottage in a few minutes time.

"Your grandmother's house is very Hansel and Gretel-esque," Ainsley gasped. "And really hard to find. I could've used a few breadcrumbs along the way."

I didn't respond, my heart sinking like a stone. "Ainsley, look!"

The front door to Hettie's cottage was open, tilted at an odd angle. Tiger, Hettie's cat, paraded leisurely across the front steps. Despite the calmness of the scene, something was wrong. The wrongness seeped into my bones until I couldn't take it any longer, and I rushed forward.

"Wait!" Ainsley called. "It's too dangerous to—"

I didn't listen, sprinting until I reached the front door. I bent down, scratched the cat's ears, looking into his eyes to see if I could see a warning. But since I wasn't a cat-whisperer, I was left with nothing. Tiger, unfazed by my presence, plopped down with a yawn.

Ainsley followed as I stepped through the front door, her words of warning silenced as her footsteps sounded a half-beat after my own. The entryway was silent as a grave. The sound of my breathing bounced off the walls as I inched forward, one foot in front of the other. I held my breath.

Another step forward, another breath, another beat of my terrified heart.

The entryway was sheathed in shadows, the starlight reaching only inches past the doorway.

One more step and I'd passed the last of the moonlight glinting against the floor. Only shadows stood before us.

Ainsley breathed in my ear. "We shouldn't be here."

I shook my head. We shouldn't be here, but we were needed. "We've got to find—"

A scream. Loud, shrill, terrified, cut me off mid-sentence. "Poppy!" I gasped. Then louder, "Poppy, where are you?"

Ainsley and I launched forward at the same time, whipping our way around the corner of the hallway.

My heart plummeted at the sight of Poppy sprawled across the floor. She held a hand to her head, her body still, her legs weakly splayed against the ground.

I ran to her, collapsing by her side. "Poppy, talk to me! What happened? Are you okay?"

Ainsley stood over us, her eyes scanning the hallways. They were empty. Except for Poppy's erratic gasps, the house was still.

I shook her shoulder. "Poppy, talk to us. Can you hear me?"

Her eyes fluttered open, her fingers reaching for me. A single word croaked from her throat. "Hettie. . . "

"What about Hettie?" I asked, my voice strangled. "Where is she?"

Poppy raised her hand, pointed down the hall toward our grandmother's bedroom. "*Help.*"

"Stay here," I said to Ainsley. "Watch Poppy."

Ainsley didn't listen, tailing me. Together, we crept down the hall. When we reached the bedroom door, it, too, was hanging open. I put my ear to crack and listened.

Footsteps padded across the floor *inside* the bedroom—slow, deliberate steps.

I gestured for Ainsley to come close. "I'm going inside."

"I'm coming with you," she said firmly. "Ready?"

There was no time to argue, so I nodded. Ainsley began a countdown from three. On *one,* she flung the door wide open and together, we rushed through.

A cry of surprise burned in my throat at the woman before us. "Zin?"

My cousin froze, hovering above our grandmother's bed. Hettie lay sleeping, her mouth open wide, snoring loud enough to wake the dead. Or the half-dead.

Zin turned toward us, but as she did, I realized it wasn't *her* standing before us. Her body, maybe, but not her mind. Zin's eyes had dilated to glittering black gemstones, vacant and hungry.

"Blood magic," Ainsley said, her voice hushed. "It's not her, it's The Puppeteer."

"Zin, put it down," I said, my eyes locked on the tiny capsule in her hand. "Give me the Poison Pill."

Zin perched over the bed, her motions robotic as she held the pill above our grandmother's mouth. She didn't speak, didn't flinch—didn't appear to hear me in the slightest.

"Zin!" I spoke louder, firmly, trying to remember how I'd latched onto Ainsley's voice when I'd been teetering on the ledge of the waterfall.

Her eyes flicked toward my face. Hope surged through me, and I tried again.

"Please, come back, Zin." I stepped closer. "You can fight this."

Then, however, her eyes iced over, a wall of stone blotting out all hints of humanity. In a single motion, she turned and set the pill onto my grandmother's tongue. Her arms moved like two-by-fours. Zin shuddered and then in a low, eerie intonation, she said, "It's done."

"No!" Ainsley cried as Hettie's snores halted.

Then everything happened at once.

I lunged for Zin. Hettie's eyes flashed open. Ainsley flew toward my grandmother, reaching for the Poison Pill.

Hettie beat us all, spitting the pill out of her mouth so that it landed with a clink on the floor. Zin didn't move fast enough, and Hettie snaked out a hand and clutched her wrist with a vice-like grip. It was enough to distract Zin until I reached her, tackling her to the ground.

Hettie sat up, stretched, and yawned. "What's a girl gotta do to get a little shut-eye around here?"

Ainsley retrieved the pill from beyond the bed, and then came up beside me. I sat on Zin's chest, my eyes stinging with tears. She struggled to get free, but I held on tighter, pressing her arms to the floor. Normally, Zin was stronger than me, but her disorientation must have given me the upper hand.

"Zin, stop it! This isn't you." I pleaded with her, begging her to listen. "It's me. Lily."

Zin's vacant eyes closed then, and she gave up. Still, I didn't move. My eyes burned, and before I could help it, a hot, salty drop streaked down my cheeks and fell onto Zin's face. It plopped onto her forehead, and then another and another.

"Zin, wake up," I said, ignoring Ainsley as she shook my shoulders. "Come on, listen to me."

One of my tears slid from my chin and dropped to her lips.

Finally, Zin's eyes flashed open. She blinked, her pupils dilated, largely unfocused as she stared into space. Then, suddenly, she focused on me, and I could see her. *Zin.*

"You're back," I said, my chest nearly collapsing in relief. I rested a hand against her cheek. "Zin, can you hear me?"

She blinked a few times. "Lily? What's going on? Why are you sitting on me?"

"You don't remember anything?" I asked, my heart sinking at the thought of explaining everything to her. "What's your last memory?"

"What are you talking about?" Zin said, blinking a few more times, as if emerging from a deep sleep. "I went to bed, and then. . . well, I woke up to you squishing me. I can't breathe, Lily, can you please get off of me?"

Ainsley helped me to move shakily from Zin's chest to stand. Zin started following suit, but Ainsley put an apologetic hand on her shoulder. "I'm sorry," Ainsley whispered. "But I need to do this." Ainsley clapped a pair of magic-proof handcuffs onto Zin. "These are Guardian-issue," she explained to me. "I never leave home without them."

"What is this about?" Zin's face crumpled in confusion, pain pinching her eyes. When she spoke, her voice rose an octave. "Somebody tell me what's going on here!"

"You tried to kill me, I'm guessing." Hettie's voice was light, a trace of a humor in her words. I could see beneath her lighthearted exterior to a layer of worry, a tremble of concern. "There are easier ways, you know, than trying to get me to swallow a pill in my sleep."

"What?" Zin flinched, backing away. "I would never. You're my grandmother! I wouldn't dream. . . " Realization hit her at once, her words trailing away.

The rest of the room fell deathly quiet.

"This is the same thing that happened to Trent. And Camden," she said finally, putting the pieces together, her voice rife with bitterness. "I understand what they mean—I almost poisoned my own grandmother."

"No," I said. "It wasn't you. It was The Puppeteer, and mind bending, and Zin... it's not your fault."

"The Puppeteer?" Zin murmured. "But I thought... she's been in jail for years."

I'd forgotten that Zin was out of the loop, locked away like Rapunzel in The Oasis. Of course she hadn't heard the news. "You know about mind bending?"

Zin gave a hesitant nod. "Most of us who grew up on the island are aware. It's illegal, of course."

"Yes, but a prisoner escaped, and it's believed that—"

"—that she's using her powers to murder Candidates."

"Candidates, and now others, too." My heart ached as I watched Zin gather the pieces together.

She sat down on the edge of Hettie's bed. She tried, but couldn't look at her grandmother. "I am so sorry."

"You don't owe me any apologies." Hettie crossed her arms, shaking her finger. "Also, you're gonna have to try a lot harder to kill me than a little pill. I raised three daughters, and I'll have you know they've nearly killed me a hundred times over from heart attacks. This is nothing, Zin."

Nobody believed her, least of all Zin. Despite my grandmother's laissez-faire attitude, the room was somber.

"Poppy!" I remembered suddenly. "We have to get Poppy. . . "

As if reading my thoughts, Poppy herself appeared in the doorway. "What's going on?" she asked nonchalantly. "I was sleeping down the hall and heard a racket."

Zin held her breath, looked to her cousin. "Poppy, I... you didn't see me, did you?"

Poppy shrugged, hiding the look of concern behind a bright smile. "What are you talking about?"

"Call Ranger X, please," Zin said to her. "Now. I need to be taken away, just like Trent."

"No, Zin," I said. "It wasn't you, it was—"

"Call him," Zin said. "If I'm a danger to my family, I don't want to be part of the Trials."

"But—"

"The Ranger program is an honor—it is about protecting my loved ones, not ruining them, and in the name of doing what's best for my island, I need to turn myself in."

"Zin—"

"Call him," she said through gritted teeth. "Now."

CHAPTER 23

RANGER X ARRIVED AT THE Twist twenty minutes later. I met him at the entrance, explaining everything as we made the trek through the labyrinth. I left out the whole journey to see the Witch of the Woods, at least for now. I didn't want to overload him when there was enough happening right in front of us.

"How did you know to come here?" he asked. "I expected you to be at the bungalow. I stopped by earlier, but nobody was there. . . "

I hesitated. "Can I please explain that later?"

"Lily." He didn't sound happy, and I didn't blame him. "What is going on?"

"Later," I said. "First, Zin. Then you can take me home and I'll explain everything I can, I promise."

"Everything you *can*? What is that supposed to mean?"

"First, Zin," I said firmly. "Please. It's hard enough without us arguing."

We made the rest of the walk in silence. There was a tenseness in the air, a disconnect between the two of us that I didn't like at all. We'd never kept secrets before, at least not on purpose. Not unless absolutely necessary.

Then I remembered Ainsley's words—to show Ranger X how I felt, especially at the moment when I couldn't say the words I wanted. As we reached the end of the labyrinth, I reached over and took his hand in mine. I held it tight, giving him a little squeeze.

A breath escaped from his lips, and as he looked over, some of the tension melted with that single, small smile.

I returned it, and he squeezed back. Together, we approached Hettie's home, hand in hand. There were secrets between us, and I needed to find a way to deal with them. But for this moment in time, our trust in each other would have to be enough.

"Zin," Ranger X said as we entered the kitchen. "Lily caught me up, but I'll need to hear everything from you."

She stood with her head hanging, the sharp black bob cutting across her chin. A despondent expression darkened her pale face as she raised her cuffed hands before her. "Fine. I'll tell you everything you need to know, but not here. Anywhere but here."

Ranger X hesitated for a long moment. He glanced around the room, and then offered a nod. "Come with me, then."

I leaned up to give him a kiss on the cheek. He held me close, his arm tightening around my back in a rough hug.

"I'm coming over later," he murmured. "Please be waiting for me."

"I will," I whispered into his ear. "I promise. I love you."

He kissed my forehead and murmured the words back.

Zin stood like a prisoner before us, her eyes averted. When Ranger X stepped away, she shuffled ahead of him down the front steps.

"Wait, Zin," I called, padding down the stairs after her. She didn't slow down, so I moved in front and forced her to stop. "It's not your fault, you have to know that."

Zin looked over her shoulder to where Poppy leaned against the doorframe. "I see the red mark on your head, Poppy. Is that from where I hit you, or is that where your head hit the floor?"

My insides twisted in distress. "Stop it."

"Take me away, X," Zin said through gritted teeth. "For everyone's safety. They were right all along. I was never cut out to be a Ranger."

My heart broke at the finality in her words. For so long, for years and years, she'd been hoping, praying, training for this opportunity. And now it was gone, washed away through no fault of her own. Zin hadn't lost the battle; it'd destroyed her from the inside out.

Ranger X exhaled a breath, but as always, he kept his mouth shut. Ever the professional, he raised a hand to her back, guided her forward. "After the events of today, I've made the decision to cancel the Trials. Until we've gotten to the bottom of this, there will be no new Rangers."

My fists clenched by my sides. Nobody—on this island, or the mainland, or in this entire universe—would destroy my cousin's dreams. As Ranger X led her away like a prisoner, I shook my head, the anger boiling inside.

"Come on," I said to anyone listening. "Let them go. We have work to do."

CHAPTER 24

AN HOUR LATER, MIMSEY HAD come and gone. I'd sent Poppy with her mother to fetch Trinket. Zin's mother needed to hear the news from us—her own family. Mimsey and Poppy would bring Trinket back, and we could break the news to her here.

This plan had the added benefit of forcing Poppy and Mimsey out of the house—they'd need to keep an eye on Trinket's six other kids for the night, leaving Hettie's house free for a meeting of The Core.

"Have you called the others?" I murmured to Hettie.

"I'll send Tiger to retrieve the gang." Hettie stood in the kitchen in her purple velour tracksuit, curlers still in her hair. She looked like she'd come from the beauty salon, not an assassination attempt. "Where is that cat?"

"What you told me a few weeks back, Hettie..." I stepped closer to my grandmother, impressed at her nonchalance. "All that stuff about the target on your head. Is that what this is about?"

Hettie patted her curlers and grinned. "Well, with a head this darn gorgeous, it's no wonder people are out for it. I'd put a target on it, too."

"Hettie. . . " My voice held a warning note.

"What, *Lily*?" She turned, planting a hand on her hip. "Do you have a problem with my attitude?"

"No, but—"

"Would you rather I just curl up and die?" She crossed her

arms. "I have limited years left on this earth, and if you think I'm going to spend them cowering under my bed, then you're mistaken. Learn to laugh when others will cry, darling, and nobody will ever be able to faze you."

"I didn't mean anything by it, I just thought that we needed to be serious here. Someone tried to kill you."

"Yes, they did. And now I have a choice. I can let life control me, or I can grab life by the cojones and be a boss." Hettie uncrossed her arms and twirled around the kitchen. "I choose to be a boss."

Hettie made a few strange mewing noises, and in an instant Tiger appeared at her feet. She reached down, scratched his ears, and hissed at the cat.

"Are you talking to a cat?" I asked.

"Of course not." Hettie stood up and gave me a look like *I* was the lunatic. "You sure are gullible, though—should've seen the look on your face. Here you go, Tiger. Get the others." She handed the cat a few treats.

Tiger took an uninterested sniff and then walked away, tail in the air.

"She doesn't like me much," Hettie said. "But she's a smart one."

"How does she understand you?"

"I'll teach you when you're older. For now, what do you say to pancakes?"

"I think we should focus on business."

"I am," Hettie said. "Pancakes are serious business."

I sighed.

"Stop your sighs! How do you expect to fight the bad guys if you have no energy? Sleep and pancakes, my dear. The secrets to success."

Ainsley wandered into the kitchen then and grinned. "Did I hear pancakes?"

"Fine," I said, mostly to avoid wasting an argument on this.

"Trinket's on her way here. We have to get her in and out before Gus and the others arrive."

"What's the plan?" Ainsley asked.

She'd utilized the break in action to shower and change, something I needed desperately after our jaunt through The Forest. However, I was too wired to stand still under a stream of water, so I settled for pacing around the kitchen while Hettie whipped up some batter.

The doorbell rang, a resounding reverberation that almost shattered my eardrums.

"That dumb bell is loud enough to wake the dead," Hettie said, surprisingly cheerful. "I hate that thing, but I suppose if I *had* died tonight, I wouldn't have stayed dead for long. That thing can rouse zombies."

I sucked in a breath. "Hettie!"

Ainsley, however, covered her mouth, her shoulders shaking with laughter.

I shook my head at the both of them and left to answer the door. If I didn't know better, I'd have guessed Ainsley was the one related to Hettie.

I pulled open the heavy front door, leaning all my body weight into it. It was so heavy I wondered how Hettie managed to do it with her eighty pounds of sass and sagginess—her words, not mine.

"Trinket," I said, greeting my aunt with a delicate tone. She stood on the front steps holding a single lily bloom in her hands. My spine stiffened, chills running down my back. "What is that? Where did you get it?"

"Is it for you?" she growled. "I nearly tripped over it on the front steps here. It would have served you right if I squashed the thing to bits. Where's my mother? I've talked to her about not leaving things on the floor, she's going to break her hip, and all her responsibilities will land on me. . . "

Trinket shoved the flower impatiently into my hands and

stomped toward the kitchen, grumbling about her "crazy mother" and Hettie's "lack of thoughtfulness."

I forgot about following Trinket into the kitchen and instead moved outside. I left the door open a crack, the sounds of Trinket and her mother arguing filtering through the small opening.

Underneath the moonlight, the white petals of the lily glinted strong, ethereal in its glow. I scanned the yard, but nothing moved. Even the wind had died down, the stillness overpowering. I looked toward The Twist, suddenly hit hard by Zin's absence. She was gone, led away like a prisoner. And with her, Ranger X.

The sense of loneliness nearly brought me to my knees. I had Hettie and Ainsley inside, and Trinket, too. Even so, the secrets I was keeping weighed me down, held me underwater as if I were drowning.

Collapsing onto the front step, I sucked in air, but my chest struggled to expand properly. Breathing was a chore. My fingers clenched the stem of the lily flower so hard I nearly broke it in half.

Forcing myself to take long, slow, breaths, I released the stem from my grasp and set the flower on the ground. It stood out against the richness of the jungle green grass. All around me the night seemed to come alive. Insects buzzed, birds flapped their wings and called softly to one another. Leaves danced on their branches, trees bent and swayed over the gurgle of the pond.

The sounds of nature eased my breathing and calmed my worries. By the time I could think again, it was clear that nobody else was around. Whoever had left the flower on the front steps had dropped it off and disappeared. It was a message, just like the first lily I'd found in the storeroom.

But how the messenger had gotten through The Twist was an entirely new question. A person needed West Isle Witch blood to navigate the maze, or they needed to use the doorbell. As far as I knew, Hettie hadn't had visitors today.

I made a note to ask my grandmother about it, if she'd

entertained anyone besides my family recently. Then I realized Ranger X had been here, but he couldn't have… A sudden thought made my spine go rigid.

I'd gone back inside the house before Ranger X and Zin had completely left the property. Could it have been one of them? Had Zin somehow left the flower while still under the influence of blood magic? And if so, was it a message from The Puppeteer? And even *if* I found out who left the flower, I still had no idea *why*.

I cradled the lily between my fingers, pushed the door open, and moved inside. Tucking the flower into a huge vase near the door, I hoped that nobody would notice it—at least for now. I needed to gather my thoughts, and there wasn't time to explain now when more urgent matters deserved our attention.

When I returned to the kitchen, Hettie was halfway through explaining the events of the evening to her daughter. Trinket sat in a state of confusion, her ashen skin outlining a stony expression.

"Mind bending?" Trinket said. "Are you certain?"

"Are we certain of anything?" Hettie waved the spoon around, flicking tiny bits of pancake batter across the stove. "It's impossible to say for certain when blood magic is involved, you know that."

"Mother."

Hettie faced her daughter. "Yes, I'm as certain as I can be that mind bending is involved, Trinket. And this isn't the first instance."

"I just meant that Zin has always been…different." Trinket folded her arms across her chest. "With the clothes she wears, her hairstyle—maybe she's finally fallen in with the wrong crowd."

Horrified, I stepped forward. "Are you hinting that Zin made the *choice* to attack Hettie? Her own grandmother?"

"I'm just saying that she moves to the beat of her own drum, and if someone had influenced her, or convinced her to—"

"No," I said firmly. "She's your daughter, Trinket. Have a little faith in her."

Trinket blinked in surprise. "I suppose you're right."

"You *suppose* I'm right?" I took another step, now inches away from my aunt. I'd never talked back to her before. Being new to the family, I'd counted my blessings just to be *included* in their homes. But enough was enough. "Look, Trinket, I'm grateful for all you and Mimsey have done for me. You brought me here, introduced me to everyone. . . but this is Zin we're talking about. She'd never hurt her family."

Trinket tried to clear her throat and botched the job. In the background, Hettie's eyes positively twinkled. Until one of her pancakes went up in flames, and she whirled around and smacked it with a spatula.

The smell of burning batter permeated the kitchen, but I didn't stop. "Zin has helped you out for years. Ever since I've been on this island she's been taking care of her siblings and helping around the home despite her own dreams—she's had her sights set on becoming a Ranger *forever.*"

"How I run my household is my own business," Trinket said, her nose tilting into the air. "She's my daughter, and I will see her now."

I let myself collapse at the table as Trinket left the room. My head sank against my arms, and I banged my forehead into the wood a few times. "I'm an idiot."

Hettie joined me at the table and elbowed me with one arm. "You're right, you know. Trinket has had that coming for years."

I didn't bother to remove my head from the table. It was too heavy, too full of regret. "It wasn't the right way to handle things. I just exploded, and now I feel worse than before."

"Uh, uh, uh," Hettie said, scooching close. "I have been waiting for years to watch someone put Trinket in her place."

"You have? Why didn't you do it then?"

"Because I'm her mother. I've yelled at her plenty. Sometimes, it needs to come from someone else," Hettie said. "Someone outside of her normal sphere."

"Outside the family," I echoed, my words hollow.

"No, of course not." Hettie put her arm around me. "You are my granddaughter, and this is my house. You are in our family whether you want to be or not."

I sighed. Since the house was empty except for Hettie and Ainsley, I spoke freely. "This business with The Core is wearing on me. I hate keeping secrets from Ranger X. He has enough stuff he can't talk about for both of us."

"Especially so early in a relationship," Ainsley chirped. "I've been there."

"You have nothing to worry about," Hettie said. "The way he looks at you is... well, it reminds me of when I was first dating Harvey."

"Really?" I look up. "You felt like this?"

"Yes, I believe I did. It was a long time ago." She smiled, her eyes light with memory. "But falling in love is one of those feelings you can't forget."

"But all the secrets..."

"You *must* keep it quiet for now," Hettie said, her words round with apology. "There is too much at risk right now. The rules are changing, Candidates are dying—our island is in chaos. We need to stay small as a group, nimble. You have to understand I'm just trying to do what's best for everyone."

"That doesn't make things any easier."

A *buzz* sounded then, and Hettie looked up. "That'll be the others out front at The Twist—I have to guide them through. Excuse me."

While she left to bring them through the maze, I stared into my glass, barely looking up as the group piled into the kitchen.

"Pancakes, planning, and pandemonium," Hettie declared, straightening her curlers. The crazy-old-lady tone she'd perfected had returned, and so had her grinning face. "We're back."

Underneath it all, however, something had changed. Even

Hettie's best attempts to be loopy were dulled to a mere shadow of her former humor and sparkle. I forced my own smile up at her.

"Something's happened," Gus said as he clanked his way into the kitchen. "Is that pancakes I smell? What's got you cooking today, you old bat?"

Hettie shuffled to the stove. "Why, tragedy, of course! Take a seat, you old nincompoop."

And so, our meeting began.

CHAPTER 25

BY THE TIME THE SUN rose, we'd come up with a game plan. It'd taken hours of heated discussion, four mounds of pancakes, and Ainsley's sense of humor to keep things in check.

Harpin had arrived with Hettie and Gus. As always, he got along with no one. Even Ainsley snapped at him once or twice, and she knew how to phrase things in a way that made everyone happy. As it turned out, she was a wonderful addition to The Core.

"So Harpin and Gus, you're responsible for tracing the blood magic," Ainsley said, bouncing a pencil against the notepad in front of her. While Hettie poured a fountain of syrup over her pancakes, Ainsley took charge of the meeting and detailed the next steps in our plan. "Whatever it takes. Start your investigation around the prisoner and work your way back from her escape. If you find her, don't do anything rash. Understood?"

After a long hesitation, the two men nodded.

"Great. Hettie, you're going to wiggle your way into the Candidate hideout," Ainsley said. "Use your position as Zin's grandmother. Be senile. Whatever it takes—find out if the Candidates have heard rumors about what's been happening."

"Aye aye, captain!" Hettie saluted so hard she nearly tipped off her chair. "Your wish is my command. Lily, I can see why you raved about this assistant of yours. She's impressive."

"The very best!" I agreed.

"And now I'm blushing." Ainsley smiled. "Unfortunately, I

have to head back to the mainland this morning. I'm going to check with MAGIC, Inc. and see if they have any information on The Puppeteer or mind bending. Don't worry, I'll be discreet and report back on any findings."

When Ainsley stopped talking, I cleared my throat. "What about me?"

"Oh, dear, isn't it obvious?" Hettie looked to me. "Make sure Ranger X does not catch wind of our investigation. He can't know about it or he'd put the kibosh on things faster than I burn pancakes."

I felt a touch of hurt bubbling up inside. "But I want to do something. . . something active. For the group. For Zin."

"You can actively distract him." Hettie waggled her eyebrows suggestively. "Can't think of a better distraction than smooching."

"I'm serious," I said. "I don't want to *just* be a distraction. I want to help. I want to look for The Puppeteer, or search for blood magic. I'm the one who went into The Forest with Ainsley, we should be the ones following it up."

"This is a group effort," Hettie said. "We are all equally involved, and we have to do what's best for all of us."

"Well, it doesn't feel very fair," I said. "I want—"

"We all want things we can't have," Hettie said. "I've been dying to touch Ranger X's butt since you brought him to my casa, but I don't go doing that left and right."

"Yes, you do," I said. "You do whatever you want."

"Well. . . " Hettie shrugged. "I'm old and senile, and with age comes the great responsibility to do whatever I want."

I rolled my eyes, but something Hettie had said rang bells in my head. If Hettie did whatever she wanted, why couldn't I? There had to be some way I could help—some small way nobody had thought of yet, while still doing my part with Ranger X.

The group began to clear out, and as I gathered my plate, the first glint of sunlight popped through the kitchen window. With it came the feeling of ice being dumped over my head.

"Oh, *no!*" I smacked a hand to my forehead. "Ranger X was going to come over last night to talk, and I forgot all about it!"

"You were busy," Ainsely said. "He knew where you were. I mean, you were at your grandmother's house—it's not a secret, and you weren't doing anything wrong."

"He *specifically* asked me to be home. I have no good reason as to why I stayed so late." My fingers shook. I was on thin ice already with him, and this wouldn't help matters.

"Tell him I was crying like a baby all night," Hettie said. "And you had to comfort me."

"Or say that you wanted to wish me goodbye," Ainsley offered. "Either way, go now. If you hurry, maybe you'll beat him to the bungalow."

I nodded. "Ainsley, I'll see you soon?"

"You better believe it." She gave me a hug, a ruffle of hair, and a kiss on the cheek. "Stay safe, boss."

I bid goodbye to the rest of the group, and then wound my way through The Twist. By the time my feet reached the sand in front of the bungalow, I'd kicked off my flip-flops and fallen into an all-out sprint.

"You're moving mighty fast." The low voice rumbled off the front porch. "What's got you flying, sweetheart?"

I stopped in my tracks, breathing heavily. I hadn't seen Ranger X sitting in the shadows. "Nothing."

Upon closer inspection, Ranger X wasn't sitting, he was swinging lightly on the hammock hung across the porch. The very same hammock where we'd met, and he'd first fixed those brilliant eyes on me. Now, he sat with his feet up and his gaze resting on my face.

"I wasn't flying. . . " I took a few steps closer, dropping any sign of an excuse and heading straight for the apology. "I'm sorry, I stayed longer at Hettie's. I should have sent you a Comm."

He glanced at the sunrise.

My shoulders sank. "I *know* you asked me to be home, and I'm really sorry."

Ranger X went back to swinging. He didn't say a word for a long time, and that scared me more than if he'd raised his voice. The disappointment in the air between us was more unbearable than anything.

I should have just kept my mouth shut, but somehow, my brain thought that if I kept talking, it'd make things all better. "How long have you been here?"

"Long enough."

"An hour?"

He shrugged. "Does it matter? You weren't here."

"I said I'm sorry!" My voice came out clogged. That sinking feeling in my stomach had appeared, the same one that arrives when a police car shows up in the rearview mirror and flashes its lights. That sense of foreboding where bad things were coming and I couldn't do anything to stop them. "I was at my grandmother's house. I wasn't doing anything wrong."

He swung his feet to the ground, his black eyes fixed on me. "I didn't say you were *doing* anything wrong."

I met his stare, but his eyes were dull. More disappointment awaited every second I looked into his irises, so eventually I averted my gaze. "What are you implying?"

"I'm not implying anything, Lily." He crossed his hands over his knees, focusing on the ground as he pushed his body back and forth, back and forth on the hammock. "I'll tell you exactly what I'm thinking."

I bit my lip, waiting, steeling myself for whatever came next.

"I'm thinking that I've specifically asked you not to run across the island in the middle of the night by yourself. Why, Lily, *why* are you doing these things? I would have met you at The Twist! I would have held your hand all the way home. I'm doing my best to keep you safe, but you're making it an incredibly hard job."

I swallowed. "I don't know, I wasn't thinking."

"I don't believe that." Still looking at the ground, Ranger X shook his head. "You're a smart woman, and I've never once seen a moment where your brain has stopped churning at a hundred miles an hour. The question is *what*. *What* were you thinking about?"

The question sounded rhetorical, but his posture demanded an answer. When he looked up, his expression was raw, cautious—like dancing on the tip of the sword, just waiting for the hurt.

"Nothing," I said again. "I'm sorry. I wanted to say goodbye to Ainsley, and Hettie. . . "

The excuses fell flat on my lips. It felt disrespectful to lie so blatantly to Ranger X, so I didn't. I didn't speak at all. "I've told you about this before, and nothing has changed."

"The thing you can't talk about," he said calmly, shifting his weight. "I thought you said you'd tell me everything tonight."

"Everything I *can*," I said. "And I will. Here is what I can tell you."

I gave Ranger X credit for sitting patiently through my tale. True to my word, I filled him in on everything from my meeting with Liam to my trek with Ainsley to find the Witch of the Woods. The only details I left out were those involving The Core.

When I finished, Ranger X raised an eyebrow. "You told me all of that, and there is *still* more that I'm missing?"

I hesitated, and then gave a single nod.

"I'm trying to wrap my head around this." Ranger X kneaded his forehead with his thumbs. "You—my girlfriend—didn't mention until now that you went into The Forest—the most dangerous place on the entire island. You fought off blood magic at the hands of a powerful witch—and there's *still* something worse that you can't explain."

"I didn't say it was *worse,* just that I'm not allowed to talk about it."

"Well, I can't imagine how your secret can be *better* than all of that," Ranger X said, slipping out of his professionalism and laying on the sarcasm. "I don't know what to say anymore."

"Don't say anything, just. . . just trust me."

"I do trust you! None of this has to do with trust."

"Then what is it about?"

Ranger X stood, stretching his long legs to their full height. He was an intimidating creature, tall, handsome—ferocious in his anger. His suit was rumpled from the day's work.

He held one hand out in front of him, gesturing toward the entire island. "I've been waiting here for hours. Waiting, sitting on the porch for my girlfriend, who said she'd meet me at home. Meanwhile, a killer is on the loose. Someone is working blood magic—the most powerful form of magic for which *we have no antidote.* We have no way to fight mind bending or to predict the next attack. We don't know who is responsible for it, where they are, or *why.*"

"That sounds worse aloud than it did in my head."

"—then I see you sprinting across the sand. Your hair. . . " He stopped, held a hand over his lips as if it'd become too difficult to continue. When he finally spoke again, his voice was hoarse. "Your hair was whipping all around and you looked like a shooting star. You are rare, Lily—so very, very rare. Gorgeous, and smart, and good. And I'm the lucky man who *gets* to hold onto you for a brief moment in time. Shooting stars are hard to catch, Lily, and they're even harder to keep."

My throat closed up, and I could barely see for the tears in my eyes.

"But now that I've touched a shooting star, there isn't another light in this entire universe that can make me happy." Ranger X's eyes glittered. "I will give everything for you. I have, and I will again, and again, and again until you understand that. But I need something back. Because if you didn't come running across that sand tonight, I don't know what I would've done."

"I'm sorry," was all I could manage. "So sorry."

"Don't apologize." Ranger X shook his head. "I'm not looking for an apology. That's the strange thing, Lily. I'd been sitting here fuming all night, angrier than I've ever been in my life. I couldn't see straight, and then out of nowhere, you appear, and I forgot about all of that. Everything. The murders, the magic, the mayhem. My anger dissolved into *happiness*. Relief, maybe, and love. But mostly, happiness."

My heart nearly burst as I listened to Ranger X's words, but my body remained frozen in place.

"My heart stopped when I saw you. Frankly, it's been doing that since the day I met you. By all accounts, I should be dead by now." He offered the smallest of laughs. A forced laugh, but a good sign. "However, if you hadn't returned tonight, I wouldn't know how to live. Maybe my body would continue to exist, but a part of me would die. Whatever it is you unlocked in here."

I stepped up to Ranger X, rested a hand on his chest. He put his hand over mine and held it there, his touch warm against the cool breeze.

He gripped the back of my head with his hand, held me close to his shoulder. "Here's the thing, Lily. I can't bottle the magic of a shooting star—it'd ruin it. A light like you needs freedom, I understand that. I understand you're smart, and that you have your own passions and hobbies and work."

His hands ran over my back. I shivered, pressing further to him.

"What I can't understand is why you won't call me. Talk to me. Tell me your secrets and let me help you with them," he said. "Why are you hiding things from me?"

I swallowed. Ashamed to admit it, I couldn't help the thought as it flew into my head. In that moment, I hated Hettie. Hated The Core. Hated that fighting for good could cause so much bad in my life, so much hurt and anger. If I was on the side of good, then why did I feel evil?

"You have to trust me for a little bit longer," I whispered. "Please."

"Lily. . ."

I didn't have anything else to say. My lips, my fingers, my very spirit trembled at the secrets I was holding inside, so I took a step back. Ranger X's arms struggled to hold me close, but I slipped away and ran through the front door, up the curling staircase, and into my room.

The tears fell freely as I reached into my closet for a nightshirt. I wouldn't have bothered normally, but my clothes were so filthy I couldn't possibly sleep in them. Sliding into the cool fabric, I listened for Ranger X's footsteps, but there were none.

I climbed in bed, sitting up, waiting. For what, I wasn't sure. I needed to lock the door, I knew, but it was essentially morning, the sun rising by the second. If I waited a little bit longer, Gus would arrive to open the storeroom.

My eyes turned heavy, and I slid under the comforter. As my head hit the pillow, the lock on the front door clicked shut.

I should have known that Ranger X would lock up. After all, he was a Ranger; safety was his first priority. Guilt weighed heavy on my conscious, and normally, I would've tossed and turned all night. Since night had nearly passed, I had no trouble letting my eyes close as I slipped into sleep.

Some time later, the bed indented behind me. I fell into a dreamlike state, neither awake nor sleeping, my eyes red from crying, lips parched.

It was him. Ranger X. He smelled like home, an unidentifiable scent that had me curling up next to him and breathing in deeply. My soul relaxed as we touched, his broad, solid chest comforting against my back.

"Gus will be here soon," I said, my voice cracking. "You don't have to stay."

"I won't leave you like this."

Ranger X's warm body against mine brought another lump to

my throat. I prayed that Hettie would change her mind and open the group to X because I couldn't do this for much longer.

He leaned over, pulled the blackout curtains shut, pitching the room into darkness. Even so, my eyes flew open and I stared straight ahead, my eyes focused on emptiness.

Minutes later, or maybe hours, he snuggled in against my neck. His lips touched my skin as he whispered. "My name is Cannon."

I shivered, my mind going blank. During my first day on the island, Ranger X had told me that he'd never reveal his real name to me. Names meant power, and he hadn't been ready to give it to me. The meaning behind his words sent tremors across my skin.

Because I understood that with this confession, he'd given me everything.

"The Ranger program is my life. I stumbled onto it during a difficult time, and. . . " He paused to clear his throat. "And it saved me from a dark future."

He left time for me to speak, but I couldn't possibly find the right words, so I did as Ainsley suggested. I rolled over to face him, and I showed Ranger X with a long, tender kiss how much this moment meant to me.

He pulled away, lingering too close. Our lips brushed against one another, the threat of a kiss looming as he continued, "I am head over heels in love with a girl. I have never been in love before, I know that now. And that is absolutely everything that you need to know about me."

My eyes stung. I longed to tell him my side, to open my soul and let all of the secrets spill out, but Hettie's promise was fresh in my mind, and I couldn't do it. So I spoke from the only place I could, the only place honest and real and raw. I spoke from my heart.

"I am a girl who's confused," I whispered. "I love a man more than anything in the world, more than anything I've ever loved combined. But I made a promise to someone important to me that

I can't break. I'm loyal, often to a fault, and I hope the man I love will trust me for just a few more days."

Ranger X brought his lips to my forehead and left his mark there. "A few days."

"Yes," I breathed. "I promise."

He wrapped me so, so close. "As long as I can have tonight."

CHAPTER 26

WHEN I AWOKE LATER IN the morning, the indentation in the bed was fresh, but a part of my heart had gone. I ran a hand over the sheets, smoothing them, trying to sort through the emotions swirling in my stomach.

Eventually, I gave up putting a name to my feelings and swung my feet out of bed. I opened the closet, grateful for the Styling Spell that supplied me with an easy, prepared outfit. I was in no state to make a decision, my brain still exhausted from the late night.

I donned a pair of loose, flowing capris and a stretchy tank top. Leaving my feet bare I took the steps two at a time. If I hadn't left my room, I would've crawled straight back into bed and allowed the world to survive on its own for another day.

Gus looked up from his work in the storeroom. He surveyed me, focusing on my eyes, which were probably red-rimmed and blotchy.

"Good morning," he said, turning back to the plant he'd been dissecting.

I wanted to ask where he'd gone after the meeting last night, if he'd begun his work with Harpin, but I didn't. Gus didn't seem interested in talking, and I wasn't interested in prying.

"There you are!" The cheeriest voice filtered through the open doorway. "How are you feeling, buttercup?"

Poppy bounded through the front door. With the minor exception of the lump on her forehead, she looked as bright and chipper as ever. She wore a lime green dress that twirled around her knees, her blonde hair glistening in the sunlight.

I forced a smile in return; Poppy had been there last night, and she wasn't moping. "Hi yourself, you look great."

"It's a new day, the sun is shining. . . " She grinned, and not for the first time, I wished for the smallest handful of her optimism. "Don't you smell that fresh breeze? Come on, let's go for a walk. Actually, nope. Scratch that. Why don't you take a shower—please—you have dirt *everywhere*. I'm going to whip us up some breakfast."

"Oh, that's not necessary. I can cook something—" I began, but Poppy cut me off with a look.

She marched right up to me, rested a hand on my shoulder, and stuck her nose an inch from mine. "You listen to me, missy. You need a shower, food, and some fun. In that order. I'm the cure for your blues right now."

"I don't think now's the time for all of that." I looked at the ground as Poppy's face fell. The last thing I wanted to do was hurt her feelings; I just wasn't in a mood for sunshine and rainbows.

"She's right, you know," Gus said. "Moping around ain't gonna get you anywhere. Listen to her."

I blinked back my surprise. The last time I'd heard Gus advocate for fun had been. . . well, never.

"See?" With renewed vigor, Poppy pinched my cheek. "Go on, girlfriend. If you're not showered, smiling, and sitting on a barstool in twenty minutes, I'm coming into the shower myself, and nobody wants to see that."

I laughed, then thanked Poppy and followed her instructions.

Twenty minutes later, I felt like a new woman. Never in a million years had I imagined a shower and a few bright words could turn my day around. I smiled as I made my way into Magic & Mixology, all squeaky clean and bright-eyed. I'd even put on mascara.

"There's my girl," Poppy said, humming to herself behind the bar. "I've prepared breakfast."

I followed her dramatic gesture to find two mimosas fizzing on the counter. "That's not food."

"It's nourishment." Poppy rolled her eyes. "For your *soul*."

"Oh, naturally," I said. "What am I supposed to do with it?"

"Drink it!"

"I have to work today," I said. "Probably not the best idea."

"Gus told you to listen to me. I'm here to cheer you up. It's not healthy to be so sad all the time, Lily Locke. It's times like these you have to remember the good."

I slid onto the barstool. "How do you do it? After everything last night, and after everything with the Trials. How can you be so positive?"

"Well, hon, if the entire world turns to crap, I can't do much about it. But I might as well enjoy the time I have left." She gave me a smile, a twist of sarcasm in her words. Then she sighed, the smile falling from her face as she slid a hand around the base of her champagne glass. "It's hard, sometimes."

I clinked my glass against Poppy's and took a sip.

"But there's still so much to be happy about," Poppy said, her voice thin, a little unsure. "I have you. I have my mother, and Trinket, and all of those rascals. Hettie and her craziness. I have two jobs that I love—I see my family every day, and I get to live on this crazy, magical island. Yes, there are terrible people here—but there are terrible people everywhere."

I looked at the bar, focusing on the whimsical way Poppy's words danced through space.

"That's nothing new, Lily. There have always been bad people. Terrible people. Worse than The Faction, I'm sure of it," she said with a sigh. "And I just have to believe that during those times there was someone—even one single person—who looked at the bright side. Who dug up hope when it was buried so far underground that nobody else could find it."

I gave Poppy a smile, a true one. "I'm sure there were people just like you."

She waved a hand. "No, not like me. I'm nothing special, but if I can make a little difference in someone's day, that's enough for me."

"You make my day," I said. "You make a lot of people's days, Poppy."

Her smile seemed ghost-like. "I don't know about that. I'm not like you, Lily. I'm not destined to 'save the world' or become the next Mixologist. I'm not destined for fame, and frankly, I don't desire it in the slightest. I'm not out fighting evil like Zin, or changing laws and rules and societies like Ranger X." Poppy shrugged, her eyes filling with tears. "I'm just me, and some days, that has to be enough."

Surprised, I cleared my throat, the lingering emotions from last night baring their heads. Undoubtedly the stress of everything that'd happened had been falling on her shoulders, and this time, she needed someone else to front the smile.

"Come on," I said, patting her leg. "Grab your mimosa, we have somewhere to be."

Poppy's watery smile grew as she sniffed. "I'm just a big, fat emotional ball of goo."

"I like goo."

She fell into my arms, her shoulders shaking, and I realized that the events of last night had affected her more than she'd let on. She'd been strong last night for Zin and this morning for me. No wonder she was overwhelmed.

"You don't always have to be the happy face," I whispered. "Sometimes it's okay to cry."

"Oh, I cry plenty." Poppy pulled back after some time and wiped her face. "Sometimes, a girl just needs a good cry."

"Do you feel better?"

She nodded. "Now, what is this work you speak of? If I can bring my mimosa, count me in."

CHAPTER 27

I LET POPPY FINISH MY MIMOSA after hers, and then together we set off through the sand. We kept to the edge of the beach, our toes dipping into the water. I carried my sandals and Poppy carried two refilled mimosas.

"I need to brainstorm," I said. "I need a potion."

"For what? Hey, whatever happened to that Glo potion you were making? The one you told me about that will replace Harpin's tea."

"It should be ready by this weekend." I winked. "I'm simmering it on low so that it'll last longer."

Poppy blew me a kiss. "You are the best wing-woman ever."

I grinned. We walked some more in silence. I let my brain puzzle through the thoughts that'd been bubbling deep beneath the surface last night.

Hettie, Ainsley, everyone in The Core had accepted difficult, dangerous jobs in order to stop the terrorizing on the island. That'd left me with *what,* distracting Ranger X? While I'd been showering this morning, a new idea had hit me. One that pleased me—one that might make a real difference.

Sitting back wasn't good enough. If The Core didn't trust me enough to share the real responsibilities, then I would make my own. First on the list? A potion to combat the effects of blood magic.

"There's never been an antidote for blood magic," I told Poppy. "It's too hard to study since the whole practice is outlawed. And when it happens, it happens so fast; for example, last night, I wasn't thinking about an antidote while Zin was being controlled. I was...

I was hardly thinking at all. When I did think, it was all about stopping Zin."

"So how do you plan on creating an antidote?" Poppy asked, sipping her orange juice and blinking at the bubbles. "Seems like it would be hard to test."

"Very challenging," I agreed. "I don't have any ideas yet. That's why I needed this walk. To brainstorm."

"I'm a good sounding board. Where do you usually start when you're brewing a potion?"

"I start. . . " I hesitated. "Well, I figure out what I need. What ingredients might work to beat a specific spell, charm, or hex."

"All right, well, let's start there. What could you need?"

I shook my head. "Mind bending is different—most spells or hexes come from the outside in, so they're easier to block with a barrier sort of potion. Conversely, blood magic works from the inside out, starting with a soul and twisting it until the person is no longer recognizable."

We walked until we reached the dock, the silence a sign that we were both stumped. Kenny, a friend from my first days on the island, was out fiddling with the boat, and I waved to him as we passed. He waved back and flashed a brief smile.

"None of the ingredients I have on hand will work," I said. "I've been going over them in my head again and again. I have enough for the base product. Herbs I can use for a starter batch, minerals that fight evil magic, but there's something missing, something I can't put my finger on. . . "

"What about something you don't have? Something you've never used before?"

"I'm sure there's something I'm missing. I've been asking around, reading, learning everything I can about blood magic." I shrugged. "Usually ingredients for Mixes aren't this difficult to find. They sort of just come to me, like a story almost."

"That's incredible." Poppy shook her head in awe. "And I suppose that's why you're the Mixologist. What does it feel like?"

I hesitated. I'd never tried to describe it before, but it was like trying to explain the smell of home, the taste of a kiss. Every instance was so unique, so different but somehow, it was always just right. "It's like a story. A fully formed story that's gifted to me from something, somewhere."

"A story? But don't you just sort of throw a bunch of ingredients together?" Poppy wrinkled her nose. "I mean, in a fancy way, of course."

"No. It's not mathematical, but it's not random either. I've never sculpted or painted, but I imagine it's something like that. The artist has an idea that they start with, but it's a big, broad idea. Then it takes lots of time and detail to get it perfect. A blend of art and science."

Poppy looked confused, so I tried again.

"I start by thinking about my goal. Right now, I want a potion that can protect someone from mind bending magic," I explained. "To achieve that, I'll need a base—silver, probably, because it's reflective. It will help to reflect evil. However, the potion has to be gentle; the magic is inside them, after all, so we can't just blast it away."

"I'm starting to get it," Poppy said. "So you've got silver, and you've got some herbs. Isn't that good enough to start?"

"I'm missing something," I said, a bit of frustration bubbling under the surface. "A crucial piece of the story."

"Well, walk with me," Poppy said. "That always helps me shake things into place. Let's head over to Sea Salt and grab some lunch. I promise I'll let you get back to work this afternoon and stop bothering you."

I smiled at Poppy. My brain hurt; it was stuck, and banging my head against the wall was only making things worse. "Lunch sounds wonderful."

"Great!" Poppy bounced ahead, her happiness contagious. "I'm going to have fish sticks, maybe a Bloody Mary since I didn't take my Vamp Vites yet today, and then for the main course…"

Poppy went on and on about the lunch menu. By the time she'd decided what I should be ordering, we had reached the edge of the Lower Bridge.

"Look at that, the flowers are blooming!" Poppy singsonged, then pointed to a patch of little white flowers near the bridge. "You should pick some! They're basically yours, anyway."

"Mine?"

"Lily of the valley, that's what they're called." Poppy grinned. "Your name's on them."

"Oh, wow." I bent down, the small blooms leaning against my fingertips. "I haven't seen these in ages—they used to grow along my neighbor's house until they tore it down."

"Take a whiff," Poppy said. "They smell like dancing."

I took a sniff. A sweet, heavenly scent drifted up to me. "I'll grab a few—I bet Gus has a use for them."

"There are tons, and they grow quickly! Take as much as you want." Poppy gestured toward the river where bright orange goldfish twisted and jumped with the dolphins. "They love water, so they're always around here."

I harvested a few while Poppy finished both of the mimosas. We continued on, my face buried in the flowers.

"Don't they smell great? Actually, brilliant idea alert! What if you make your mind bending potion smell like these flowers?" Poppy turned to me, her eyes wide. "I'd totally drink it, just for the perfume. You know, you could even *make* a perfume with your name in it—personalized perfume. You could make one for me and Zin, too."

My spine stiffened. "Personalized perfume?"

"Even an alliteration," Poppy chirped happily. "Poppy's personalized perfume. Maybe you should—"

"Poppy, that's it!" I whirled around to face her, changing directions so fast my head swam with stars. "You solved it!"

"What did I solve with perfume? The problem of body odor? I'm pretty sure someone else figured that out first."

"*No*, the personalization piece. That's what I was missing."

"My brain doesn't work as fast as yours. Catch me up."

"I can use lily of the valley as the missing ingredient for the antidote! It makes complete sense!"

"Total sense," she said dryly.

"Blood magic is dangerous because it starts inside and changes a person until they don't remember who they are," I said, remembering Ainsley's voice grounding me to reality while I was under the spell in the Library of Secrets. "If there were a way to remind the person of who they really are, it might pull them back from The Puppeteer's control."

"Zin woke up when you held her," Poppy said. "When your tears hit her face. Maybe that snapped her out of it, knowing you were there. That you were her family."

Excitement coursed through my veins. "I'm sorry, we have to turn around—lunch can wait."

"I have a question though. Will you need to make a personalized potion for everyone? That doesn't seem economical."

"No, I don't think so." I held up the lilies. "I'm the Mixologist; I need to blend this potion in a way that makes sense to me, but I don't see why it shouldn't work for everyone else. The goal of this potion is to make people believe so strongly in themselves that they can't be persuaded to act in a way untrue to their own beliefs."

"Well, sounds like you have a plan," Poppy said. "I'll tell you what. Make it mimosa flavored, and I'll even be your tester."

I hardly heard Poppy as I grabbed her hand and pulled her back toward the bungalow.

Unfortunately, we only made it a few steps before an unwelcome visitor blocked our path.

"Lily," Harpin drawled, edging me off to the side of the path. "Just the woman I needed to see."

We were still near the East Isle, the Lower Bridge within sight when Harpin blocked our path.

"What do you want?" The snark in my voice came effortlessly. "My cousin and I are busy."

"You don't say?" Harpin raised an eyebrow at Poppy's empty mimosa glasses.

I crossed my arms. Hettie had said it was important to keep up the facade that Harpin and I didn't get along. Oddly enough, I didn't even have to fake it.

"May I have a word?" Harpin shifted, his long black robes swishing across the ground. "Alone, please."

"Whatever you want to say, you can say in front of Poppy."

"I don't think you'd like Poppy hearing what I have to say." He glanced at my cousin. "It's privileged information."

"She said she's busy." Poppy marched forward and stopped inches away from him. "If she's busy, she's busy."

Harpin sniffed, and then turned back to me. "It's quite urgent."

My hands balled at my side. I warred within myself over my own distaste for the man, and Hettie's instructions to work with him.

"I'm sorry, Poppy. Can I have a second?" I blew out a frustrated sigh, casting a glowering stare at Harpin. "Make it quick."

Poppy's eyebrows knitted together, but she grudgingly agreed.

Harpin rested his fingers lightly on my elbow as we stepped off the path. I shrugged him away, following a few paces behind as he led me toward a small cluster of trees.

When we reached the shade, he turned. "I need information."

I glanced over my shoulder to Poppy. She was too far away to hear anything, but when she saw me glance, she waved. Then she curled her lips at Harpin.

"What sort of information?" I met his squinty gaze.

"On The Puppeteer."

I couldn't keep my mouth from opening and closing. "Your task is to find out about blood magic and The Puppeteer, and you come to *me*? My job is just to be a distraction, remember? And why didn't you ask last night?"

"You know more than you're letting on." He stepped closer, his voice low, his breath oddly scented—like old tea leaves. "You might fool the others, but you're not fooling me."

"What makes you think that?"

"Your little boyfriend. He spent the morning with you. I don't get the same pillow talk as you, and that puts me at a disadvantage. Do what's best for the group, Lily."

"Are you watching me?" I hissed.

He sneered at my horrified gaze. "I can't do my job if you're withholding information."

"I'm not! I don't know where The Puppeteer is holing up."

"What did your boyfriend have to say?"

"Leave him out of this!" My voice rose and I turned slightly, catching sight of Poppy stepping toward us. I raised a hand, and she retreated again. "He doesn't know anything either; but even if he did, he wouldn't tell me."

"Work and play don't carry over?" Harpin tapped a long, thin finger to his lips. "That's a shame. I really could've used a leg up here, Lily. Or is there something else? Trouble in paradise, perhaps?"

"Shut up, Harpin." I hated that he was getting to me. "Do your job, and I'll do mine. I don't want to see you again."

Poppy didn't need to hear what we were talking about to interpret the expression on my face. She stepped forward, shoving the two empty mimosa glasses in Harpin's hands. "Hold these, please," she said, and then marched me away from him. "Don't look back."

I didn't have to look back to feel Harpin's eyes on us as we left, his lips curling into a smirk.

CHAPTER 28

"THAT SHOULD BE EVERYTHING," I said, dropping the last of the little white bell-shaped flowers into a gurgling potion. "Lily of the valley."

Poppy inhaled deeply, her eyes closed. "I'd definitely wear that perfume."

"You don't need to. Blood magic doesn't work on vampires."

"Oh, that's right." Poppy looked crestfallen. "Well, what if you take out all the magic and just slather me in the scent? I don't care about the antidote, I just want to smell nice."

"I'll add it to the Glo I'm making for you."

Poppy plopped down at the bench. "What are you going to call your new potion?"

I bit my lip and stirred, the potion bubbling into a milky white color with a bit of an iridescent sheen to it like the most glamorous of pearls. "I'm going to call it Jinx and Tonic."

"Oh, sexy."

The familiar *thunk* of a cane sounded on the front steps. "Oh, *no*. It's Gus." My heart stuttered, and I looked with horror at Poppy. "Not a word about Jinx and Tonic."

"I'll distract him."

"You're a lifesaver," I whispered, hurling ingredients back into their jars and putting out the tea light flame under the small cauldron. I tossed the majority of the supplies back onto the shelves, finishing just as Poppy initiated a titillating conversation about nail polish with Gus. *Some distraction,* I thought.

It wasn't that I wanted to hide the potion from Gus—I was proud of it, my own tiny way of fighting back against The Faction. But he'd been at Hettie's meeting, and he *knew* I hadn't been tasked to make a potion. A part of me was worried he wouldn't approve of me taking liberties on Hettie's rules.

"What do I care?" Gus growled as he pushed past Poppy. "Rip your nails off for all I'm concerned. It'd save you time from painting the stupid things."

Poppy beamed as she followed Gus into the room. With a quick scan of the place and a look at my face, she could see that she'd stalled him long enough for me to hide just about everything.

"Hey, Gus, you're back early," I said. "What's up?"

He'd slipped away, and a part of me had wondered if he'd gone off to meet Harpin. I didn't ask; it wasn't my business.

"What is that foul odor?" Gus waved a hand in front of his face. "Smells like a funeral."

Poppy sucked in a sharp breath. "It smells gorgeous!"

"What are you Mixing, Lily?"

"I'm just working on the Glo potion." I called as I left the storeroom for the bar. "You told me it was stupid."

"It's not stupid," Poppy said, then relaunched her argument about nail polish.

I zoned out, distracted by a movement from the bar area. Moving across the room, I recognized a distinctly orange feline shape.

"Hey, kitty, I said. "What are you doing here?"

Tiger strolled his way across the bar, leaping from stool to counter easily. I gave him a quick scratch behind the ears. Out of habit, I went to the fridge and poured a little saucer of milk. I set it out, petting his soft fur.

"I should really keep some real food for you around here, I suppose. But then everyone would know I like you."

Tiger lapped up the milk faster than parched dirt. I reached for a refill, but apparently the cat wasn't having it because he leaped from the bar and landed hard on my arm.

"Okay then," I said. "Just trying to be helpful."

I moved the dish to the sink. In the background, Poppy was still laying into Gus, and Gus had gotten busy rearranging the vials on the shelves. Surprisingly, he wasn't arguing back.

"What do you want?"

Tiger purred loudly.

"Are you trying to tell me something?"

As if he understood what I was saying, he flicked his tail at my knees, suggestively leading me forward. He took small steps, waiting until I followed. When he made it onto the beach out front, he turned and looked back, his eyes piercing.

"I'm coming!" I glanced back, but according to the sounds emerging from the storeroom, Poppy and Gus wouldn't be done arguing anytime soon. I hustled out to follow the cat. "Where are we going, Tiger?"

CHAPTER 29

THE TREK TO THE TWIST was brief. I wasn't surprised to find Tiger leading the way back to Hettie's treehouse. As I climbed the rope ladder, it dawned on me that Gus hadn't been invited. Otherwise, Tiger surely wouldn't have left the bungalow without both of us.

Pulling my way up, I swung my legs onto the platform and stood tall. Below, Tiger mewed, and then scampered away into the bright, exotic flowers.

"Hettie?" I called. "Are you around?"

"Up here!" My grandmother called down from the table at the very tippy-top of the tree. I looked up to find two pairs of feet. She had a visitor. "Come up, we've been waiting for you."

I continued my climb, wondering if Ainsley had returned, or even Harpin. I hoped desperately for the former. Surprisingly, it was neither.

"Liam?" I asked. "What are you doing here?"

The handsome man offered a smile. He looked comfortable sitting next to my grandmother at the table, but then again he fit in anywhere. It was one of his many skills, a reason he was so successful in his line of work.

"He's here because he has information," Hettie said quickly, leaving out all mention of The Core. "And I trust him to never abuse the knowledge of this meeting place. Right, Liam?"

"I'd never."

"Good," she said. "Well, since that's settled, let's get started.

Liam came to me asking what he should do with a certain piece of information. I thought you should know."

I dragged my gaze to meet Liam's. "Did something happen after we last talked?"

He cleared his throat and, for the first time, looked uncomfortable. "I left a few things out."

"Okay," I said slowly. "May I ask why?"

His eyes shifted toward Hettie first, and then down to the table where someone had laid out a variety of crackers, cheeses, and meats. "Because of its personal nature."

My heart twisted at the look on his face. Traces of a distant, old pain that'd been dredged to the surface marred his usually calm, stoic features. "What happened?"

"The Puppeteer." He swallowed, met my gaze evenly. "A long time ago, I knew her."

I reached across the table. His fingers grasped the edge of the wood. Resting my hand on one of his, he finally released his grasp, his fingers regaining some color.

"She was a friend?"

"No, not exactly."

Even Hettie was silent. Her lack of retort was unusual in itself, but the way her lips were pursed in thought, her wrinkles on display and exposing her true age, made me nervous.

Liam tapped his fingertips against the table. "She was my fiancée."

I blinked, the surprise so thoroughly flooding me I couldn't hide it. "Oh, I didn't. . . didn't know you'd ever been engaged."

Liam gave a slow nod. "Once."

I kept my eyes on Liam. "Do you want to talk about it?"

"No." He reached for the platter, crafting a small sandwich with one cracker, a slice of brie, and a bit of salami. He didn't eat it, just set it back on the table. "But I suppose you should know about it."

"Why now?" I shook my head. "We just talked the other night, and you didn't mention it."

"Because she contacted me."

"The Puppeteer? When?"

"Her name was Ilinia." He sighed. "I suppose her name is *still* Ilinia, but no one has called her that since she went to prison."

"Tell me what you can, Liam. I don't need to know everything. Did she say why she tried to contacted you?"

"I'll explain everything," he said, his eyes meeting mine. "I have nothing to hide. It started over ten years ago."

Hettie reached over and built herself a sandwich in the ensuing silence. Liam waited for her to finish before continuing.

"I was here on a business trip. Long enough ago that I wasn't as successful as I am now, and my business relationships weren't set. Believe it or not, I was doing a lot of the dirty work myself." He gave a pitiful smile. "It was on this trip that I'd set up a meeting with the Witch of the Woods."

"Liam knew The Forest like nobody else," Hettie said. "He had those creatures eating from the palm of his hand."

"I had to learn the hard way, just like anyone else. Years and years and years of blood, sweat, and tears." He paused, his eyes distant with memories. "I'm getting too old to traipse through The Forest nowadays, though. I've been there, done that."

"I didn't know—"

"Not many people know my history. Even the ones who knew me back then seem to have forgotten how hard I worked. Days on end without sleeping, journeys through The Forest and beyond, trips that nearly stole my life. It is what it is, however, and on this particular trip I stumbled upon a lagoon. The most beautiful place in the world."

"Where is it?"

"You'll never find it, and I'll never tell." Liam shook his head, his lips tight. "It's too dangerous. Too beautiful—deathly beautiful. That's where I met Ilinia. Once upon a time, she lived there."

"*In* the lagoon?" My mouth hung open. "A *mermaid*?"

"No," he said with a ghost of a smile. "A human, though the rumors say her grandmother was a mermaid who became human. However, this means that Ilinia has mermaid blood. Which makes sense—she has the most beautiful eyes, the color of the lagoon. She belonged there, blended with the water."

"What happened then?"

"I stayed for three days. Talking, befriending her. . . falling in love." The look in Liam's eyes was torn between equal parts tragic and hopeful. Love had found him, and it'd been taken away. The scar was still fresh, though years had passed. "Eventually I had to leave; it was the hardest thing I'd ever done in my life."

"But you went back, I assume?"

"We used to communicate with lights. Flash a light into the sky four times—red, white, green, yellow. That's how we'd set up our times to meet. I made many journeys deep into The Forest to see her. It was on one of these trips that she asked if I would take her away, bring her fully into the island culture so we could be together forever."

A looming sense of foreboding filled the room. "And you did?"

"I proposed to her on our next visit. I couldn't imagine living without her." Liam pressed down on a cracker until it shattered into pieces. "She told me *yes*."

"But something went wrong?"

"We weren't ready to marry right that second; she lived in the lagoon, and at that time, I was at the height of my traveling. My primary home was on the mainland, but that was just an address. I bounced around every continent once a week."

"Building your business?"

"Forming relationships, working odd jobs, anything I could get my hands on." Liam folded his arms across his chest. "I knew where

I wanted to be in five years, ten years, and I knew that it'd take a lot of work to get there. I was putting my time in while I was young and able, so I could relax when I got older."

"Are you there now?" I asked, gently brushing the cracker crumbs off the table. They fell between the tree branches, whirling into the air. "Where you want to be, I mean."

A shadow passed over his face. "In some senses, yes."

"You mean in business?" Hettie asked. "Or love?"

"In business, I am happy," he said through gritted teeth.

"Leave it alone, Hettie," I warned. "Now's not the time."

"It's fine." Liam uncrossed his arms stiffly. "This happened years ago, I'm over it."

That was a lie, but nobody commented on it.

"I asked her to give me a year," Liam said. "Within that year, I would either make my own business work, or I would get a job with MAGIC, Inc. on the mainland—a stable job—to support a family."

"I think that's fair," I said. "It was a big decision, and—"

"We didn't make it a week," he interrupted. "She was arrested three days after I proposed."

"What?" I gasped. "Why?"

"They say she used blood magic," Liam said, his words clipped. "As far as I'm concerned, it has still never been proven. She's been locked in jail ever since."

My reaction was delayed. "Sorry, I'm trying to work out the details. How could she have been thrown in jail if nothing was ever proven? Are you telling me that The Puppeteer might never have performed blood magic?"

"It was reported that there was one witness," Hettie interjected. "However, the name of this witness was never revealed for safety reasons. The first Ranger on the scene made the arrest."

"Was the Ranger the witness? What if he lied?"

"No," Hettie said. "He showed up too late. The witness was on the ground, unconscious, according to this Ranger. He then suspected Ilinia of using blood magic—the signs and symptoms were all there. He arrested her, searched her home near the lagoon. There, he found mind bending paraphernalia, though her dolls had been hidden away. He found one or two practice ones and enough materials to suggest that she'd been working on a collection of dolls to encompass the entire island."

"Her arrest stuck. Blood magic is difficult to prove, but a jury of islanders voted that there was enough evidence to keep her locked away," Liam said. "For the greater population's protection."

"And what do you think?"

"I think. . . " he hesitated. "I loved her. I didn't think. I'm not sure I could believe it then, and I'm not sure I do now. If there was a witness, why wouldn't the Ranger expose the witness?"

"For safety?" I suggested. "Who was the Ranger?"

Liam met my gaze. "You are dating him."

"Ranger X made the arrest?" My heart pounded in my chest. "But... he must have been so young! How long ago was this?"

"It was his first year on the job," Liam said. "And the arrest stuck, I had no say in the matter."

"No, this doesn't make sense. So X knows the name of the witness?" I was reeling in shock, stumbling to get my bearings. "He never mentioned it."

"I'm sure he didn't."

"He was so upset when he heard she'd escaped," I said, "but he never explained. . . Oh, no. What if she goes after him?"

"She's not going after anyone!" Liam stood up. "She's in trouble, that's why I called you here!"

"In trouble? She escaped from prison!"

"She signaled me late last night," Liam said. "The same way we used to do it, using lights in the sky. I know it was her. She's in trouble."

I looked to Hettie for her opinion.

My grandmother shrugged. "I don't know the answers, dear."

"What makes you think she's in trouble?" I asked. "How do you know it's not a trick?"

"She's been misunderstood for all of these years. What if none of this is her fault? What if someone from The Faction is holding her captive, forcing her to use mind bending against the Candidates."

I bit my lip, my mind fuzzy with the onslaught of information. "It seems a little far-fetched, Liam."

"They must be threatening her with something." Liam ran a hand through his hair. "Not her own life, surely—maybe someone else's."

"Maybe yours," Hettie said. "If she loved you as much as you loved her, maybe she's doing these things to save you."

"We have to find her. I'm going to help her," Liam said. "I'm sure she'll be near the lagoon. Maybe she's escaped, hence the warning lights. I'm sure she needs help."

"What do you think?" I asked Hettie. "I don't know what to say."

"This is between me and Ilinia," Liam said. "I'm going to help her, but I thought you should know."

"Do you want me to come with you?" I asked quietly. "Is that why you brought me here?"

Hettie snorted. "He won't let me come, good luck with that."

"Lily is the Mixologist," Liam said, turning a careful expression toward me. "If Ilinia is in trouble, you might be able to help. I don't know who else to ask for assistance. I'm the only one who believes her."

I stood up, stalling as I paced around the room. "I think we should bring Ranger X into this. An escaped prisoner is part of his jurisdiction."

"Absolutely not," Liam said. "He arrested her in the first place. He'd never give her a second chance now."

"You don't know that," I said, my voice rising. "He's the most fair, honest man I know. If he arrested her, he had a good reason for doing it. He's *seen* mind bending before, the effects of it on a person. One of his Rangers fell victim to *her*. And he never recovered."

"Well, it's me and you, or it's nobody," Liam said. "I know you want to get to the bottom of this as much as I do—I heard about what happened with Zin. The Trials are cancelled. How long can this go on?"

Both of our tempers flared high, and it was Hettie who finally waved her hands around and quieted us. "Stop it, both of you. Don't lose sight of the end goal. We need to find out who's behind the attacks on the Candidates. For Raymon, we need to bring the responsible party to justice."

"There is only one way to find out the truth." Liam stood, turning to face me. "If you come with me, Lily, you'll know for sure one way or another."

"I'll go with you under one circumstance," I said. "Hettie stays here, and if she doesn't hear from us within a few hours, she's allowed to divulge everything—absolutely everything—to Ranger X. And if he arrests Illinia again, so be it."

Liam's eyes flashed, but he gained control of his emotions and extended a hand. "Fair."

We shook on it, the heated temperature of the tree fort slowly cooling to a more manageable level.

"How far away is it?" I asked. "What do I need to bring?"

"We can make it in one hour if we leave now," Liam said. "Bring whatever you like, but don't pack heavy."

"Best to take some defensive spells," Hettie said. "And maybe a few snacks. Want some power bars? I make them fresh with granola and cranberries. Really tasty. It goes great with a sip of my delicious homemade lemonade—lavender flavored. You'll have energy for weeks!"

I reached into my pockets and fingered the tiny vial of single-serve Jinx & Tonic that I'd stashed before disappearing with Tiger.

"I have what I need," I said. "Let's go."

CHAPTER 30

"WHAT DO YOU KNOW ABOUT lilies?" I asked Liam as our feet swept through the soft grass of The Twist. "Where they grow, things like that."

We'd just finished a small meal at Hettie's treehouse—her idea, not ours—and then prepared for our journey into The Forest.

Liam shot me a surprised look. "Lilies? Well, they are challenging to grow on the island. They're considered a relatively rare plant to find in the wild."

"That's what Gus told me. On the mainland, lilies aren't particularly rare."

"The soil here is different, flowers grown on the island have magic infused through their core," he said. "You could use lilies from the mainland in potions, but they wouldn't be as strong."

"So if I wanted to find calla lilies on the island, where would I go?"

Liam stopped walking, ran a hand over his forehead. "I'm confused. Has Trinket run out of them?"

My back straightened. "Trinket?"

"Gus gets a somewhat regular supply from your aunt. To grow a lily here on the island takes exacting care—it's a lot of work, but Trinket's managed to get a successful garden going behind her house. I thought you knew."

I caught sight of my face in the reflection of a pond outside The Twist. "I didn't know."

"I'm sure there's a reason Gus didn't tell you." Liam resumed walking, and I followed. "It's not a secret."

I bit my lip. "Does anyone else grow them?"

"They *might* grow wild in The Forest, but I don't know anyone who harvests from there. It's difficult and dangerous to grow lilies without constant attention. In the wild, they are even rarer. If anyone ever asks me, I direct them to Trinket."

"Oh, I didn't realize—"

"Are you low on your supply?" Liam frowned. "What makes you ask?"

A new thought dawned on me. "Have you sent anyone to Trinket for calla lilies lately?"

"Why the sudden interest?"

"It's personal."

"As is my business," he said. "I've said it before, I'll say it again; I operate with the utmost discretion."

"It's important," I said. "I think someone's been threatening me."

Liam reached out, his hand grasping above my elbow. "Who else knows? Have you told Ranger X?"

I shook my head as his fingers dug into my skin. "No, I haven't told anyone. I don't even know if it *is* a threat."

"Explain, and I'll give you any relevant information."

I hesitated, but when I couldn't come up with a better option, I nodded. "There have been two instances so far when someone left a lily for me—no note, no explanation, no clues."

Skepticism radiated from Liam's face, so I continued.

"You're not understanding. Someone *broke in* to my storeroom. They must have wanted me to see the flower badly since the bungalow was locked. Everyone was at the Trials. After Raymon. . . " I cleared my throat. "When I returned home, I found the flower."

"Are you sure there's not a simpler explanation?" Liam shook his head. "Maybe Gus left it out, or Ranger X left you a romantic surprise."

"Nope. Gus came into the bungalow to find the flower, and he seemed genuinely confused. Ranger X came with us in the morning, and he stayed in the public eye until the evening. It couldn't have been him."

"What if it's not a threat? What if someone is trying to send you a message?"

"Could be. But what?"

"Well, I'm not a mind reader."

"I need to pay a quick visit to Trinket," I said. "The lilies were fresh. And on the second time…" I paused. "Trinket picked up the lily from Hettie's doorstep."

"It's none of my clients," Liam said. "Someone either went to Trinket privately or stole from her. The last person requesting fresh lilies was over a year ago. If it's important, we can swing by Trinket's on the way to the lagoon."

I nodded and took the lead, realizing that Liam had stopped walking. We were still in The Twist, and he'd never be able to find his way out. So I picked up my pace, leading him through the foliage.

"You know, I've never been inside Trinket's house," I said once we reached the edge of the labyrinth. "She's not the inviting type."

"Neither have I," Liam said. "And I've known her a lot longer than you."

"I suppose there's a first time for everything."

CHAPTER 31

BOTH MIMSEY AND TRINKET LIVED relatively close to The Twist, their houses forming a neat little triangle.

The house was tidy on the outside, reminding me of mainland suburbia, without the cookie cutter–style of housing. Trinket's home was built from stone, the windows lit from the inside as carefully pruned flowerbeds added a pop of color to the exterior. A wooden picket fence formed a perfect square around the home, the yard carefully trimmed.

Though seven children lived in this house, there was no real sign of life anywhere. No trucks littering the yard or toys strewn on the path leading to the arched wooden doorway.

The two-level house itself was long, built wide instead of tall. There were clear dividers between sections, as if a new addition had been tacked on every time a child had joined the family.

"Do I just knock?" I looked at Liam. "This is very Anne of Green Gables."

"I suppose so," Liam said. "That seems to be the normal way of announcing oneself."

I gave Liam the eye. "Are you coming with me or waiting here?"

"It's not my business," Liam said. "I'll be waiting here if you need anything."

I narrowed my eyes. "Chicken."

"Me?"

"You just don't want to face Trinket."

"That, too." Liam exhaled. "Go on, Lily. Ten minutes, or I'm leaving without you."

I swallowed. "Yes, of course. I'll be quick."

With a feeble wave, I turned and approached the dainty house. I raised my hand and knocked. It took three tries before someone opened the door. The figure in the entryway was small, one of Zin's younger siblings. The male half of "the twins."

"*Mom!*" he yelled, before I could say anything. "Company!"

Then he ran off, leaving me standing in the doorway, my hands clasped awkwardly in front of me.

Trinket yelled a few things about cleaning up to her children. Then she appeared around the corner, wiping her hands on a towel. "Lily," she said, unsurprised to see me. "Hello."

"Hi," I said, not making a move to step inside. "Beautiful. . . entryway."

"Thank you." Trinket took a few steps closer. "What brings you around?"

Indeed, the entryway was nice; clean, and well kept. Warmer than I expected, likely due to the shadows of firelight licking up the walls. Wooden floors gleamed, highlighting the sitting areas while richly colored rugs spruced up the space.

Seven jackets lined hooks on the wall, and a small mahogany table held a bowl of keys next to the door. A small bouquet of flowers added a dash of welcome.

I swallowed, taking a tentative step forward. Trinket set her towel on the table, placing one hand on her hip. She still didn't invite me inside.

"The lilies," I said. "What do you know about them?"

"What lilies?" Trinket's voice came out monotone, and it was difficult to tell if she was completely clueless or pretending.

I cleared my throat. "You brought me one the night Zin. . . at Hettie's."

"I gave it to you," she said. "It was on the front steps."

"Yes, but who put it there?"

Trinket's eyebrows shot up. "Good question."

"Do you know the answer?" I hadn't meant to accuse my aunt of anything, but her dodginess was wearing on me. "Before you deny it, I've been talking to people. You're the only person on this island who's managed to successfully grow lilies. Either someone is stealing from you, or—"

"Nobody is stealing from me."

The sureness of her words took me by surprise. "Oh, then. . . " I blinked, gathering my thoughts. "That means. . . "

"Why are you here, Lily?"

"Why are you leaving me flowers? What are you trying to tell me?"

Trinket's mouth pursed as she sized me up. She watched me for a long, long time. "I thought you were ready. You're not."

"Ready for what?"

"I'm sorry, Lily."

"What are you talking about?" My anger began to flare up. "You've been sending me messages, worrying me that something was wrong—breaking into my house! And now I'm not ready to hear what you have to say?"

"Yes." Trinket's mouth was in a firm line. "I was wrong."

"Wrong? You sent me those flowers for a reason. What are you trying to tell me?"

"I'll explain one day. Good evening, Lily."

"No!" I flung my arm out as Trinket tried to shepherd me. "I want to know."

Trinket moved so close to me I could smell a light, spicy scent coming from her apron, as if she'd just baked cinnamon rolls. "As I said, you're not ready."

I held my ground. "That's not a good enough answer."

Trinket held my gaze, her eyes burning with knowledge that she'd held secret for a long, long time.

"You owe me this at least," I said. "Why did you send me the flowers?"

A light flickered on in Trinket's gaze, and if I wasn't mistaken, it was some sort of approval. She took a step back. "I see now that if I tell you, it will destroy you."

My stomach sank to my knees, my blood chilling. "Why would you want to ruin me?"

"I don't."

"If it's so horrible, I need to know."

"And you will—when you're *ready*, Lily, I won't tell you again."

"How will you—how will I—know when I'm ready?"

Trinket bit her lip, flicking a glance over her shoulder. The hallway was empty. "You'll be ready when you trust yourself."

"But—"

"No." Trinket blinked, and then to my surprise, she took a step back and ran a hand across her eyes. "Your past is difficult, Lily. You're strong. You're intelligent and talented. But it's too soon. I'm sorry. I promised your mother I'd wait for the right moment."

"Please!"

"Go," Trinket said. "Now."

At a loss for words, I turned and took lethargic steps down the front path. Trinket watched me go, her gaze burning into the skin of my back. I moved like a sleepwalker, ready to be woken from my nightmare.

Liam wrapped his arm through mine, and the door behind us closed. "It'll be okay."

CHAPTER 32

"IT'S CRUEL," I CONCLUDED THIRTY minutes later as we crossed through The Forest. "I can't believe my own aunt could do such a thing to her niece."

Liam remained silent. I'd awoken from my shocked haze, digesting all that had happened as we followed an invisible path through the brush. Liam had clearly been this way hundreds of times before. Like muscle memory, he maneuvered the path without hardly paying attention.

"What did she mean?" I said, more to myself than to Liam. "If I'm not ready, she should've just kept quiet. Of course I'm ready. I'm part of. . . " I trailed off, remembering just in time that Liam had no knowledge about The Core. I sighed, reining in my frustration before I said something I shouldn't.

Liam hadn't said anything for the entire journey so far. He pushed back branches from a weeping willow and formed his words carefully as he spoke. "Have you considered that she might be right?"

"Right?" I reached a hand out, grabbed the branches of the willow, and stood still. "What are you talking about?"

"Maybe you aren't ready to hear whatever it is she has to say."

"Fine! Then why'd she tell me in the first place? What's the deal with the flowers?"

"Maybe she was testing you, maybe she didn't expect you to figure things out so quickly," Liam said. "I don't know. But I think you need to consider that she's got your best interests at heart. Maybe she's right, and now's not the time."

I let the branches droop as I pushed past, staring at the ground and fighting not to snarl at my one friend who was around to listen. "I have seen murder. I've experienced blood magic. I've navigated The Forest and fought The Faction. If anything, I need to know all that I can before it's too late."

Liam raised a hand in surrender. "I'm not arguing with you, and I'm not trying to pick a fight."

I sullenly stomped behind him, aware I was acting childish. "You're on her side."

"I'm saying she might be right, that's all. Maybe she made a mistake. Everyone makes mistakes, and maybe you're being a little harsh toward her."

"But—"

"I didn't say she handled it well, and Trinket is a tough pill to swallow on a good day. She's probably not happy with how things went either."

I considered it, wondering if Trinket was back at her cottage having the exact same thoughts. "Maybe," I finally relented. "I'm sorry. I'm frustrated and I'm stressed. And I'm nervous about what's so horrible that she has to hide it from me."

Liam faced me, darkness surrounding us as the sun slid behind the tree branches. "The lagoon is just ahead. We have to put this behind us for now and focus on the present."

"I understand."

"That's the spirit." Liam gave me a smile, his lips tight, the light not shining in his eyes. "Last warning. I doubt that we'll see any of the mermaids; they avoid the surface when there are visitors. But should you hear any music, plug your ears as quickly as possible, and don't let up until I give the all clear."

"Music, like singing?"

"Music of any sort. Singing, or shells. They make instruments from seashells, and the effect can be just as powerful."

"Powerful in what way?"

"They lull a person into a dreamlike state, easily influenced by outside suggestions."

"Like hypnotism?"

"A mild form," Liam said, hesitation lacing his words. "It's in the same family of magic as mind bending, though not technically illegal. It's their best defense. As with all weapons, it can be misused."

"Do you think. . . " I turned the question over in my mind before I finished it. "Do you think that's why people assumed she was behind it? Because she has a natural inclination for it?"

"Those are the rumors."

Before I could ask any more questions, he led the way through a twisty, narrow path under a row of low-hanging branches. We scaled a monstrous pile of rocks, then picked our way down the other side. After taking tiny steps across a flimsy log over a rushing river, we finally made a steep descent across a sandy beach and came upon the lagoon.

The place was even more beautiful than Liam had described.

He must have heard my gasp. "Don't forget, Lily. For every inch of beauty, there is an inch of danger. Pay close attention to everything."

I nodded, too busy absorbing the scenery to respond. We stood in The Forest where, for a breath of time, the world fell quiet. Before us sat a lagoon filled with water so blue, it was as if the sky had pooled together to form liquid.

Hills leaned high above us, the water trickling down the slopes and forming divots in the sand as it rolled into the lagoon. Through the water, rocks glimmered—deep reds and blacks with a glint of gold.

Though achingly beautiful, an air of something darker hung over us, something looming beyond the brilliant blues and vibrant greens. Flowers hung from branches, just a little too bright. The air was chilled, just a little too pure. The calmness was quiet, and just a little too still.

At the center of the lagoon was a dark swirl of water. I pointed, and turned to Liam. "What's that?"

"It's deep—very, very deep," he said. "Don't go near it."

The warning in his voice told me there was more to the story, a lot more, but I didn't press.

Liam moved briskly toward the water. I followed, my eyes darting between every little detail.

"Do you hear that?" I asked as we reached the edge of the pool. I held out a hand to touch the water. "What is that noise? It's not *singing,* but it's—"

Liam caught my arm just before my fingers brushed the water's surface. He pulled me back so hard I let out a cry of pain.

"*Don't* touch anything!"

I rubbed my elbow. "Don't you hear. . . "

I stopped as Liam tilted his head. We both heard it now; the sound grew steadily louder.

"Over there." I pointed toward one of the thin falls trickling over the edge of a rocky cliff high above us. The sheet of water was almost transparent, a curtain masking us from the darkness behind it.

"It's. . . " he hesitated, taking a few tentative steps forward, his eyes razor sharp in their focus. "It's *her.*"

"Liam," I called, rushing after him. "Wait!"

He didn't listen, and I wasn't fast enough. Liam had been here many times before, it was evident in the way his body moved over the rocks. Though years might have passed, his legs remembered the path, his feet steady on the uneven ground. When he sprang, it was graceful, quick, and I had no chance of keeping up.

I scrambled over the rocks behind him, swearing under my breath as I skinned a knee, scraped an elbow, bashed a hip into the sharp stones. He might move like a jaguar, but I moved like a drunken elephant.

"Ilinia," Liam called, his voice hoarse as he landed on the sandy beach next to the waterfall. "Is that you?"

A soft response came from the shadows. It must have been the right response because Liam moved forward despite my cries. He took one step straight through the shimmering sheet of water and disappeared.

By the time I reached the beach, I was bleeding from at least three different locations. I pushed through the falls, my scrapes stinging from the crush of water on my shoulders. When I stopped on the other side, I was drenched.

My breath caught in my throat. Liam had fallen to his knees, his arms wrapped around a stick-thin figure. Her hair was a tangled black mess, her clothing ragged and torn. She'd closed her eyes, her skeletal fingers digging into Liam's back as they hugged.

I stepped away, hiding myself in the shadows. *Have I been wrong about everything?*

Liam must have sensed my presence because he broke the embrace, keeping one hand on her shoulder. "Lily," he said, turning around. "Meet Ilinia, my... my fiancée."

My heart nearly stopped in my chest as she looked up at me. Her eyes were blue, the color of the lagoon—big and bright, just as Liam had said. She stared up at me with a wild sort of hunger, and it was then I realized the cut rope around her hands and feet. Liam must have freed her from a set of bindings.

"Hi," I said, my voice hoarse. "I'm Lily."

She smiled, a shy smile, and despite her bedraggled appearance, I could see the signs of former beauty. Her hair, stringy and clinging to her cheeks, might've been rich and shiny once upon a time. She was hungry, too, I could see it in her face, her eyes. Her waiflike figure might have been curvy once, back before she'd been locked away.

"Ilinia," she said in a raspy voice. She tried the name on for size, a wan smile crossing her face. "I haven't been called that in forever."

Liam ran his hand up and down her arm, clearly in a daze. He looked into her eyes, and I could feel him trying to draw out a semblance of the woman he'd once known. Liam had come here expecting to find his fiancée, and judging by the look of shock on his face, he'd found another person entirely.

"I'm sorry you have to see me like this. . . " She interrupted herself with a coughing fit. "So very sorry, Liam."

"How long have you been here?" I stepped closer, pulling off my shawl and handing it to Liam so he could warm her. "You've got to be freezing. Who kept you here? You probably have pneumonia, or worse, sitting around in the water for so long."

Liam wrapped my shawl around her shoulders, rubbed his hands up and down her biceps to warm her.

"You need to leave—we need to leave," she said, ignoring my questions. "He'll be back."

"Who will be back?" I scanned the lagoon, but it appeared empty. "Who took you?"

"It was. . . he works for The Faction," she said. "I don't remember his name—I don't think he told it to me."

"Start from the beginning," I said, trying to sound encouraging. "Quickly. We need to know who we might run into as we get you out of here."

I hadn't made up my mind whether I believed her story. She looked tired, worn, distraught. Even so, the image of Raymon flashed through my mind, and a whiff of anger pointed me toward caution. Liam clearly wasn't thinking straight, so I needed to think for both of us.

"I didn't break out of prison," she said, a shiver wracking her body. "He was there, he showed up in my cell and took me away. He brought me here."

"How did *he* know about the lagoon?" I asked. "Liam told me nobody knows about it except the mermaids. It's how he met you."

"I knew about it, and this man—he knew of my background. He knew me, everything about me, though I'd never met him before." She shook her head, blinked those huge blue eyes. "He made me give him directions to this place, and I agreed because he threatened to kill me if I didn't. I asked him why he'd picked here."

I waited as her eyes glazed over.

She shook herself back to reality. "He told me it was because nobody could hear me scream."

"Where are the mermaids?" I asked. "Couldn't they help you?"

She scoffed. "They abandoned this place years ago. Ever since they found out Liam knew of its existence, it wasn't the same. They've moved on."

"Where is he now?" I asked. "The man who broke you out of jail? What does he look like?"

"Dark hair, big muscles. He's strong—strong enough to carry me. When he broke me out of jail I was weak, so weak he had to carry me. . . "

As her voice trailed off, Liam held her closer. "Enough questions. We need to leave."

"What happened after?" I pressed on, ignoring Liam. "The blood magic—was that you? With the Candidates?"

She paused, her lips quivering. They were colored a dark purple, dry and cut and bleeding. Running her tongue nervously over them, she glanced at Liam and then back to me. "Yes," she said softly. "And I am so very, truly sorry to say it."

Liam froze. His arms went stiff, yet he couldn't seem to let go completely. "How could you, Ilinia?"

"*He made me.*" Her voice cracked. "He threatened my life first, and I told him I'd rather die than participate in his plan."

"That wasn't enough, so he threatened someone else's life," I said with a quick glance at Liam. "Whose?"

She raised a hand, brought her fingers to Liam's face and traced a thin line down his cheek. Tears spilled freely from her eyes. "I had to do it, for you, for us. I'm sorry."

The horror in Liam's face twisted my heart. I ached for him, for Ilinia, for their dangerous affair. There was love between them, I could see it, feel it in the air, but there was also death. And loss. To be surrounded by so much love and loss all at once—Liam's face crumpled in pain.

"You shouldn't have," Liam said. "I could've saved you, I would have found you. I can protect myself, and you, and us. You should never have agreed."

"I had no choice."

"You always have a choice," Liam said, his eyes the color of slate. "You should have let me die."

I stepped forward, exhaling a shaky breath. "Liam, stop—she was trying to save you."

"A Candidate is dead," Liam said flatly. "It should have been me."

"It's done and it's in the past. Right now, we need to get out of here," I said. "Ilinia, can you walk? You can tell us the rest on the way."

She nodded, struggling to her feet. She leaned against Liam. His face had taken on a grayish sheen, and his expression told me he hadn't decided if he should hold her close or push her away.

"Liam, can you get us out of here?" I asked. "I'll take one arm, you take the other. . . "

We hobbled through the sheet of water. Our drenched clothes made the journey long and treacherous, the rocks skittering beneath our feet, the clothes heavy on our backs. We'd made it almost into the shade of the trees when Ilinia stiffened.

"He's coming. We need to hide."

I didn't hear anything, but I didn't wait for another warning. I pulled her quickly to the side, and Liam followed us. Soon enough, a whistling noise approached from deeper within The Forest.

"Ilinia," a deep male voice called, "we've arrived! The mind bending wasn't enough to knock him out, but we helped it along!"

I turned to Ilinia, a prickling sensation creeping down my spine. "What is he talking about?"

Her eyes were wide, and she gave the smallest shake of her head. But something in her eyes, the smallest sense of disappointment, gave her away. My heart understood before my brain, but once my mind figured out that everything Ilinia said had been a lie, I moved like lightning.

Diving for Liam, I pushed him out of the way as Ilinia leaped to her feet. She went from weak to able-bodied in the blink of an eye, her blue gaze full of energy, her lips curled into a smile. Liam and I tumbled to the ground.

"I told you to be discreet, idiot," Ilinia shouted to the man now standing on the rocky beach. "What part of you *screaming* through The Forest is discreet?"

From the ground, I could see the figure of a man holding the arm of an even bigger man who was slumped on the rocks. Two additional men accompanied the first, helping to carry the unmoving figure. *A familiar figure.*

"X!" I screamed, lunging for the group of men. They were much too far away for me to reach them, but I couldn't help it. "X, it's me!"

The men dropped Ranger X's body to the ground. He was bleeding from his head, bruised on his arms. He didn't move as his body hit the beach, clearly unconscious.

"What did you do to him?" I yelled, turning to face Ilinia.

She stood with her hands held out in front of her, her hair whipping behind her in the rising wind. I fought against Liam as he tried desperately to hold me back while I struggled toward X.

"Let him go!" I shouted, but Liam won our battle and held me to the ground.

Ilinia took a few steps toward us, her hair wild as my shawl flapped against her skeletal figure. "I'm sorry you had to find out like this."

Liam's breath was hot against my neck as he hissed at The Puppeteer. "What is this, Ilinia? What are you thinking?"

Her face contorted in what looked like genuine pain. "I wish things didn't have to be like this."

"Have to be like whaaa. . . " The word didn't make it from his mouth before Liam jerked to attention, his eyes going vacant as the words disappeared into thin air.

Ilinia twisted her hands, the blues of her eyes going almost milky white as she muttered words at the speed of light. Liam didn't react when I shook him, so I set his body against the ground.

Before I could lunge for her, she stopped speaking and Liam slumped into unconsciousness. I knelt over him, listened for breathing. Shallow puffs of air slipped from his mouth. He was alive, but just barely.

When I looked up, Ilinia was breathless, her lips turning black, her eyes still white as snow. With her hands dancing like a puppeteer's, she muttered the curses that would trade a piece of her soul for control over my mind.

The world began to dim, the familiar sensation of blood magic taking over. My mind faded to black as the names, the faces of those I loved, disappeared into nothing.

CHAPTER 33

WHEN THE HAZE CLEARED, THE world returned in full force. Once again, the colors struck me as too bright, the noises too loud, the taste of air on my tongue too strong. I blinked, stretched, tried to understand how I'd ended up on top of the waterfall staring down at the lagoon below.

The sun pierced the trees and warmed my skin. As I stretched, the skin of my wrists twinged in pain. It was then I realized that my hands were bound behind my back with rope, and it bit into my skin as I struggled. The Puppeteer was nowhere in sight.

But I wasn't alone, either. Liam and Ranger X were near, our backs touching one another, forming a triangle in our cross-legged positions on the ground. We were each bound individually, with a larger rope tying all six of our wrists together.

"Are you both okay?" I asked, trying to keep the worry from my voice. I could hear two sets of breath—at least they were alive. "X, are you awake?"

"Lily," he said, relief in his voice. "I'm fine, but you—"

"I'm fine, too." I looked down at my legs and found them dusted with scratches. A raspberry burned on my elbow, and I could sense a bruise forming on my hip. "How did I get up here?"

Ranger X clasped his hand around a few of my fingers. It was all he could reach. "You walked."

"I walked?" A pit of dread weighed heavy in my stomach. I had no recollection of anything after Ilinia had worked her magic on me. My memories were a complete and utter void.

"Mind bending," X said. "She used it on all of us, but it looks like she can use it on only one person at a time."

I cleared my throat, feeling a rush of sympathy for Camden and Trent. The feeling of waking up, of not knowing how I'd gotten here sent shivers down my spine. "Did I do anything else?"

"No," X said softly. "They tied us and left."

"How long ago?"

"Just a few minutes," he said. "It took you awhile to come out of the trance, but it was your first time. It hit you hard."

"No, there was. . . there was the time I went under with the Witch of the Woods," I said. "I fought it off."

"That wasn't real blood magic," Ranger X said. "Nobody can fight this off—don't blame yourself."

"But—"

"It worked on me. Ilinia's mind bending magic hit me while I was home alone, preparing to meet with the Candidates. I don't remember what happened after that. The men hauled me through The Forest while I was out."

"I'm so sorry." I ran my fingers along the palm of his hand. "I wish I could have done something to stop it."

"No, I'm the one—I should've done something," X argued. "I shouldn't have left you alone. If only I'd—"

"*You* should've done something?" Liam's voice rose in pitch. "What about me? I walked Lily straight into a trap and exposed her to the worst form of magic in the world. And even then, I didn't protect her."

"She used you," I said. "It's not your fault. You cared about her."

"If I'd listened to Ranger X years ago, this never would have happened. From day one, he warned me against her. Then he arrested her, and still I fought him on it." A shiver wracked Liam's body, his words bitter. "This has all happened because of me. I'm so sorry. To both of you."

The apology felt directed toward Ranger X, so I waited for his response. Instead of speaking, he moved so quickly I hardly knew what was happening. Then I felt the ropes loosen on my wrists and I realized that somehow Ranger X had sliced through our bindings.

"How did you do that?" I asked, leaping to my feet and staring at him.

Instead of responding, he reached out and kissed me with a desire so overpowering I couldn't breathe. My heart soared, my stomach on fire with emotions for him as his lips pressed to mine.

And then Liam cleared his throat.

Ranger X's hands latched behind me, hovering just below my waist as he glared over my head.

"I'm sorry to ruin the moment, but I think we should figure out a plan," Liam said. "And then I will leave you alone. I promise."

"I already have a plan," Ranger X said, stepping into business mode with a resigned glance at my lips. "Sit," he instructed, "and wrap the rope around your hands—loose enough to throw it off when the moment arrives."

"Let's go now," Liam said. "Why wait?"

"If we go now, she'll get to us first. We need to let her come to us, let her guard weaken before we attack. I don't want to run from her; I want to end this."

Once we'd all slid to the ground, adjusted our positions, and looped the rope over our wrists, I scooted as far back as I could. I touched both men's hands, the motion small but purposeful.

"I'm scared," I whispered, my heart racing. "I *hate* mind bending. If she does it to me again..."

"She won't," X said. "I won't let her."

"Wait!" I hissed. "I have something. I almost forgot."

Quickly slipping my hand out from under the rope, I pulled the small vial from my pocket. "Split this," I said, handing it to the men. "It'll help."

"What is this?" Ranger X asked, palming the vial. "A potion?"

"I call it Jinx & Tonic," I whispered. "It protects against blood magic. I think. It hasn't been tested, but there's no time for that."

"No." Ranger X pressed it back into my hands. "You take it."

"I have another for me," I lied. "Which means that you two will have to share. It's a half serving each, and hopefully it'll lessen the effects."

"Lily—"

"Now!" I hissed. "They're coming, don't waste it."

"Are you sure this works?" Liam asked.

"Fifty percent."

"And what are the chances it's deadly?"

"One percent?" I flinched. The sounds of The Puppeteer returning could be heard in the distance, now echoing off the rocks of the lagoon. Even so, we didn't have long. "I don't think it's deadly, just drink it. It's your only chance."

Ranger X lifted the small vial to his lips. He took a few sips before passing it to Liam. He finished it, and then both men returned their hands behind their backs. Conversation filtered up to us, signaling the arrival of Ilinia and her gang.

"You didn't take your potion," X whispered as he shifted into position. "Do it now—she's coming."

"I don't have any more," I said, my voice barely audible. "Don't argue now, X, please. I can fight it off—I've done it before. I wasn't ready this last time, but I'll be ready next time," I said, praying it would be true. "Trust me."

"Lily—"

"Let's get out of here now, and we can argue about it later. Deal?"

The footsteps thumped closer. With each step, the beat of my heart flew a little faster. My muscles tensed with anticipation. I inched a little closer to the warmth behind me.

"I'm holding you to it."

It was the last thing he said before The Puppeteer crested the hill. Gone was the flimsy, weak woman whom Liam had found cowering behind the waterfall. Back was The Puppeteer in all of her beauty, in all of her terrible, dangerous glory.

"Why, hello," she said, her voice lilting over us. "How are we this afternoon?"

Though she had never been a mermaid, her heritage ran strong. Her words sounded like singing; when she spoke, remnants of the mermaid magic lingered in her voice, the effect calming, almost hypnotic.

She knew it, too. She stood tall and proud, formidable. She'd let her hair loose and it tumbled in long curls down her back. Her black hair and blue eyes made for a startling combination.

She wore a gauzy, emerald green dress, and the finished product was stunning. I could hardly blame Liam for falling in love with her; she was gorgeous and dangerous, all in one.

"Have you made yourselves at home?" The Puppeteer carried a straw bag over her shoulder. She set it on the ground, peeked at the contents inside, and then looked expectantly at us. "Well? I asked you a question."

"We're wonderful," Liam said dryly. "Just awaiting your return."

"Oh, good, my dear." She left her straw bag on the ground and strode forward.

She circled us. Her eyes, sharp and calculating, landed briefly on our wrists. The fake knot must have been good enough to fool her, because her gaze slid past it. Finally, she came to a stop in front of Liam.

Reaching out a hand, she smoothed the back of her fingers over his cheek; I watched out of the corner of my eye. "I'm sorry it's come to this," she whispered to Liam. "I didn't mean to fool you, my love."

"You've been fooling me from day one." Liam tipped his chin upward. "Whatever I couldn't see back then is clear to me now. You never loved me, Ilinia."

"I did," she said with a pout. "I loved my Liam."

"You don't even understand what the word means," Liam said. He slumped forward, letting his gaze drop, his words stemming from a corner of pain in his heart, more sad than angry. "I was stupid then. So very, very stupid."

"It was love," she argued. "When you asked me to marry you, I said yes."

"You wanted something, and it wasn't me," he said. "I don't know what you were after then, or what you're after now. I don't know who hurt you or why, but it has ruined you. I'm sorry you couldn't learn to love me, and I'm sorry I couldn't help you more. I'm sorry about it all."

I reached out, squeezing the hand closest to me. Liam's disappointment, his realization that everything he'd loved had been a lie, was devastating, even to an outsider. Now was not the time to feel sympathy, yet I couldn't seem to help myself.

"Only you and I know what we had back then."

"Why'd you end up in prison?" Liam asked. "I fought for you. All these years, and I never once considered that you were guilty. I never gave up on you."

"Not until now."

"Not until now," he agreed. "When you gave me *no choice*. I love you, I still do, but I respect Ranger X and I love Lily, too. I can't let you hurt them."

Ilinia's eyes flashed toward me, hatred and jealousy in her glare.

"I don't love her in that way," Liam said. "I could never love anyone like I loved you. But she *is* part of my family on this island now. She's our Mixologist; by nature, she is good, and it's my duty to protect her."

"She's nothing," Ilinia said. "With her power, just *think* if she learned the art of mind bending. She'd be unstoppable."

"I'd never—" I started.

"Stop," Liam warned. "What do you want with us, Ilinia?"

Ranger X, to my right, was fidgeting with something, but I

ignored him, hoping Ilinia wouldn't notice. I craned my neck even farther to watch the interaction between The Puppeteer and Liam.

However, Ranger X spoke next, sounding resigned. "I think it's time he knows why you went to prison, Ilinia."

Ilinia didn't bother to glance at him, her eyes focused on Liam. "It was necessary," she said. "I had to do it."

"Do what?" Liam leaned forward, and I grasped tighter at his hand. The last thing we needed was to give away our only advantage. "What did you do?"

"It was *you*!" she cried. "You are the reason I went to jail! I trusted you with everything; I told you my plan to rule this island, and you tried to stop me. I *had* to make you forget—you gave me no other choice."

"You never told me any such thing," Liam said. "Where is this coming from?"

"She did," Ranger X said. "Liam, you *were* the witness. I caught Ilinia using blood magic on *you*, and that's why I refused to reveal the name of the witness. I didn't want to hurt you; I could see how much you loved her."

Liam shook his head. "No."

"You have a scar on your head," Ranger X said. "Just above your temple. You fell then, while under her spell, and she told you it was from sleepwalking that night."

Liam stiffened, and I sensed he'd heard that story before.

"The truth is that she used mind bending on *you*. I found you under her spell, unconscious on the ground, and *that* is why I arrested her." Ranger X sighed. "And it's why she'll go back for hundreds more years."

"Is this true?" Liam whispered, his eyes locked on Ilinia.

"Of course it's true," Ilinia said, her emerald green dress billowing in the wind. "But I didn't mean to hurt you. I had a plan, Liam, and you fought me on it. Together, we could've ruled this island but no—you threatened to expose me, and all of my plans. You left me with no choice."

"You wiped my memory?" Liam echoed.

"Don't you see?" She fell to her knees, inching closer to Liam. "I wanted to marry you. I wanted to marry you so badly I used my magic on you, and it *worked*. And if it weren't for *him*, we'd be together. We'd be happy, and we'd be the king and queen of The Isle."

His next move happened so fast I couldn't stop it. Liam freed his hands from the ropes, lunged forward, clasped his fingers around her neck.

Ilinia made a strangled noise, her arms coming up to pull him away from her, but Liam didn't budge. He held her tight, cutting off her air.

I wanted to move, to tear Liam away, but Ranger X was faster. He leaped for Liam and pulled him off her.

"She's not dying like this," Ranger X said, kneeling next to her, holding her back.

A shot rang out then, whizzing past me and connecting with Ranger X's shoulder. He spun backward, never letting go of The Puppeteer, even as his shirt was soaking with blood.

I reached for him while Liam rushed for the attacker. In all of Ilinia's explanation, we'd forgotten about her travelling companions. There was only one man now, the other two assistants having departed while we were unconscious.

"X," I said, shaking him, my voice trembling, on the verge of falling apart. "Stay with me."

"I'm not going anywhere." His face pinched with pain as he reached a hand up and pushed the hair back from my face. "I love you."

"Stop it," I said, reaching into my pockets for my teensy vial of Aloe Ale. "This isn't meant for serious wounds, but it should help accelerate the healing. It's only a patch, and it'll—"

"Shh." Ranger X's fingers pressed against my lips. "You're shaking. I'm going to be fine."

A shadow appeared over my shoulder. I could feel it was her. But I needed to focus on covering Ranger X's shoulder with the Ale, so I slipped a hand under his shirt. The wound felt clean, as if the bullet—magic or otherwise—had gone straight through.

My stomach roiled, nausea darkening my vision, but from somewhere I pulled the strength to continue. The world slowed down, every motion exaggerated.

When I finished, X breathed easier. He squeezed my hand before he closed his eyes.

"He won't die from it, you know," Ilinia said, coming to stand behind me. "The Ale will patch him up."

"I know," I said, turning to face her. "Why are you using weapons like a human? Magic isn't enough for you?"

A look of annoyance crossed her face. "I didn't use it—*he* did."

I glanced over her shoulder. Liam, his face more battered than before, was pressed nose-first against the ground with a shoe on his back. Over him stood one of the last people I'd ever expected to see holding a gun.

A Candidate.

One of Ranger X's very own Candidates—a person X had taken under his wing, guided and instructed, and given every opportunity in the world—had turned against him.

"Hello, Lily," Dillan said. "It's nice to see you and Ranger X. Again."

CHAPTER 34

A FEW MINUTES LATER, THE THREE of us were piled together under the watchful eye of Ilinia and her accomplice. Bindings weren't necessary, but Dillan fastened them around our wrists anyway.

Ranger X was forced to lie on his side because every time he tried to sit up, he'd spiral toward unconsciousness. I sat next to him, with Liam on my other side.

"What are you doing here?" I asked, glaring at Dillan. "What could you possibly be thinking?"

He smiled, that handsome smile now oily, the glint in his eyes suddenly terrifying. "I'm thinking big. Very, very big things are happening, Miss Locke, and this is just the beginning."

"What beginning? And your broken arm—what happened to it? I watched you fall in the first Trial. You were in pain when I stopped by The Oasis. You should still be in a cast, not carrying a weapon."

The former Candidate stretched, flexing his muscles. He didn't look injured in the slightest. "Ilinia healed me. Blood magic is powerful. It can be used to help, too. To heal a person when nothing else works. As for the help in the tent. . . that was a setup. I, in fact, needed something from *you*."

"From *me*?"

"I didn't have a doll for you, my dear," Ilinia said, a giddiness to her voice. "But thanks to Dillan, thanks to the blood he obtained from your paper cut, I had all the materials I needed. Your doll is complete, Lily."

I didn't care if she had a hundred dolls of me. I was stuck on the idea that blood magic could heal. The possible consequences had my mind reeling. I glanced at The Puppeteer. "You healed Dillan?"

She stood in the background. The emerald green dress whipped around her legs and gave an ethereal quality to her figure as she watched us all.

"I don't believe you," I said when she didn't respond. "Prove it. Heal Ranger X."

Her fingers twitched, as if she was dying to demonstrate how very wrong I was. But Dillan interrupted before she could do anything. "Don't," he said. "Let's get rid of them already."

"Why?" I asked. "At least tell us why."

"Why?" He gave a mirthless laugh. "Why what?"

"Why *everything*? Why are you working with *her*? Why are you murdering Candidates?" I ran my fingers through Ranger X's hair. "Some people spend their whole lives dreaming about joining the Ranger program; you, however, have the opportunity, and you turn around and hurt the man who gave it to you....*why*?"

The smallest glimmer of discomfort flickered in Dillan's eyes. "It's nothing personal." He spoke to Ranger X's chest. "But he's not the *only* one who trusted me. My uncle trusted me, and he's far more powerful than any old *Ranger*. He holds a key position in The Faction."

"Is this true?" I asked Ranger X. "I thought you carefully vetted each Candidate."

"We do," Ranger X said, his teeth gritted in pain. "We knew about the link between Dillan's uncle and The Faction. What we *didn't* know was that Dillan *knew* his uncle. Your father hates his brother more than anything, doesn't he?" Ranger X asked Dillan. "He kept your uncle a secret from you."

"My father doesn't know what's good for him," Dillan said with a frown. "No, I didn't know about my uncle until just before the Trials. But that's when everything changed. My uncle came to visit me, and he told me the *truth* about my father."

I knew Dillan's father—not personally, but I knew Gus purchased a good chunk of fresh fruit from the man. He was a farmer, a jolly man with red cheeks and a quick smile. Gus had no problems with him, and Gus had problems with *everyone.*

"The Faction tried to recruit both my uncle *and* my father. My uncle leaped at the opportunity while my father *turned them down.* He chose to stay here on this stupid island and live as a farmer. A *farmer!* He could've had the world at his fingertips, just like my uncle, but no."

"Your father is a good man," Ranger X said, pulling himself into a sitting position. "I took a chance on you, Dillan. I thought you had a brighter future than your uncle."

Dillan's hand trembled. I couldn't tell if it was from anger, uncertainty, disappointment—his eyes darkened, and he stepped forward. "I'm stronger than my father will ever be. When my uncle searched me out, he told me about everything we could accomplish together."

"He was lying." Ranger X's voice was soft, cutting. "If your uncle gave a damn about you, he would've entered your life years ago. He *knew* about you. He knew where you lived. He's using you, and you're letting him."

"That's not true."

"Of course it is," Ranger X said. "And you know I'm right, or you wouldn't be this upset. He's chosen not to be a part of your life since the day you were born. This is a decades old fight, and he chose sides before you existed."

"Well, my father didn't tell me he had a brother, either," he snapped. "It goes both ways."

"Because your father didn't want to lose you to The Faction,"

Ranger X said. "Like me, he hates The Faction more than anything in the world, and *that* is why I gave you a chance."

"How could you know that?" Dillan's accusatory stare dropped, a note of genuine curiosity in his voice.

"Because your mother was kidnapped by The Faction, and your uncle did nothing to save her," Ranger X explained. "Just after you were born, they came for her. She's believed to be dead."

"My mother died," Dillan said. "Freak accident."

"There was never a funeral because to this day, she's still considered *missing*. As a child, it was easiest to explain that it was an accident."

"But—"

"Argue all you want. I have no incentive to lie to you," Ranger X said. "You will understand when your uncle throws you away, forgets about you like he has the past twenty years of your life. He's using you to get at the other Candidates, to access The Puppeteer. When you've served your purpose and he's done with you, don't come back to me. I don't give second chances."

"No, I helped Ilinia escape from jail." Dillan backed away, fear blooming where anger had been moments before. "We're going to work as a team. My uncle promised me that the two of us could rule this island together. The Faction asked us both to maintain control of The Isle for their cause." He turned to Ilinia, his eyes widening. "*You* promised me."

She wrinkled her nose, black hair billowing behind her as the wind picked up. "Apologies," she said. "But I lied."

"No..." Dillan moved away like a caged animal. He raised his hands, his gaze darting from one person to the next. "No, you can't. . . my uncle will find out you lied."

"Your uncle and I had a little deal," Ilinia said. "You see, I'm selfish, and I don't want to share control over this island. Though I appreciate all of your help and rabid enthusiasm, your work here is done."

"No!" He screamed, but halfway through the scream Ilinia extended her hands and twisted her fingers, muttering a spell under her breath.

Dillan's body went rigid. Stone still, straight as a statue. Then, he began to march like a toy soldier who, once wound up, never stopped moving. He marched and he marched, straight toward the edge of the cliff—not the lagoon side, the far side where there was no water to break his fall at the bottom. It was a hundred-foot drop onto sharp rock.

"No!" I cried. "Stop!"

Ilinia's eyes were hollow, a glow around her blueish pupils as her irises faded to white and her lips drained to black. With intense focus, she directed her hands like the puppeteer for which she'd been named.

I tugged at my restraints, but they were too tight. Ranger X could hardly move he was so weak, and from what I could tell, Liam was only half conscious.

I leaped forward, but the restraints held me back. I couldn't budge the dead weight of the two men fastened to my arms.

My cries sailed off the cliff as Dillan continued his march toward the ledge.

Marching and marching until finally his feet no longer hit firm ground. Taking one final step, he hit thin air. His stride broke with a flail of his arms, a twitch from his legs. Not a peep from his lips.

And then he was gone.

CHAPTER 35

MY EARS RANG, THE SILENCE deafening.

Ranger X's breaths rasped, while Liam was hardly lucid enough to be useful. Ilinia watched me carefully as I leaned closer to X, as close as my restraints would allow.

"It's you and me, isn't it," Ilinia said with a wry smile, her feet nudging the two men before her. "I wish you'd consider working with me, Lily, I really do. You and I could be unstoppable. Rule this island like nobody before us."

I couldn't tear my eyes away from Ranger X. "What good would that do?"

She laughed, an indulgent, high-pitched giggle. "That's why you and I could never be business partners. You just don't *get* it."

"I don't," I said evenly. "But I'd love to try. Enlighten me."

"No."

"No?"

"I'm sick of questions, sick of explaining myself. Sick of *nobody* understanding my plan. Stand up," she said. "I have a use for you, and as long as I need you, you'll stay alive."

"How?" I gestured to my position on the ground. The rope holding my wrists together was looped to the same rope holding Liam and X captive. "I'm tied to them."

"Well, let's fix that," she said. Stretching her fingers, she moved them gently, delicately, as if playing a melody on the piano. The black lips returned, the blue of her eyes fading to the white of the clouds.

In sync with her murmurings Ranger X began to rise, his movements stiff. From somewhere, he withdrew his knife, slicing his own ropes.

Ilinia, still controlling X, walked over to the bag she'd been carrying. "You made an antidote," she said, her voice flat. "I can feel his resistance. He didn't take enough of it, but I can sense it, and I don't like it. You're making my life difficult, Lily."

Despite the horridness of the situation, a piece of hope soared through my veins. I'd concocted a potion to fight the strongest, the most powerful form of black magic. Ranger X had only taken a few drops but maybe, just maybe, Liam had ingested enough to keep himself immune.

She bent over the bag, her dress shielding my view. When she stood, she held something in her hands. A doll. I'd recognize that black hair, those dark eyes anywhere—it was Ranger X, constructed from yarn.

"To use mind bending at its strongest form, I need my Puppets. Usually, I don't need them for simple mind bending, but with your new potion..." She paused, stroking the doll's hair. "It is more difficult than I expected. Lucky thing this will help. Just *wait* until I pull out miniature Lily—she's my best work yet."

Sure enough, as soon as her hand touched the doll, Ranger X reacted. He stood straight, waiting for further instructions, any semblance of fight in his eyes gone. I pulled at the bindings, struggling to stand, but Liam's dead weight was too heavy.

Meanwhile, Ilinia picked her way across the rocky cliff, reaching Ranger X in a matter of seconds. She hooked her arm through his, and together they strolled toward the edge of the cliff. She held her head high, one hand on his chest, almost delicately, as if they were on a leisurely stroll.

"There we go," she whispered. "Good boy."

"Ilinia, stop! I'll do whatever you ask. Whatever you need me to do, just let him go. Let X and Liam leave," I panted, my body exhausted, muscles straining to break free. "You have my word."

"Sorry," she said. "Promises mean nothing to me, as you might've guessed by now."

She reached the edge of the cliff, and it hit me that no matter what, there was no stopping her. The pair stood at the cliff's ledge, the deep lagoon below them.

"Goodbye, dear." Ilinia pressed a kiss to Ranger X's cheek. With a dainty push, she let go of Ranger X's arm, and he fell.

At the same moment, a rage I'd never known soared. I stood, dragging Liam with me, and that's when I spotted it—the knife Ranger X had used to break us free. He must have dropped it when he'd moved under Ilinia's spell.

I snatched it and cut myself free. Liam murmured something, slowly regaining consciousness. Adrenaline burned through me as I flew across the face of the cliff toward Ilinia, but even then, I was too slow.

I grabbed her, yanked her back as I leaned over the cliff, watching as Ranger X hit the water with a splash. Bubbles pricked the surface. He was alive, but for how long? He was injured and sinking fast beneath the surface of the water.

"The fall might not have killed him," Ilinia said. "But I will, don't you worry."

Then she murmured the dreaded spell, hitting me hard and sending my body flying backward. I couldn't stop it. I landed with a *crack* against the stone. Something softened my fall, and as the spell lifted, I realized it was Ilinia's bag that had broken my crash landing.

Her dolls had spilled out, scattering across the rock surface. It couldn't have been all of the dolls; there were hundreds of people on the island and only a dozen dolls in here. There, in the mix of yarn and fabrics, I spotted a black haired doll wearing a green dress. *Ilinia had a doll for herself.*

My pulse raced. I knew what I needed to do. Ilinia held her

hands out, murmuring her horrid spell, holding Ranger X captive under the water. I needed to get to Ranger X before he drowned. Time was running out, and my options were limited.

So I didn't think, I acted.

Reaching for the Ilinia doll, I swiped it, squeezed it tight.

Then I closed my eyes and extended my hands. The spell from the Library of Secrets came back to me in a rush. I took a breath, braced myself, and invoked blood magic of my own.

The power ripped through me, my body nearly seizing with the effort. I wasn't ready for the rush of power, not even close. My stomach cramped and I bent in half, my soul feeling like it was breaking in half. Through the pain, I kept my arms wide, murmuring the spell over and over again, never once losing sight of The Puppeteer.

Ilinia crumpled on the ground, her eyes vacant. She was under the spell. I should have stopped, but I didn't. The uncomfortable sense of pleasure at the power coursing through my veins was addictive; I'd tasted the capabilities of mind bending, and I couldn't seem to stop.

I directed Ilinia until she'd wound herself in the same ropes that'd held us captive. It wasn't until she slumped over Liam that I shook myself free of the spell, my breaths coming in huge waves, a sense of emptiness taking over my body as Ilinia's eyes lost their vacant gleam.

I barely stopped to think, wondering briefly if my lips had gone black, my eyes white. I pushed the thought away—it was a dangerous path to go down, wondering if I was just as evil as *her*.

"Liam, are you awake?" I cut his hands free of the rope. "Liam, it's me."

"Fine," he murmured. "Go."

I didn't waste another second. There was no time to climb down the rocks, to pick my way through the stony path. Grasping the

Ranger X doll to my heart, I crossed my arms, moved a few steps backward, and took a running start toward the edge of the cliff.

When I reached thin air, I kept running, my body hurtling straight toward the lagoon.

CHAPTER 36

THE WATER STRUCK ME HARD, the *clap* of impact stinging against my skin. It was cold, freezing even, but I'd landed in the dark spot at the center of the lagoon and been spared death by rocks. My body plunged deeper, deeper below the surface.

I kept my eyes wide, my body going into shock. Something—a fish, or something worse —nipped at my leg. Seaweed brushed against my toes, a big, black shadow moved beneath me.

X, I thought, kicking deeper. My lungs burned as I reached for him, his torn shirt flapping around his body. Grabbing hold I yanked him higher, higher, until my chest nearly collapsed.

Finally, just as my vision began to explode into a realm of stars, we pierced the surface.

"X!" I cried. "Can you hear me?"

I held the real Ranger X in one hand, his Puppet in the other. Struggling to shore, I pulled him onto the closest rock that I could find. The sun beat down on us as I hauled him halfway out of the water. His lips had turned blue, his face ashen. He wasn't breathing.

"X!" I cried. "Wake up!"

I defaulted to CPR, compressing his chest, giving him air. Nothing helped. I dropped the doll next to me, and I could feel him fading by the second. If I didn't do something, he'd leave me forever. If he left me forever...

My last resort became my only option. Terrible and horrible and inevitable. Grasping the Ranger X doll, I laid it out on the rock next to the real thing. For the second time, I closed my eyes and whispered the forbidden spell.

My fingers danced across the doll's chest as I murmured the spell over and over and over, bringing back the rush of mind bending until tears streamed down my face and the world vanished into blackness.

I didn't stop, not even as a hole emptied inside me. The cost of the spell—a little piece of my soul going to Ranger X. If I could, I'd give him everything.

"Cannon," I said, using the name he'd entrusted to me just hours before. I funneled all of my energy into healing him, allowing my hands to do the work that would keep him alive. "Wake up, X."

My body was drained—mentally, physically, emotionally. . . I had nothing left to give. Finally, I let go of the doll and let the spell lapse. The power poured from me, leaving my body a frail shell of what I'd been before.

It was then that I heard it. A breath. Shallow and raspy, but it was there.

My eyes flew open. "X!"

Another breath, this time followed by a cough.

I collapsed onto him, covering his chest with my arms, resting my face against his. "Can you hear me?"

"No," he breathed, the sound of his voice sending tremors of joy over my skin. "Come closer..."

I curled next to him, resting my head on his shoulder. I adjusted his view so he stared straight into my eyes. "Better?"

"No," he rasped again. "Closer."

I inched closer, our lips hovering apart.

"There," he said, his eyes regaining their light with every smile. "Much better."

Then he closed the tiny gap between us with a kiss. Cold, brittle, and a little fragile, but perfect nonetheless.

"I love you," he said. "And my arm hurts. Take me home."

CHAPTER 37

MONITORS CLICKED, EQUIPMENT BEEPED. EVERY SO often, Elle stopped by to refresh my cold mug of coffee and give me a sympathetic pat on the shoulder. And still, Ranger X didn't move.

"He'll be okay, you know." Gus's voice echoed off the black stone walls of the room. "They only sedated him as a precaution."

I cleared my throat, keeping my focus on X. "I know that."

"You look like death."

I finally turned to Gus. "Is that your attempt at comforting me?"

Gus stood in the doorway of a state-of-the-art room in the Ranger HQ infirmary. When a Ranger got sick, the group preferred to take care of their own.

The old man wore a frown on his wrinkled face. A tiredness hung from his shoulders that belied his normally stoic expression. "He's—"

"I know he'll be fine," I said, pulling myself to my feet and facing Gus. "The doctor has told me a hundred times, and so have the nurses. It doesn't make it any easier."

"I'm sorry."

I paused, halfway turning to face Gus. "Sorry, what?"

He raised a hand to his forehead, massaging stress from his temples before speaking. "I said I'm sorry, Lily. I'm sorry you have to see X like this. I'm sorry you had to be there when it happened, and I'm sorry I don't know how to help you. I'm not good at this sort of thing."

I blew out a breath and crossed the room in a few steps. Offering up a smile, I waited until Gus returned it. "You're doing just fine. It would've been worse if you hadn't arrived when you did."

After I'd pulled Ranger X out of the lagoon, we'd barely begun the trek back through the woods when Gus, Hettie, and Harpin had appeared at its rocky edges. It was thanks to them that we'd been able to bring X, Ilinia, and even Dillan back to Ranger HQ without additional help.

It was Harpin who'd discovered that Dillan was still alive; injured, but alive. Instead of crashing to a rocky death when Ilinia had forced him over the cliff, his clothing had snagged on an overgrown tree, trapping his body within its branches. Despite the horrible plan he'd been a part of, I had been relieved by the news.

"How did you know where to find us?" I asked. "You showed up at the lagoon right when—"

"We were too late," Gus said, a flicker of regret in his eyes. "If only we'd been faster, maybe this. . . " he gestured toward X, "wouldn't have happened."

"Gus, you can't blame yourself."

"I'm not blaming myself, I'm just stating facts."

"You never said how you knew where we were," I said. "Did you—"

"Let's step outside if you'd like to discuss this." Gus reached out, pulling me to the side as a doctor pushed his way through the door.

"We can talk right here." I crossed my arms, my eyes following the doctor's every movement as he took X's vitals.

"It's probably best if you take a minute." The doctor looked up, his voice tinged with exasperation. "Watching me like a hawk will not help things along. X will be out for the next hour. Get a cup of coffee, Lily. Drink it. Talk with your friend, I'm begging you."

"But—"

"I'll personally find you the second he wakes up." The doctor shooed me out of the room. "I promise."

Pushed by the doctor, pulled by Gus, curious to find out information, I watched Ranger X for one last second. Then the doctor closed the door in my face, and Gus dragged me down the hall to a small conference room. Except the room wasn't empty.

"Lily." Hettie rose from her chair, a sleek leather thing that matched the decor of the upscale space. "How is he?"

"He'll be fine." I returned my grandmother's hug, breaking away quickly to address the others in the room. "Ainsley, you're back?"

"I have a few hours before I need to get going, but I heard what happened and I had to come." She grasped my forearms and scanned my face. "I'm sorry I wasn't here sooner."

Harpin didn't offer any such greeting. His eyes were locked on the floor, his expression one of indifference.

"I guess we're all here," I said quietly. "The Core."

Hettie waved a hand and the door flew shut. "Yes."

"Now can someone please tell me how you found us?" I focused my attention on Gus. "How did you show up at the edge of the lagoon just in time to help us back?"

"We were just doing the jobs Ainsley laid out at our last meeting," Gus said. "Harpin and I were tracing blood magic. We realized that Ilinia would've needed help with her agenda—if not in breaking free from jail, then once she'd made it to the outside world. She'd been locked away for so long she wouldn't have had enough resources on her own. So we began there, while Hettie—"

"While I played my senile card and looked into the Candidates," Hettie interrupted. "I snuck into The Oasis."

"They let you talk to the Candidates?"

"No." She looked smug. "But I didn't need to—I realized one of them was missing. Then I overheard the guards muttering about how you had gone off into The Forest with Liam. They were talking about getting ahold of X for instructions, but by then, he was already missing. Since I had heard Liam's description of the lagoon, I had a good idea where the pair of you would be heading."

"It was around that same time that I arrived at the bungalow to ask you a question about your potion in progress. The mind bending one." Gus gave me a knowing stare, but he didn't wait for a response. "You weren't there."

"And when the three most important people on the island go missing," Harpin chimed in, his voice oily with sarcasm, "of course the alert is sounded."

"We put our heads together and realized that Dillan was in on it. I recognized your potion as an attempt to fight blood magic, and we figured you'd gone looking for her," Gus said. "We connected the rest of the dots with Hettie's help. The timing, that was a lucky break. If we'd been luckier, we would've been there before this happened."

I swallowed as Gus nodded toward the hallway where Ranger X lay motionless behind closed doors.

"Why'd you hide it from me?" Gus asked, startling me from a haze. "The potion. Why hide it?"

"The potion?" I stalled. "I wasn't hiding it."

Gus tapped his cane against the floor. "I know when you're lying, and I know when you're hiding something. You're doing both."

"Do tell us more about this wonderful potion," Harpin said, the request a mix of genuine curiosity and morbid fascination. "Something *wonderful*, I'm sure. Everything Lily touches turns to gold, we all know that."

I turned to Harpin, ready for war. But Gus prevented it by speaking louder than both of us combined.

"It was good. A damn good potion." Gus's voice cracked with surprise. "Why'd you hide it? I've never seen anything like it. You left a tiny batch of it in a corked bottle, and I saw your ingredients. I put the rest together myself. When you went missing, I forced Poppy to confirm my suspicions."

"Because!" My chest tightened as I turned to Gus. "Because of this group, and because of my stupid assignment!"

"Lily, we were worried about you." Ainsley frowned. "You had so much on your plate that when we decided on the assignments, it was agreed to keep you out of harm's way if at all possible. Not that it worked."

"If I'm staying in this group—if The Core is going to do its job—a few things need to change."

I stopped for a breath and scanned the group. My chest heaved with exertion, fear hovering just on the edges of frustration. I'd never been so confrontational, so demanding of anyone in my life.

"I'm telling X about us," I said. "That's my first condition."

"If you can convince me why we should loop him in," Hettie said, "I'll agree to it."

"Because he cancelled the Trials." I pointed a finger toward the doorway. "He's lying in a hospital bed because he will do anything to protect this island. You were worried about him having a conflict of interest with us because he's a Ranger and we're The Core. Well, I think we have the same priorities. He put the island above the Ranger program when he cancelled the public events, and that is good enough for me."

Hettie's face remained unreadable. Harpin looked at the ground, an amused smirk on his face. Ainsley and Gus made themselves busy staring at the ceiling.

"Fine," Hettie said again. "You have a week to invite him into the group, and then the offer expires."

"A week?"

"I'm making big plans, Lily. I need to know if X will be joining us. Soon."

"Thank you." I gave a curt nod at my grandmother. "The second thing that needs to change are my responsibilities. If you are all out investigating blood magic, I want to be there, too. I am not sitting around all day in my bungalow like some princess kept in a tower. Understood?"

A few mumbles sounded from the group.

"Understood?" I pressed again, until each of them agreed. "Great. Lastly, I want to go to prison."

"Uh, Lily?" Ainsley stood up, pressing the back of her hand to my forehead. "Have the doctors taken your temperature?"

"No, the jail where Ilinia is being kept," I said with growing agitation. "Now. While Ranger X is sleeping."

"You're afraid he won't approve." Harpin gave a slow smile. "He'd keep you locked away, like that princess in a tower you're worried about."

"Shut it, Harpin," Hettie said again. "Why do you want to go, Lily?"

"I need to understand why. Why she tore Liam apart. Why she murdered a Candidate. Why she had my boyfriend shot and why. . . " I couldn't speak the last part of the phrase. "I need to talk to her—will you accept my terms, or not?"

Hettie glanced around at the group. Save for Harpin's thin smile, the rest of The Core had stern expressions. "Gus?"

"I'll take her," he said. "And I'll have her back within the hour."

"We will be there as long as it takes," I said. "I am getting my answers."

Hettie walked me out of the room, her arm looped through mine while Gus retrieved his cane.

"Why'd you agree with me?" I asked. "You accepted my terms without argument."

She faced me. "I'm a reasonable woman, and I understand a reasonable request when I hear one. Lily, we've been waiting for you to step up—to step into your role. When you know something is right, go after it. Trust your instincts."

"Come." Gus pulled me away from Hettie with that one simple word. We left, marching down the hall, past X's room, away from The Core. A few minutes later, he turned abruptly. "In here."

"This isn't the exit."

"We're getting there. We have one stop to make before we leave this place."

CHAPTER 38

"I NEED TO SHOW YOU SOMETHING before we head to the jail," he said. "And I apologize if I overstepped my bounds in doing this, but it was necessary."

"Is that why you volunteered to take me?" I asked. "So you could show me something else? Are we even going to see Ilinia?"

"We'll get to the jail. You have my word."

I waited patiently as Gus pressed a button that buzzed us through a doorway. We stepped through into a place I'd been before. Blinking lights lined the ceiling, the walls, and the floor of the otherwise dark tunnel. It looked as if the solar system had been bottled up and splashed through the tube.

We passed through to more familiar settings. "There," Gus said. "You recognize it?"

He gestured through a maze of clear walls to the lab. Inside, scientists in white suits and goggles moved between beakers and bowls, jars and vials. Small fires in every shade of orange and blue glowed underneath pots and pans of all sizes. One experiment in particular caught my eye.

"Jinx & Tonic?" I twirled to face Gus. "Is that what I'm looking at?"

Gus stared over my shoulder at a tall, slender tube of bubbling liquid the color of pearls. "I'm not sure."

"What do you mean?"

"Like I said, I found the leftover corked vial you'd stashed in the supply closet," Gus said. "I must have walked in on you and Poppy while you were creating it, and I'm guessing you hid the supplies from me while Poppy blabbed on and on about her nail polish. I only know the name because I quizzed Poppy when I realized you were gone. She didn't know much, but she knew enough to get me started."

I tilted my chin a little higher. "And?"

"And it got me curious." Even as Gus's eyes darkened with apology, a light shone in his irises. Nothing in this universe excited him more than his storeroom and the potions created there. "Maybe I shouldn't have, but I pieced together the spell. Silver, to reflect the unsavory spells back outside the body. Gentle herbs so the spell won't injure the user. And most importantly, lily of the valley. To remember yourself, when the rest of the world goes blank."

I swallowed.

"I'm right, aren't I?" Gus's voice softened in reverence. "It's brilliant, Lily."

"What is this?" I nodded toward the lab. "Why are they trying to recreate it? I would've helped. I would have explained it to you, Gus, you have to believe me. I'd only just figured it out—I didn't even have time to make a batch large enough for more than one person."

"I know that."

"Well?"

"Well, I'd already pieced together the necessary ingredients, and I had just the smallest of starter batches left in the vial. From there, I brought the sample and the ingredients to the lab once I realized something had happened to you."

"Why?"

"The Puppeteer is one of the strongest forces on this island, and if she'd taken you out already. . . " Gus stubbed his toe against the floor. "There was no help for the rest of us."

"That's not true—"

"If she wanted to take over The Isle and you hadn't stopped her, she might very well have done so. Unless. . . "

"Unless you had a potion that made her magic useless," I finished. "You got Jinx & Tonic brewing in case neither of us came back."

"I left them instructions to use it only in the direst of circumstances," Gus said. "After all, it wouldn't have been tested. But if something happened to both of us in The Forest, it would've been better than nothing. I sent instructions for a large batch to be made. Then I gathered Harpin and your grandmother, and we went after you. From there, you know the rest."

"May I?" I pointed toward the potion.

"I hoped you would ask." Gus knocked on the door to the lab. "We have a use for it still, you know. With your approval."

"What sort of use?"

Gus didn't respond because a man in a white coat who resembled a mouse with his pointed nose, sharp widow's peak, and shiny little eyes behind circular spectacles, showed up at the door.

"Yes?" He looked at Gus first, then to me. "Ah, the Mixologist. Do come in, Miss Locke."

"Lily," I said, shaking his outstretched hand. "How is everything going?"

"We believe the batch is ready to go. It's been brewed precisely to Gus's instructions, and it appears to match the sample sent with it."

"May I?"

"Our lab is always open to the Mixologist." The scientist bowed his head, backed away. "You can find both samples to your right."

I moved to the place he recommended. Two samples sat before me. One of them was hardly more than a few drops on a tiny, rounded plate, while the other, larger sample, bubbled in a beaker.

I first inhaled it, the lily of the valley scent potent, strong against the otherwise sterile air of the lab. "How much silver did you use?"

The scientist rattled of his ingredients list without notes, his detail exact to the last measurement. "Even so, we couldn't have made the potion ourselves," he clarified. "Not without your starter batch. Without your Mix, ours would be nothing but a pile of herbs and ingredients. The silver shouldn't even blend with the rest of the potion." His voice increased with excitement. "It's amazing, really—whatever you've done here, I've never seen it before. When we Mix the potion with your starter batch, the magic you created bleeds into our supply."

"So you can use a starter batch to make more, but you can't create it from scratch?"

"Nobody can create it from scratch except you," he confirmed. "Which is why I'd like to request a larger original batch from you at your convenience. To keep with all of the other Mixologist potion starters."

I followed his pointed finger to a large, sturdy-looking door. "What's in there?"

"Show her," Gus instructed.

The scientist paused for only a second before agreeing. "Just one moment, it requires special permissions."

A few minutes later a shorter, mousier-looking man with even larger glasses and an even larger white coat appeared. "Hello, Miss Locke—"

"Lily," I corrected as I shook his hand.

"I'm Herman Mort, and I run the lab." He blinked rapidly. "You'd like to see inside the Mixologists' vault?"

"Yes," Gus said. "First time for her."

"It's overdue, I suppose." Herman pulled out a key as long as his forefinger and inserted it into a huge lock on the door. He twisted it, a loud click sounded, and then we were inside. "Look around, Miss Locke, but please do not touch."

I began to correct him again and insist he call me Lily, but when the door swung open, I lost interest in what he called me. The lab's vault was a huge refrigerator, as long as a hallway and as wide as a city block. It was completely black inside, save for individual spotlights along the wall. Each light was situated under a jar that had been meticulously labeled with the name of a potion.

"There are lots of legacies in here," Herman said, his voice thin, cutting like a knife through the darkness. "The potions here are. . . they're irreplaceable. The hexes guarding this vault are some of the strongest we have on the island."

I turned to face Herman. "What are these?"

Along either side of the black walls sat one shelf. It reminded me of a museum—each potion a piece of artwork to be displayed.

"Similar to Jinx & Tonic, there have been potions created in the past that take a Mixologist's touch in order to work. We keep the starter batch here. We can often expand on these potions, but once the last drop of the starter is used. . . "

"The potion will cease to exist," I said. "Unless another Mixologist can create it."

"Which is why we cherish this room, and we open it only in cases of need." Herman turned to me, pushing his glasses up onto his nose. "Miss Locke, I'd like to put in a formal request to add Jinx & Tonic to the vault." His fingers danced over an open space near the front. On the wooden shelf, there was an empty space. A lamp had already been placed above it, the light shining onto a blank plaque.

"Of course." This vault had the air of a church; old, precious. . . somber, even. Like an ancient city that, if destroyed by war or natural disaster, could never be recreated. "I'd be honored."

Gus and Herman nodded, then stood still as I made my way through the rest of the hallway. I stopped to read a few of the potions along the way. There was a batch for the Elixir, a potion that stole one's soul in exchange for extra time after one's death.

I continued walking, walking, until I found it. The potion I'd been seeking.

I raised a hand, running my fingers along the edges of the wood. I left the beaker untouched, the light shining into the bright, blood red liquid. Vampire Vitamins, the sign read, followed by a list of ingredients used to meet Poppy's nutritional needs. But it was the name underneath that caught my attention. Harvey. My grandfather.

I swallowed past the lump in my throat. He'd created this, molded the potion from his very own hands. I bowed my head and closed my eyes, letting the sensation of closeness wash over my shoulders. Even though he was gone, even though there was no chance of us ever meeting, I finally felt a kinship with him.

I felt close to the man who'd held the position before me—the man from whom I so desperately wanted advice, encouragement, and wisdom. I was afraid to walk this journey alone, to uncover my role of Mixologist without the guiding hand of someone who'd experienced the trials, the decisions, the horrors before me.

After a long while, so long I lost track of time, Gus cleared his throat. "It's time to go, Lily. Ranger X will be waking up soon, and I imagine you want to get back before then."

His implied meaning—that we must get to the jail quickly— was not lost on me. I looked at the blood red potion one last time, brushed my fingers over my grandfather's name, and then followed Herman from the vault.

"It's good," I told him. "Your potion will work."

To my surprise, Gus reached out a hand and shook Herman's. "She's approved it. Send it now."

"Send what? Where?" I looked between them. "Gus?"

"Better to show you," Gus said. "We have forty minutes. Will that be enough time, Herman?"

"It'll be ready in five minutes."

CHAPTER 39

WE TOOK AN ELEVATOR DOWN for what felt like an eternity. The doors finally opened to reveal a long passageway flanked by guards. Gus and I were frisked by three different Rangers at three different stopping points in what served as the lobby for the jail—not the normal island jail, but the maximum-security cells dug far beneath the ground at Ranger HQ.

"A little much, don't you think?" I mumbled, brushing off my clothes. I straightened my shirt and waited for Gus.

It took him an additional minute to retrieve his cane, which had been all but torn apart by security. "I'm walking through naked next time to spare them the hassle of undressing me," he growled. "I don't have a secret left in me."

"Is it always so intense?"

"I can't imagine an escaped prisoner looks good on their track record." All humor left Gus's face. "They'll be on high alert forever. I imagine X wasn't thrilled when The Puppeteer escaped, and they're trying to make up for it."

"And now she's back," I said.

"And now she's back."

We took a few steps forward, the dampness settling in around us. Torches lined the roughly cut walls. We were deep underground and even though the rock around us was solid, the sensation of being under hundreds of tons of dirt was suffocating.

Rocks paved the way ahead. The stone, naturally an off-white color, was now marred by dirt and debris. I sidestepped a stain on the ground that turned my stomach. Unlike the pristine nature of the rest of Ranger HQ, this place was dark, dank, and reserved for only the worst criminals.

"You never asked me why I wanted to come here," I said to Gus, the tap of his cane swallowed by the oppressive, stale air. "To visit her."

"No, I didn't," Gus said.

We continued walking for quite some time. Something small and furry skittered through the hall and sent my pulse skyrocketing. Eventually, Gus inhaled a breath. Before us, a dull glow lit the path though the source of the light was hidden behind a curve.

"You don't have to come," I said, eyeing the twisty passage before us.

We were getting close. The temperature dropped, the pressure rose, and all signs of life faded away.

"Neither do you," Gus said.

Together, we rounded the bend. My heart thudded, my ribs nearly cracking from the intensity. There, before us, sat a cage. Thick, steel bars formed a square, the inside of which was dark, musty, and seemingly empty.

Around it was a cavern with high, rocky ceilings and an echo for every breath. The faint outline of crystals shone from the ceiling, affixed there to dampen the effects of spells.

Another set of pillars stood beyond the steel bars of the cage. These, however, were made from glass. It was inside these glass tubes from which the source of light radiated outward. Liquid bubbled, coursed through the pillars, sending a glow through the underground.

"Is that—"

"Jinx & Tonic," Gus cut in. "Do you think it'll work?"

I took a step forward, admiring the handiwork. Before I could comment, however, a raspy wave of laughter came from the darkest corner of the cage.

I waited until my eyes adjusted to the darkness before I cleared my throat and spoke to Gus. "You're hoping that having the antidote surrounding the cell will prevent her from using blood magic?"

"Yes."

"It'll help, but I wouldn't count on it working completely." I kept my chin up, ignoring the sounds of hysterical laughter now coming from the cage. "Tell Herman to add wax to the potion and a wick. Light a candle in here; that will help. Anyone who enters will inhale bits of the potion and it will add a layer of protection."

"She'll inhale it, too," Gus said.

"Good."

Gus bowed his head. "Consider it done."

"May I have a moment alone with her?"

He hesitated, the sound of shrieking growing louder by the second. "Lily—"

"Please."

He raised a hand, scratched his head, and shrunk away. "I'll be right around the corner if you need anything."

Once Gus had gone, I waited until Ilinia's laughter faded to a gasping noise, her voice shredded to bits. From the glow of the potion, I could make out her stringy hair, her waspish figure. A ghost of the woman who'd stood above us in her emerald dress, powerful and strong. Now, she was broken, vacant looking. The misery was gone from her eyes, replaced by a sharp glint of hate.

"Welcome to my home," Ilinia said, crawling forward into the light. Her skin was pale, so very pale that the tiny veins in her arms shone blue through it. "Pleasant, isn't it?"

"Why did you wait so long to escape?" I stepped closer to her, refusing to be intimidated. "You used blood magic to get out of here; there was no defense for it until now. Why sit in here for all those years?"

She moved closer, her motions like a snake. When she reached the edge of the cage nearest me, she stopped. Her beauty had morphed into something so terrible I could hardly bear to look into her eyes—at the same time, I couldn't look away.

"You needed a partner," I answered for her. "Once you had things set up with Dillan, that's when you made your move. This whole time you were planning. But why?"

Ilinia smoothed her dress, eyed me with curiosity. "You really *don't* understand do you? The thrill of control. Of royalty. Of being the most powerful person in this realm just because you can."

"Is it worth all of the effort and deception and lies? You spent years in prison over this when instead, you could've been happily married to Liam."

Her lips turned into a pout. "I've been waiting for this moment for years. You see, my grandmother was the Queen of the Sea. She was the last great ruler of the water. She made sacrifices, and so must I. She changed for the sake of power. She made the transition from mermaid to human. In comparison, my sacrifice of a happy life with Liam is nothing. If only my mother hadn't ruined our momentum, we would've succeeded by now."

"How did she ruin everything?"

She laughed, the sound grating on my ears. "My mother was a flimsy excuse for a person. She didn't have a streak of ambition in her. My grandmother took the burden of changing from mermaid to human for the sake of power. Do you know how difficult that process is?"

I shook my head.

"Similar to a vampire changing a human." A smirk turned her lips upward. "Many times, the human dies before they change. The same goes with mermaids. My grandmother though, she survived. She was strong. There is only so much life to conquer in the sea, you know. My grandmother ruled it all; she wanted to expand, to take the land. But she needed her daughter's help. It was more than one lifetime of work."

"But your mother didn't want to give it to her."

"No, she wanted a boring life, to marry and live happily ever after." Ilinia shook her head. "Quite tragic. My grandmother died, and so did my mother. Age catches up to even the strongest of us. The burden falls to my shoulders—the weight of our family's legacy. I'd do anything for her, for me. For my heritage."

"You don't have to do any of this! Your mother wouldn't have wanted you to."

Ilinia's face darkened. "Shut up about her. She never liked me, said I was bad from the moment I was born."

I didn't respond, I couldn't.

"How do you think that feels? Your own mother saying she wished you'd never been born. She said I was too much like my grandmother, but little did she know, I took that as a compliment. I am just like my grandmother. I am strong, and I will rule this island someday, just like she wanted. I'll fulfill my family's legacy."

"But—"

"It would've all worked out perfectly. You and your friends wouldn't have been alive to deny my story, and the loss of Dillan would have been sung as a tragedy. He would've died a Faction hero, and I would've gotten my island. Everyone would've won. Shame you spoiled it."

"What about—"

"You'll go back to it, you know." She looked through the bars, her face changing. Her laughter faded into silence and her breathing sounded painful. All the while, her eyes gleamed, her lips forming a thin barrier, barbed with the secrets she held inside. "You won't be able to resist it."

"What are you talking about?"

"The power. You tasted it, didn't you?"

My blood boiled, the rush of anger so intense my mind spiraled out of control. "I don't know what you're talking about."

"Yes, you do." She hissed. "The scent of power, of control. . . you've inhaled it. You love it, just as much as I do—I can see it in your eyes. You'll always be different now, Lily. There's no coming back from the edge."

As hard as I tried, I couldn't push away the image of me on the cliff, twisting Ilinia with my power. She had been mine. My vision began to blur, the memory almost overtaking me. I collapsed to my knees, the taste of honey-sweet power cut with the burn of whiskey. *Sweet and powerful, and. . .*

"Lily." Ranger X's voice rocked me from the haze as his hand came to rest on my shoulder. He shook me until I stood. "You shouldn't be here."

Trembling, I brought myself to my feet. Hatred spiraled with shame, and I couldn't look at either X or Ilinia.

"You know it, don't you—pretty girl, you'll be just like me!" Ilinia murmured through the bars. "You and I will work together someday, just you wait."

My flash of rage sent all rational thought from my head as I tore at the cell. Ranger X held me back, his hands steady on my waist.

"Let's go," he said again. "That's enough, Ilinia."

"You two make a beautiful couple," Ilinia said. She flicked her tongue out at Ranger X, the motion suggestive and grotesque all in one. "He's even worse than you. Ask him about it, won't you? He knows it, yes, yes, yes he does. It's written on his face. Ask about his secrets, Lily."

Ranger X hauled me from the room without another word.

We passed Gus on the way out of the tunnel. "Get rid of the candle idea," I told him. "Make it a torch. A bonfire. Burn her cell down with the potion, for all I care."

"You don't mean that," Gus said. "Lily!"

"Not now, Gus," Ranger X said. "Do as she says. If she wants a torch, give her a torch."

"Where are we going?" I stumbled before Ranger X, a flurry of emotions blurring my view. "You're hurt! You need to be at the infirmary."

"Not until we talk."

"But—"

"When we were tied up, you said we could argue later." He didn't stop moving. "Well? I'm ready to argue."

CHAPTER 40

WE EMERGED BETWEEN TWO TREES somewhere near the edge of The Forest.

"Where are we going?" I asked. Ranger X had remained silent on our journey out of Ranger HQ. Speaking only when necessary, his sentences were short and clipped. "I need to get back to the bungalow."

"I'm taking you home with me."

I walked in silence while Ranger X fumed ahead of me. His normal movements were that of a panther—smooth, silent, controlled. Now, he moved like a bear, swinging his arms and punishing the ground with every step. A blaze burned in his eyes that'd never been there before.

"What did she mean back there?" I nearly had to jog to keep pace with him. "You should slow down. Your shoulder. . . "

It was bandaged where he'd been shot. "I'm fine. I was released from the hospital."

"Were you released, or did you sneak out?"

"I didn't sneak."

"Oh, even better. You terrified the doctor into letting you go." I reached for his hand. When my fingers encircled his wrist, he stopped walking. "What was she talking about back there?"

"What does it matter? Is it going to change what you think of me?" His words were biting, but I could see the fury in his eyes. It wasn't him. It wasn't my X.

"No, it won't change anything! But it's got you upset, and I want to understand why."

"I'm sorry," he said finally, studying me with a long gaze. He shifted his weight from one foot to the next.

"She hit a nerve." I shrugged, trying to seem nonchalant. In reality, I was surprised by his reaction. I'd never seen anyone affect X like Ilinia just had. "She got to me too. I mean, you had to carry me out of there! But if you don't want to talk about it, that's fine."

"I do, I will."

"Actually—" I raised a finger and pressed it to his lips "—wait."

Confusion flashed through his eyes. "You just asked—"

"I know what I asked." Cupping the side of his face with my hand, I continued. "But before you explain what she meant, I need to tell *you* something."

"Before you've heard what I have to say?"

I narrowed my gaze at him. "I told you whatever Ilinia referenced won't change how I feel about you. Trust me, X, please."

"You don't know what I'm capable of."

"But I know you, and that's far more important."

He closed his eyes, his lips softening from their frown. Suddenly he'd turned innocent, childlike almost, with his face tipped into my palm.

"The Core," I said. "It's a secret society. Hettie leads it. My grandfather started it, and then passed control along to his wife before he died. Now it's just Hettie, Harpin, Gus, Ainsley, and me. That's where I've been sneaking off to these last few weeks."

Ranger X had frozen, his hand pressing mine to his face.

"I'm sorry I couldn't tell you sooner, but Hettie swore me to secrecy. I've hated to keep this from you, and eventually I told Hettie enough was enough. That if she wanted me to remain a part of the group, she had to invite you into it, as well."

"You stood up to your grandmother?"

"I did what I had to do." I hesitated. "My grandfather started

The Core to fight back against The Faction. Now, it's our turn to help keep the island safe, and nobody cares more about The Isle than you."

Ranger X took my hand, lightly kissed the outside of it. "I know."

"Know. . . what?"

"I know about The Core."

"What?"

"I didn't know what you called yourselves, nor did I know the names of the members. But as Rangers, we are everywhere. I knew something was going on, and I took a guess. I'm not surprised, Lily."

I shook my head. "You knew this whole time?"

"It doesn't change anything. I still want you to be careful. Everything I said stands—I don't want you running around in the middle of the night, and I want you to talk to me. To trust me with any of your secrets. That is why I must decline."

"Decline the invitation?"

"Yes."

"What?" I took a step back. "I thought. . . I thought this is what you wanted. To be a part of it with me. I stood up to Hettie for you."

"Lily, please—"

"I don't understand."

"Please." He spoke softly. "I never wanted to be a part of The Core. Hettie kept it a secret from me for a reason, didn't she? Because our priorities are different."

"That's what she claimed."

"Well, she's right." His eyes washed over my face, full of warmth, a gentle expression. "My loyalties lie to the Ranger program and I cannot do anything to compromise that. Ever. That's the life path I've chosen. Lily, when I asked where you were going, I wanted to keep you safe. I've never wanted to control you or to invade every aspect of your life."

"You're not invading anything."

"You're the Mixologist, Lily. You protect this island on a whole different level than I do. I will never pretend to understand what you do, or how you do it. I want to protect the island as a Ranger. I want to love you, and to be a part of your life. That is all. I'll support you, collaborate with you and The Core whenever possible. I'm sorry, but I cannot join you."

"You'll collaborate with us?"

"Of course." He pulled my hands toward his chest, bringing us inches apart. "All you have to do is ask. And talk to me. Tell me what's happening. You're right that the safety of the island is my top priority. The Rangers and The Core have overlapping goals, and we'll be stronger working together. That doesn't mean I need to join."

I swallowed, blinking back a few unshed tears. "I'm sorry about keeping secrets."

"Sometimes, it's necessary." A shadow flickered over his eyes.

"She said I'll be back." I blurted the words out, the tears that hadn't fallen now stinging against my eyelids. "She told me that I've tasted power, and that the scent doesn't go away. When I was using mind bending back there, when I used it on you. . . " I dragged my expression up to meet his. "I know what she means, X. I liked it. I liked knowing that Ilinia was mine, that I had the control."

X didn't say anything.

"When a person uses blood magic, they give a piece of their soul to the other person," I said. "She told me that I'd always be different. That I wouldn't be able to say 'no' to the feeling. What if. . . " I shook my head, taking a second to breathe. "What if I become her?"

X leaned close, his lips inches from mine. "You'll never become her. The darkness inside of her is a choice, Lily. She chose that route. Nobody forced her down it—she didn't taste the power and *fall* into it, she decided to go after it. You'll never do that."

"How do you know?"

"Every person has dark and light inside of us." X's voice rumbled softly through the night. "Every day we make decisions about which side to follow. Ilinia picked darkness far more than she picked light. You're not like her."

"I don't know." My hands shook in my lap. "I always thought so, too. But in that moment, it's like I lost myself. I didn't know who I was or what I was doing, but I liked it. I liked the control." I raised my gaze to face Ranger X. "I'm scared, Cannon. I'm scared of myself."

"Me, too."

His words took me by surprise. "You're scared of me?"

He shook his head. "Of myself. The mind is a dangerous thing, Lily Locke. I know that more than anyone else. Let me explain what Ilinia meant back there."

"You don't have to tell me." I rose up on my tiptoes and kissed his lips. "You can leave some things unsaid. I trust you."

"All Rangers have a Uniqueness, as you know."

"Yes."

"I've never told you mine."

My heart pounded as X led me to a fallen log and perched me on the edge of it. He sat next to me. "X, you don't have to—"

"I hurt somebody once, I hurt them badly," X said. "I didn't mean to do it. I didn't feel like I had control. It's when—and why—I left my home."

"Oh, X."

"There was a break-in at our house one night. It was me, my mother, my father, and my brother. My brother was away for the weekend, or so I thought. The window to our shared bedroom opened, and I sat up in bed and attacked the intruder."

My heart ached as I anticipated his next words.

"It wasn't until it was too late that I realized it was my brother. He'd forgotten something and didn't want to wake our parents, so he snuck in through our window." X took a rattling breath. "He spent two months in the hospital recovering. He's alive, but for two months, I had to watch my brother—my own blood—breathe through tubes because of me. I bring this up because you asked me if you'd be different now that you've used blood magic."

I gave a tentative nod.

"When you healed me using mind bending, you gifted me a piece of your soul." X leaned in, his words brushing against my cheek. "And now you'll always be a part of me. There is nothing dark about that, Lily." He pressed my hand to his chest. "We'll always be connected, and I promise to protect that piece of you until the day I die."

Tears slid down my cheeks. He'd turned my worries, my horrible fears into something so good, so sweet, I couldn't speak. "Thank you."

"No, thank you." He leaned in and kissed the wetness on my cheeks.

"But what about the part of myself I gave to Ilinia?"

Ranger X looked to the ground. "You gave her a piece of something good."

The tears kept coming, and he kept holding me, rocking me, and then the tears came harder. I cried and I cried until my chest felt like it was crushed, until my breath came in ragged gulps and my very spirit tired.

Only then did Ranger X sit back, a contemplative look on his face. He watched me cry for another minute before he raised his hand and held it before him. His eyes turned blacker than coal, his focus entirely on me.

My tears stopped. I watched him as something else took over. A force inside him, a concentration so thorough he seemed to be in another world entirely.

Then it happened. One by one, the tears left my cheeks. He moved his fingers like a musician, hand-selecting which notes to play and in doing so, he dried my face. The tears hung, suspended as individual water droplets, in the palm of his hand.

I gaped, watching as he moved his open palm before his lips. He waited until he was sure my attention was on him, and then he moved his fingers until the water combined to form the shape of a flower. A lily made from nothing but tears. He held it there, glistening under the stars.

And then he closed his eyes and blew. The teardrops sailed through the air and drifted like orphan balloons cut free from their ties.

My eyes followed them until the water had disappeared from sight, fading into the blackness of night. When I turned my attention back to Ranger X, his eyes were fixed on me.

"You call it telekinesis on the mainland," he said. "I have the power to move objects with my mind."

"That is your Uniqueness?"

He nodded.

"That's how you hurt your brother," I said. "He climbed through the window and—"

"And I reacted. I didn't have control over my power then. I was too young, too stupid, too reckless to be trusted with such responsibility. It's a rare trait. Very, very rare."

"It's like mind bending," I said. "You are as powerful as Ilinia."

"I could be."

"But you choose not to be."

"After I injured my brother, I never used my power again," X said. "I was recruited to the Rangers and I joined under one condition—my Uniqueness would remain a secret. And unless utterly necessary, I wouldn't have to use it."

"And you haven't until now?" I asked. "Why now?"

Ranger X blew out a long breath. "When I use this power, it makes me weak. I'm at my strongest, but I'm also at my most vulnerable. It takes all of my energy to maintain concentration, and if someone were to catch me off guard while I focused, I'd be unable to defend myself."

"That doesn't explain why you showed it to me."

"Because you needed to know. You are a part of me now—in many ways." Ranger X brushed a kiss against my cheek. "You know my name, you've seen me at my most vulnerable. You have the power to cripple me unlike anyone else, Lily Locke. I never trusted anyone until I met you."

"I'd never abuse it."

"I know."

I couldn't resist asking, "And your family?"

"Still living. I ensure their safety, but our ties are cut."

"They don't know you look after them." I read between the lines to the things he didn't say. "You chose to cut ties."

"It's for their safety."

"But—"

"It's late and we're exhausted. Stay with me tonight."

I swallowed, took his hand, and followed as he led me to his house in the woods. As we crossed under the darkened sky, the rain started. Individual, tiny drops, as if the very sky itself had begun to cry.

CHAPTER 41

IT WAS EARLY, STILL DARK the next morning when I made my way back to the bungalow. The first fingers of morning light stretched from the depths of the horizon.

As much as I'd wanted to stay at X's and lie around all day, I had work to do, people to talk to, potions to create. The island would be abuzz today, which meant that I needed to be at the bungalow where I belonged.

To my surprise, the bungalow wasn't empty.

"Liam?" I approached the front steps, quickening my pace. "What are you doing here?"

He sat dressed in his normal business attire, his posture rigid, a stoic expression masking any real emotion. Only a briefcase and a hat rested on the stairs next to him. "I've come to say goodbye."

"What? Where are you going?"

"I must go away for some time." He rose to his feet, the only sign of distress his lightly ruffled hair. "I'm sure you understand. After all of this. . . "

"None of this was your fault. You did the best you could, and—"

"I'll be back, don't worry."

"Wait!" I reached out as he took a step past me. "Answer me one thing."

He turned, his gaze searching. "Yes?"

"You told me that. . . well, you had a vested interested in my safety. Why?"

A shadow of a smile crossed his lips. "Another day, Miss Locke."

"But—"

"Goodbye." He leaned in, pecked me on the cheek with a chaste kiss. "Until next time."

And then he was gone.

I stared after him for a long while. He headed toward the dock, but I lost sight of him somewhere along the way. Eventually, I pulled myself into the bungalow and opened the storeroom. Gus joined me shortly after, and the day began as if Liam had never arrived.

Hours passed, and I nearly forgot about the Liam incident as the minutes ticked by. Gus and I had been particularly busy serving breakfast, drinks, and minor potions all morning, so when X strode into the room, I was surprised to see it was almost lunchtime.

"Hey," I said, greeting him with a kiss. "How are you?"

To my surprise, he pulled me into the staircase leading up to my bedroom. "No," he said when I continued walking. "Stay here—I don't have a lot of time."

"Why not?" I traced my steps backward until we were standing eye to eye. "Are you leaving, too?"

"Too?"

I sighed, and then told him about Liam. When I finished, he simply nodded.

"I need to leave. The note you found in Dillan's pocket. . . I believe I've solved it."

"Solved what?"

"It's a code."

"So it wasn't from his mother?"

"It is from her. . . If I'm correct, it will point us in the direction of The Faction. I must depart today."

"I'm coming with you."

"No."

"But—"

"I'm bringing the Ranger Candidates." X gave me a level gaze. "They need this after everything that's happened."

I exhaled. Ranger X had cancelled the rest of the Trials, but I wondered if this wasn't his way of issuing one last test. "Will Zin be going?"

He gave his first genuine smile of the day. "She was the first to volunteer."

"Well. . . " I shrugged. His mind was made up, and there was nothing I could do about it. "Be safe. When will you return?"

"When the job is finished." He leaned in and pressed his lips to mine with an intensity that told me this trip wouldn't be easy. "Be careful. Poppy will stay with you while I'm gone. I don't know if I'll be able to receive communications where I'm going."

I nodded and walked him to the door. I didn't let go of his hand until he gently peeled my fingers back with his own. As he walked toward the dock, I couldn't help the deep sense of loneliness as it settled into the space. The room quieted, and even Gus didn't have a smart comment.

When Poppy arrived a few minutes later, she took one look at my face and gave me a hug. "He'll be back," she said. "I promise."

CHAPTER 42

TWO WEEKS LATER, THE MORNING of the masquerade ball dawned sunny and bright. The rest of the public Trials had been cancelled, but we were moving forward with the celebrations, the ball, and the naming of new Rangers.

On this particular day, the bungalow was filled with chipper guests. The sweet scent of toast and melting butter blended with steam curling from dark Caffeine Cups.

Rumors swirled as I served lunch, rumors about the return of Ranger X and his posse of Candidates. For two weeks, I hadn't seen or heard from X. According to Poppy, the group of Rangers had been on a communication ban while they were in the field. Which was why I lingered with the bungalow guests, taking seconds longer than usual clearing plates away. At the first mention of anything Ranger, I tuned in and listened for news. For any tidbit that might've slipped past the radio silence.

"I think that table's clean," Poppy whispered over my shoulder, startling me. "You've been wiping it for five minutes."

"You almost gave me a heart attack!" I dropped the rag on the table as I turned to face my cousin. Her eyes were shining, and she had a smile on her face. "Good news?"

"Zin's back." Poppy clapped her hands.

"That's great!" I smiled. "How is she?"

"I haven't seen her yet. I hear from my sources that she got back around three this morning. I stopped by her house before coming here, but Trinket pushed me out and said Zin was still sleeping."

"Well, it sounded like a tough job." I picked up the rag and resumed wiping the spotless table. "And the rest of the Candidates?"

"They all made it back. Probably still sleeping. They cut it close with the masquerade ball being tonight, don't you think?"

"At least they're safe," I said.

"You can ask about him, you know."

I sighed, twisting the rag around my hands. "Have you heard if he's back?"

Poppy reached out to squeeze my shoulder. "Ranger X didn't arrive with the rest of the Candidates," she said softly. "Nobody's said a peep about what happened. I asked everyone."

My heart plummeted. "Not even Zin knows?"

"I asked Trinket if Zin had said anything. Not a word." She exhaled a long breath. "Look, I'm sure it's fine. He probably had to tie up a few loose ends after the Candidates came back. I know he'll get in touch with you the second he steps foot on this island."

"I haven't heard from him in two weeks."

"I told you they were on a communication lockdown," Poppy said. "I personally put the order through at Ranger HQ—nobody had heard from X or the Candidates until they got back this morning. It was a top-secret mission and these things are strict." She shrugged. "You know how it goes."

"I suppose." I straightened and pasted a smile on my face. "Well, I should get back to the customers. I'm closing early today to get ready for the ball, so I should get to work on the dishes. I need to fix up a few potions, too, before Gus leaves."

"He'll show up, I promise," Poppy said. "I promised before, and I never lie. Meanwhile, come with me to Hettie's this afternoon."

"I have to get ready for the ceremony."

"I *know*. Our crazy grandmother has hired a stylist to help us prepare for the ball."

"A stylist?"

"Let's go. Gus can take care of things, I'm sure. It's one afternoon away from your storeroom." She hesitated. "And you could use some friendly company. Zin will come by, too."

"I don't know…" I wanted to go, wanted to question Zin about her trip. Maybe she had some insights about Ranger X's location. "It'll be busy here. I shouldn't leave Gus alone."

"Gus!" Poppy yelled over my shoulder. "I'm taking Lily. Close up, will you, please?"

He grunted in agreement, and before I could argue, Poppy had grabbed my arm.

"One second," I called, stumbling back into the storeroom to snatch a vial. "Here."

Poppy took one look at the neon green potion. "Glo! You did it!"

As she dragged me out of the bungalow, towel and all, I laughed. "I thought you could use it for the ceremony."

"Just wait until Glinda sees this," Poppy said, her eyes lighting with excitement. "She'll be so jealous she'll sic her Forest Fairies on me."

Once outside, it was hard to deny the beauty of the day. Blue waters twirled with green accents, and a single cotton ball of a cloud hung high in the sky. Flowers bloomed from every branch as if even the trees were celebrating. I inhaled the fresh air, trying to push thoughts about X out of my mind.

"There you are! I was just about to send out a search party for you two." Mimsey flung open the door to her mother's house before I had the chance to knock. "It's almost your turn, Lily—Glinda's working on Zin now, and then it's Poppy and you."

"Zin's here?" I said. "Already?"

"You hired *Glinda* as a stylist?" Poppy raised an eyebrow. "She'll use glitter *everywhere*."

Mimsey shrugged. "It was my mother's idea. Plus, her services are free. She even brought her own glitter."

"Wonderful." Poppy said. "I'm sure Zin was thrilled, too."

I was so anxious to see Zin that I let the glitter comment slide, stepping past Mimsey and into my grandmother's house.

"Hi, dear. What do you think?" Hettie twirled, blinding me with all the pizzazz on her body. Sequins from head to toe. From her earrings to her shoelaces, there wasn't a place on her body that didn't involve sparkles, including the mask strapped to her face. "Beautiful or what? It was all Glinda's idea."

"Gorgeous," I said, meaning it. The outfit embodied Hettie's very essence. "I love it. How's Zin coming along?"

"She'll be ready in a few minutes." Hettie grinned. "I know you're excited to get your dress, but patience. We have plenty of time."

Her grin was muted somewhat by a barrage of loud, rude expletives shouted by Zin, followed by some soothing sounds from Glinda.

Hettie winced. "Maybe it'll be sooner than we thought."

Thirty seconds later, Glinda appeared in the bedroom door, a disgruntled look on her face. "Lily, you're next." She crossed her arms. "I'm sick of fighting Zin. If she doesn't want to wear a dress, I can't make her."

"Maybe I could talk with Zin for a minute before we get started?" I asked.

"No." Glinda's hand clamped down on my arm. "She's locked herself in the room and demanded to be left alone. Come with me."

Poppy gave a helpless shrug when I looked to her for assistance. Since I couldn't get to Zin anyway, I let Glinda drag me to her lair.

She took me into a spare bedroom that she'd set up as Glam Central, where she proceeded to tug on my hair for the next half hour. Then came the clothes, the makeup, the polishing. By the time she finished, even I was surprised.

Glinda had chosen a dress the color of red roses for me, paired with a thin string of diamonds sparkling around my neck. A black lacy veil shielded my eyes, draping over half my face to fit the masked ball theme.

"Ranger X is not going to know what to do when he sees you," Poppy said, whistling as she gestured for me to twirl around. "You look great."

"Poppy. You're up." Glinda took Poppy away then, and Hettie tagged along.

For the first time all afternoon, I was alone. However, now that I had a moment to myself, the kitchen felt crushing. The four walls seemed to close in as I sat at the table. I stood up and moved to the backyard, a private space just beyond the screened-in porch. An apple tree stood tall, glistening red fruit threatening to fall from every branch.

Underneath the leaves stood a familiar figure.

"Zin!" I stopped walking the second I saw her. "I'm sorry, did you want to be alone?"

She turned, a sweeping black gown slinking against her thin frame. The fabric shone like fur, and a pop of a golden necklace brought out the flecks of yellow in her eyes. She wore a mask that gave off a highly feline vibe, and black gloves that covered her arms from fingertips to elbows.

Her eyes softened when she saw me. "Of course not. I was hoping I'd find you."

My feet carried me the rest of the way, bringing me into her outstretched arms. I hugged her for a long time, and even when I spoke, I didn't let go. "You're back."

"I'm back." Her fingers were cold against my spine. "We all made it. Except—"

"How was the trip?" I interrupted, stepping away. "You look great."

"X stayed behind." Zin shrunk away from me. "He sent us all home and said he'd join us later. I can't tell you the details of the trip—it's confidential, of course—but I *thought* we'd accomplished our goal. And then when the boat returned to The Isle, he wasn't on it."

"Nobody noticed?"

"We didn't *forget* him, if that's what you're implying. He gave the orders for us to come home."

"But why?"

Zin shook her head. "I don't know, but obviously there was something left that he needed to accomplish."

I nodded slowly, trying to understand. "But he needs to be here. Tonight is the ceremony. Who is going to announce the new Rangers if he's not on the island? He needs to be present for the masquerade ball. For his job, for *everything*."

A complicated expression crossed Zin's face. "For you, too."

I let my arms fall helplessly to my sides. "Maybe."

"I promise you he'll be back." She shook her head, the complexity fading to admiration. "Working with him, training with him on this trip was an incredible experience. He can take care of himself, Lily. He'll be fine."

"So the trip was a success? Did they announce anything to the Candidates yet about who will get an offer for the program?"

"X confirmed that they'd made their selections. Two new Rangers will be announced tonight at the ceremony."

"Only two?"

Her gaze turned to the ground. "Don't get your hopes up. I haven't made it. They never take more than that, and I'm not one of the selected."

My stomach churned. "They told you already?"

She shook her head. "But they don't need to. I've had almost two weeks to come to terms with it."

"Zin, you have as good a chance as the rest of the Candidates." I rested my hands on her shoulders. "You've worked harder than anyone."

"The jaguar isn't my final form." Her eyes flashed up at me.

Still tinged with gold, they filled with tears. "The second day of the assignment, I shifted into a bird. A tiny little bluebird as fierce as a stuffed teddy bear."

"Oh, Zin." I couldn't move, my hands frozen onto her shoulders. "I'm so sorry. But maybe that doesn't mean anything."

"You know the rules as well as I do. Shifters without a final form are not considered for the Ranger Program."

"Well maybe the rules have changed. They never used to allow women, either."

"It's for safety reasons," Zin said. "X wouldn't jeopardize anyone's life like that. It's not safe for me to be changing into random creatures left and right. It's foolish."

"How did it happen? Did you try to do it?"

Zin shrugged. "We needed some intelligence from a small Faction camp, and I found myself wishing that I could fly. A few seconds later... it just happened. I was flying."

"And?"

"And I got the information we needed," Zin said with a sigh. "So I suppose it was a success."

"Did you tell X about it?"

"It was the right thing to do." One big, round tear slid down Zin's face. "At the time, I debated not telling him the information. Nobody was around to see me shift—I could've kept it a secret. Kept myself in the running."

"But you didn't."

She shook her head. "I had to tell him. He needed the information I'd overheard, and there was no other way to explain it. Keeping quiet wasn't an option."

I pulled my cousin into me, held her close. She was stiff in my arms. "I don't know what to say."

"You don't have to say anything."

I held her until she relaxed, and she wiped her eyes.

"I guess some things aren't meant to be," she said, pulling back with a watery smile. "I've had two weeks to sort myself out, and I'm okay. Really. Now we should get to the ball before Glinda sprinkles more glitter in my hair."

I watched my cousin stride toward the house, her thin shoulders held tall. She looked fragile, like a china doll on the verge of shattering. As if she was freefalling toward the ground, and there was nothing I could do to stop it.

CHAPTER 43

"THERE, DO YOU SEE IT?" Mimsey pointed. "I hear music."

A few more steps, and Mimsey, Poppy, Zin, and I arrived on the doorstep of the party. Glinda had gone ahead to get her Forest Fairies ready for the evening. They were on guard duty, tasked to zoom around the island and report any unsavory findings back to the Rangers.

Fairy lights twinkled from the treetops, lighting a dance floor that extended the length of a football field. At one end sat a gorgeous array of sweets, the fruits and crackers and cookies centered around a huge chocolate fountain cascading into a mouthwatering display.

A server from Sea Salt—the fanciest restaurant on The Isle— had set up a bar along the other side, serving drinks that flamed and wine that smoked. The whole ambiance was surreal.

"Well, does anyone want to eat?" Poppy asked, glowing like the moon. The Glo potion had given her an almost angelic aura around her face, and she couldn't stop looking at herself in every mirror, dinner plate, or silver utensil we passed. "Or dance? I could dance, too."

"I'm hungry," I said, surprised as my stomach growled. "I haven't eaten all day."

"Go on, girls," Mimsey said. "Zin, I'll go with you to find Trinket and check in—I want to get a good seat. She's with her children, so that crowd should be easy to find."

"Look at this." Poppy loaded her plate with one of everything.

"How do they expect anyone to dance after putting out a spread like this? You'll have to roll me around the floor."

I laughed, helping myself to a plate equally full. "I think the point is to dance, and then work up more of an appetite and. . . is that apple pie?"

"It's fresh," a voice spoke behind me. "I picked the apples this morning."

I turned to find a familiar face behind me—a face I'd never seen in person, but one that'd graced many a newspaper the last several weeks. "Oh, Mr. Dartmouth—hello."

Dillan's father attempted to smile, but his efforts fell short. "I hope you enjoy it."

The way his shoulders hunched forward in pain, maybe shame or guilt—gave me an ache in my stomach so strong I reached out and rested a hand on his arm. He looked up, his cheeks red, his eyes a slightly dulled version of his son's. His clothes weren't expensive, nor were they flashy, and his hands looked clean but rough—the hands of a farmer.

"I'm so sorry, about everything." I couldn't imagine all he'd been through—first losing his wife and then a son to The Faction. Dillan might be alive, but he'd be locked in prison for a very, very long time. "Is there anything I can do?"

He twisted his hands together. "Miss Locke, you've done so much for this island in your short time here. I'm just sorry for my son's actions. The things he did, the things he said. . ." Mr. Dartmouth paused and shook his head. "I hid my brother from Dillan so this could never happen. I should've known better."

"You couldn't have known," I said. "Everyone chooses their own way. You did the best you could."

"If I'd just realized it sooner, I could've stopped him somehow. It was hard enough to lose her."

"Your wife?" I asked gently. "I've heard she was quite a woman."

"She was smart and so very beautiful." Mr. Dartmouth looked

up, his face pained in the same way as Liam's when he'd realized that his fiancée was no longer the same person he'd once loved. "I miss her."

"I'm sure you do. I can't imagine."

"We never had a funeral, you know," he said, as if he hadn't heard me. His eyes had taken on a haze as if he were in his own little world. "Never found her body, never heard a word from her. Do you know why they kidnapped her?"

I shook my head.

"She was good with languages. She could speak ten or more of them. The Ranger program was considering opening up a space for her—even back then, when female Candidates weren't a passing thought."

"The Faction took her for her skills?"

"Turns out that being good with languages made her very, very valuable. In a society where communication was difficult, she could create nearly unbreakable codes. The Ranger program wanted to use her for their communication team and had even hired her on for a few projects, but then. . . before the Trials, The Faction took her. I woke up one morning and she was gone."

"But she left a note," I said, remembering the code X had cracked. "She *had* left a code to try and get in touch."

"A code that nobody could crack," he said sadly. "I took it to the Ranger HQ, but nobody had any luck with it. Eventually, I let Dillan have it as a keepsake. I only wish it'd meant something."

"It did," X's voice sounded from behind us. "Mr. Dartmouth, there's someone here to see you."

CHAPTER 44

THE DEEP, MELODIC SOUND OF his voice sent butterflies through my stomach. I turned to face X, my face warming as I scanned his solid, unscathed body from head to toe. I wanted to leap into his arms and kiss his cheeks, but I couldn't. He wasn't alone.

X stood before us, a woman on his arm wearing a dress the shade of lilacs and a mask that matched. Though it covered most of her face, her lips parted in a shy smile lined with age.

"Hello, Bristan," she said, her voice paper thin, her lips quivering.

Dillan's father stood still for a long moment, and when he turned to face the woman with X, he dropped his plate on the ground. A perfectly good piece of apple pie hit the floor, splattering everywhere.

Bristan Dartmouth took a step forward, his hand extending to pull the mask up and over his wife's face. She peered back at him, unsure and cautious, as they viewed each other for the first time in too long. He let out a cry that burned the line between pain and happiness, pulling her to his chest.

I slipped my hand into Ranger X's and dragged him to the side. The moment felt too personal to intrude on, so I turned my back on the reunion to give them some privacy.

"You're here," I whispered once we were standing close enough to touch. "You came back!"

"Of course. Did someone tell you I wouldn't?" His forehead creased in concern. "I'm sorry I couldn't communicate with you—I thought Poppy would've told you we put a freeze on all transmissions while we were in Faction territory."

"She did." I stubbed my toe against the ground. "I still worried."

He held me at arm's length. "You are the most remarkable woman I've ever met. And the most beautiful. How could you think I wouldn't come back?"

"It sounded like you stayed behind when the rest of the Candidates returned."

"Because my business wasn't finished. Theirs was." He pulled me close to kiss my forehead. "There is no force in this world strong enough to keep me away from you."

My heart skipped a beat or two, and I leaned my head against his chest. He smelled like home, and I inhaled deeply. "Where was she?"

"A little town tucked into the mountains of Colorado. As it turned out, that town was communication headquarters for The Faction."

"They made her work for them?"

"She was crucial to their communication system. Now that we have her back, The Faction will be hurting. The town is completely disbanded."

"You sent the Candidates home after you took over the town," I said. "Why did you stay?"

"I wanted to find Mrs. Dartmouth by myself."

I brushed my lips against his neck. "I'm proud of you, I hope you know."

"I'm sorry I worried you."

"Well, I suppose now we're even."

He leaned in and kissed me, wrapping one hand behind my head and holding my face in his palm. The fairy lights faded to the background, the music a dull murmur against the night.

Eventually, X stepped back. "I want to continue where this

is going, but I have to get to the stage. We're announcing the new Rangers."

"About that," I said. "Zin told me—"

"Sorry, I have to get going." He gave me an apologetic look. "I can't discuss this now."

"But Zin—"

"Find a seat, Lily. Sit with your family." He frowned. "My decisions are final."

CHAPTER 45

"WE STARTED THIS JOURNEY WITH ten Candidates," Ranger X said, pausing as the audience shifted in their seats, plates of appetizers spread before them. "To qualify as a Candidate is already an accomplishment. A great feat of physical, mental, and emotional strength."

I pushed food around my plate. Dinner would be served as soon as the Rangers were announced, but I could hardly stomach a bite of appetizer. Poppy sat on one side of me, Hettie on the other. Trinket and her children sat at the table next to us with their faces all turned toward X. Beside him sat the remaining Candidates.

"We now have seven left. Seven Candidates accompanied me on a mission deep into Faction territory over these past two weeks—a mission I am quite pleased to announce was successful."

He paused as the audience cheered and clapped. Hettie whistled loud enough to break my eardrums.

"However, we are left with only two Candidates who will receive positions within the Ranger program."

I counted the seven Candidates on stage. Dillan obviously wasn't there, and neither was Raymon. After everything that'd happened in the Trials, Trent had also dropped out of the running.

Ilinia had freely admitted her role in controlling Camden, Trent, and Zin with blood magic. While Trent had chosen to remove himself from the running, Camden had elected to continue his quest, just like Zin.

"The first Candidate who has been chosen for the Ranger

program is someone who, in the face of horrible circumstances, showed true bravery." Ranger X tilted his chin upward as he surveyed the crowd. "As a Ranger, sometimes things happen beyond our control. Horrible things. The ability to put the past behind himself, or herself," he quickly corrected, "is essential."

Zin sat on the edge of her chair. Her face was a sheet of white and, despite her claims that she had come to terms with everything, she was clearly upset.

"Camden Lyons." Ranger X turned to face the handsome Candidate. "Please approach center stage to accept your offer."

Camden's face drained of color. He didn't move. It wasn't until the Candidate in the next chair gave him an elbow to the ribs that he struggled to his feet. Women in the crowd cheered everywhere, their golden boy taking his place in the elite Ranger program.

X extended his hand and shook the newly minted Ranger's outstretched fingers. Somehow, Camden managed a firm handshake. Then he accepted a long, furled scroll that detailed every aspect of the Ranger program.

Finally, the news seemed to reach Camden's brain. He turned to face the crowd and raised the scroll to the sky. The audience erupted, cheering wildly. The only silent one in the room was Zin, her gaze fixed on the floor.

"The next Candidate is someone who—" X's speech was interrupted by a loud, screeching noise that ground any remaining applause to a halt.

"What's happening?" I mumbled to Hettie. "That noise is horrible."

Her lips tightened into a line, her head giving the smallest shake.

In the sky over Ranger X's head, a face appeared projected onto blackness. I'd never seen the man before, but judging by the scream from Mrs. Dartmouth, she knew him. And he wasn't a friend.

"That's Ellis, Dillan's uncle," Hettie whispered to me. "He

doesn't run The Faction, but he was one of the founding fathers. You could say he's influential in their world."

Dillan's uncle stared down at us, a bored, almost uninterested look in his gray eyes. "Somebody misplaced my invitation for the party this evening. Shame, isn't it?"

The crowd stilled.

"No matter, I forgive you all," he said, turning up the charisma and appearing almost jolly. He pulled a party hat from off screen and placed it on his head, snapping the rubber band below his chin with a resounding *thwak*. "I'll have my own party. You see, I don't mind the celebrations, but I do mind the way you've treated several of my friends." He laughed, an almost gleeful sound. "And we all know what that calls for, don't we? *Revenge!*"

"He's crazy," I muttered as the man on screen sipped from a crystal glass.

Hettie nodded. "Whatever the Rangers did these last two weeks, it was big. The Faction has never been so forward with their messaging."

"I won't keep you lovely people from the festivities now, as I am just here to say a quick toast." The man raised his glass, smiling as if congratulating a pair of newlyweds. "Celebrate now, and savor the memories. Because your precious island will pay, and the day is coming. It's coming soon, soon, soon!" Another high-pitched giggle followed. "Cheers!"

The projected image exploded into pieces, thin material raining down over the dance floor. One or two screams erupted from the tables, but they were quickly shushed. Ranger X stepped forward and demanded calmness.

It took a while, but eventually the crowd settled down again. When Ranger X spoke again, his voice was like ice. "We have two options now." He took his time scanning the eyes of everyone in the crowd. "We can dissolve this meeting and go home. We can run from this and hide in our basements."

The silence throughout the room was absolute. Not a single utensil clanked against a plate.

"Or I can announce the next Candidate to become a Ranger." He gestured vaguely all around him. "The Isle is safe. We have guards everywhere—this image was nothing more than an attempt to scare us. If anyone is worried that's not true, you may leave now."

Nobody moved, though one or two folks in the back shifted.

"Fine. Then we will continue. Anna, let's get dinner served while I make my announcements." He nodded toward the caterer from Sea Salt. "This last announcement won't take long because the Candidate's actions speak for themselves."

Zin hardly moved, her hands intertwined with one another, her eyes focused on a world different than ours.

"This Candidate is honest. Fierce in morals and fiercer in loyalty." Ranger X took several deep breaths. "Someone who will follow the rules implicitly, but even more importantly, someone who will break those rules when they need to be broken. I've never met a Candidate more deserving of the title of Ranger."

A lump appeared in my throat.

"These past two weeks were difficult, trying weeks. The only reason we succeeded and escaped alive—all of us—is because of her." Ranger X looked up, his gaze locked on Zin. "As the head of the Ranger program, I am honored to extend an offer to Zinnia Dixie."

Tears ran down my cheeks as Camden hurried to her side. He reached out, helping Zin stand. She leaned against him as the two moved toward the center of the stage, a thin smile on Zin's lips.

"If I'm correct," Ranger X said, "We have a shiftling in our midst."

The audience stilled as everyone listened closer, myself included.

"What is a shiftling?" He looked toward Zin. "It is a shifter whose final form is fluid. A rare breed, an incredibly rare treasure. A Uniqueness of the highest order. With this offer, I hope she'll join our team."

Ranger X extended a second scroll to Zin. She accepted it with shaking fingers, and then the two new Rangers faced the crowd. Hettie leaned over, pulling me into a hug so intense I could feel the beat of her heart. As she rested her head against mine, I felt the tears staining her cheeks, too.

"Let dinner be served," X said. "And let us welcome these new Rangers to our team. To those who were not selected, we thank you for your dedication to the island. Your work has not gone unnoticed, and you will be invited back to the next Trials."

The night was silent. Nobody moved, all of us waiting to hear X's final words.

"We are stronger than ever before." He paused for a long moment, surveying the crowd with pride on his face as he raised a glass of blood red wine. "If The Faction comes to us, we will be ready. This is our island!"

Epilogue

S OMETHING PULLED ME FROM THE bungalow toward the grave, the way it had every day since Ranger X and the Candidates had returned to the island. In my hands I carried a fresh bundle of flowers—roses, tulips, lilies of the valley. The most colorful, sweetest smelling flowers I could find.

My feet led the way, one step in front of the other. It was early, barely sunrise, and Gus hadn't yet arrived at the bungalow. For some reason, I kept my visits a secret. It felt private, personal, and somehow more meaningful.

The grounds were quiet this morning, as it always was at sunrise. Set just inside the edges of The Forest, not far from Ranger X's house, it was a private cemetery reserved only for Rangers. Only now there was one exception: Raymon.

I removed the flowers I'd brought the previous day and replaced the bouquet with a fresh one. The initial burst of wreaths and plants that'd followed Raymon's funeral had withered away, and now it felt too bare and desolate. I told myself that was why I continued my visits.

Kneeling down, I cleared away the extra growth around the headstone. I sat back on my heels in silence, not quite knowing what to do or what to say. If I should say anything at all. I couldn't explain why I'd been drawn here in the first place, or why I kept coming back.

"It takes time."

I leapt back, startled by the familiar voice. "X," I said, resting a hand over my racing heart. "You scared me."

"The dead don't talk, Lily. No matter how many times you sit. No matter how long you wait. No matter how hard you cry."

"I know," I whispered, surprised at the tremor in my voice. "I don't know why I come here, to be honest. The stupid flowers keep dying, and Raymon shouldn't have dead flowers at his gravesite. Maybe that's why. He shouldn't have died, X—"

Ranger X grasped my fingers in his with a touch as faint as a breeze. He guided me to a nearby bench and sat first, pulling me onto his lap. I rested my head against his, my body melding to his chest as he wrapped strong arms around my back.

"I just need to sit here a minute," I said. "Please stay."

"I'll always stay."

He held me for a long while. Closer and closer until I couldn't hardly gasp for air, until every breath of mine inhaled the scent of him and together, we were one. The hurt, the despair, the destruction, all of it was no longer mine to bear alone. And neither was the joy, the hope, the love. It was ours, together.

He raised a thumb and pressed it lightly to my cheek, separating our faces until he could look into my eyes. "We all have a shadow side. A dark side, a piece of ourselves we don't want anyone else to see. You have to accept that. You are not *her*. You never will be."

My chest felt hollow as I inhaled a rattling breath. "But—"

"You're not alone," he said. "I, too, wonder how anyone could possibly love me after they've seen the edge of darkness inside my heart. But you do, Lily. You love me."

"Yes," I whispered. "More than anything."

"You've seen all of me, and I've seen all of you. I've seen the good, the better, the beautiful, and everything that is Lily. Don't walk alone. Trust me."

I swallowed and managed a nod. "I love all of you."

He smiled, a tinge of sadness glinting in his dangerous eyes. "I know."

"I think I'm done here." I hesitated, glancing at the grave. "For now."

He nodded, sliding me off of his lap and onto the seat. "I'll give you a few minutes alone. Join me at the cabin when you're ready, and I'll cook you something to eat."

"Wait." I sat on the bench under his looming height. "Kiss me."

A glint in his dark eyes lasted for all but a second before he bent over, clasping my face between his palms. He tasted like mint and smelled like danger, and when his lips softened and his hands came around my back, the world, the good, the bad, all of it disappeared like magic.

When he pulled away and the blackness subsided, he brought me to my feet. We stood a foot apart from each other and watched, breathless.

"I'll be waiting for you," he said. "Don't be long."

I nodded, watching him go before I returned to the edge of Raymon's grave. Kneeling, I whispered a few last, private words before brushing my hand over his name. I blinked, but the tears didn't fall. Finally, I sighed and dragged myself to my feet.

As I turned to go, a blade of grass caught my eye. Big and lanky, it drooped over Raymon's name. I bent to pull the stray strand I'd missed when, before my eyes, it grew. Bigger and bigger until I realized it wasn't a piece of grass, but the stem of a flower.

I stumbled back, watching as the stem grew taller and taller, until eventually it bloomed. The flower was a lily.

"It wasn't me, you know." Trinket spoke from behind me, sending my pulse racing. "It wasn't me who delivered the flowers to you."

I turned to find my aunt standing there. She was dressed in all black, a single pearl hanging from a silver chain around her neck. "How did you know I was here?"

"Your mother fell in love with a man," she said. "He wasn't from here; he was exotic and dangerous and handsome and intelligent." Trinket's hands shook as she fiddled with her necklace. "He came to this island for one summer, his last summer before he started at Cretan in the fall."

"Are you talking about my father? I thought nobody knew his identity. Hettie said—"

"I know what Hettie said." She cleared her throat. "Their romance was secret. Nobody knew—not even me, not until it was too late."

"Why are you telling me this?"

Trinket ignored my question. "Autumn rolled around after that summer, and your father went off to school. He was scheduled to start his studies at Cretan. Naturally, your mother remained here. Her future was on the island with her family. She told me later that Lucian had promised to return when he graduated."

I blinked, still trying to catch up. "He never came back."

"No." She gave a faint smile. "None of us West Isle Witches have much luck with men."

I shook my head, a hot streak of anger flooding to my lips. "Do you know his last name?"

"We thought he died, Lily. In his dorm, the night before he was scheduled to start school."

Too many thoughts competed for my attention. "I don't understand. What do you mean you *thought* he died?"

"Your mother found out she was pregnant the day after your father left. She packed up all of her belongings and prepared to follow him to Cretan." Trinket blinked a few times, struggling to keep a level voice. "She arrived there, only to find out that there'd been a fire in his dorm room the night before and your father hadn't escaped."

I swallowed, taking a minute before I trusted myself to speak. "An accident?"

"That's what they say."

"What who says?"

"There's more to the story, Lily." Trinket bowed her head. "He's alive, I know it. Your mother knew it. He leads The Faction."

"No."

"It might sound unrealistic, but it's not—The Faction is sharp. Many people don't believe he's still alive. Think about it. Who better to lead their team than someone who died twenty-six years ago? He's impossible to find. A ghost."

"You're saying he faked his death?"

"Yes. He made a deal with The Faction and staged the fire. Then, The Faction took him under their wing and groomed him for leadership."

I sat in silence. The scent of the roses—once sweet—had turned almost dizzying. "How do you know?"

"Your mother."

"What?"

"She came exactly one time in her life to confide in me, and it was the night after the funeral." Trinket blinked several times before I realized she was crying. She glanced at the locket around my neck before continuing. "That night she told me he wasn't dead. That something darker had claimed him."

"Did she have proof?"

"Enough for me to believe her."

"But what about me?" I stood up, my voice entering shrieking territory. "I need proof, too! You can't tell me all of these things, and then—"

"I didn't send the lilies—I lied about it. I took credit for it because you weren't ready to know who sent them."

"Was it him?" I couldn't help the anger rising. I jabbed a finger at the now fully bloomed lily. "Did he do this?"

Trinket gave a succinct nod. "I believe so."

"Why?"

"I believe he's going to pay you a visit," Trinket said, her voice next to a whisper. "I was trying to protect you from this as long as I could, but I can't anymore. You need to be prepared. I don't know how he knows about you, I don't know why he's doing this, but—"

"You don't need to protect me," I snarled. "It's my history. It was wrong of you to hide it from me."

"I'm sorry." Trinket's voice was so frail, so thin that I couldn't find it in me to argue with her anymore.

I sat down, watching as the lily fluttered in the breeze. Trinket stood over me silent, waiting.

"What does this mean for me?" I asked quietly. "For The Isle?"

"I don't know," Trinket said finally.

"So you think..." I stood up to face her. "Do you think it's a part of me? Whatever it was that turned him to The Faction?"

Trinket shook her head, the curve of her lips too sad, too tender to be called a smile. "No. You're very, very good, and that is the one fact of which I am certain."

"But—"

"I don't know the answers." She stepped away from me, turning to leave. "And you don't have to know them all either. The only thing you have to figure out is who you are and who you want to be. Everything else will follow."

"I don't know how to do that."

"You're not him," she said. "You don't have to be him, and you never will be. But you will have to be ready because there will come a day, Lily, when you will have to choose between him... and us. And when that day comes, nobody can make the choice except you."

And then Trinket was gone, and I was left alone.

With one perfect, blooming lily.

The End

Author's Note

Thank you for reading, Islanders! Your enthusiasm for this book means everything to me. I hope you enjoyed the story!

Love,
Gina

P.S. If you are curious to see what our good friend Ainsley Shaw has been up to since Lily left for the island... you're in luck! You can read her adventure called *The Undercover Witch,* available on Amazon in January 2017!

For other news on upcoming releases, sales, and events coming soon, please sign up to my newsletter at www.ginalamanna.com.

❧

Gina LaManna is the USA TODAY bestselling author of the Magic & Mixology series, the Lacey Luzzi Mafia Mysteries, The Little Things romantic suspense series, and the Misty Newman books.

Books By Gina LaManna

Here is a list of other books by Gina
LaManna: http://bit.ly/GinaLaManna.

Magic & Mixology Mysteries:
Hex on the Beach
Witchy Sour
Jinx and Tonic

Reading Order for Lacey Luzzi:
Lacey Luzzi: Scooped
Lacey Luzzi: Sprinkled
Lacey Luzzi: Sparkled
Lacey Luzzi: Salted
Lacey Luzzi: Sauced
Lacey Luzzi: S'mored
Lacey Luzzi: Spooked
Lacey Luzzi: Seasoned
Lacey Luzzi: Spiced
Lacey Luzzi: Suckered

The Little Things Mystery Series:
One Little Wish
Two Little Lies

Misty Newman:
Teased to Death
Short Story in Killer Beach Reads

Chick Lit:
Girl Tripping

Gina also writes books for kids under the
Pen Name Libby LaManna:

Mini Pie the Spy!
Mini Pie the Christmas Spy!

WEBSITES AND SOCIAL MEDIA:

Find out more about the author and upcoming books online at www.ginalamanna.com or:

Email: gina.m.lamanna@gmail.com
Twitter: @Gina_LaManna
Facebook: facebook.com/GinaLaMannaAuthor
Website: www.ginalamanna.com

About the Author:

Originally from St. Paul, Minnesota, Gina LaManna began writing with the intention of making others smile. At the moment, she lives in Los Angeles and spends her days writing short stories, long stories, and all sizes in-between stories. She publishes under a variety of pen names, including a children's mystery series titled Mini Pie the Spy!

In her spare time, Gina has been known to run the occasional marathon, accidentally set fire to her own bathroom, and survive days on end eating only sprinkles, cappuccino foam and ice cream. She enjoys spending time with her family and friends most of all.

Made in the USA
Lexington, KY
05 September 2017